NEW JERSEY NOIR

NEW JERSEY NOIR

EDITED BY JOYCE CAROL OATES

Gerald Slota

Published by Akashic Books
©2011 The Ontario Review Inc.

Series concept by Tim McLoughlin and Johnny Temple
New Jersey map by Aaron Petrovich
All photographs inside the book by Gerald Slota

Hardcover ISBN-13: 978-1-61775-034-2
Hardcover Library of Congress Control Number: 2011902727

Paperback ISBN-13: 978-1-61775-026-7
Paperback Library of Congress Control Number: 2011922958

Akashic Books
PO Box 1456
New York, NY 10009
info@akashicbooks.com
www.akashicbooks.com

ALSO IN THE AKASHIC NOIR SERIES:

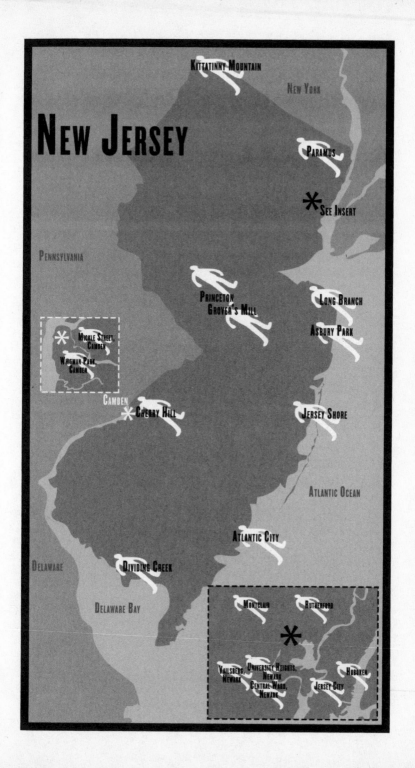

TABLE OF CONTENTS

Miles of black turnpike and parkway pavement
scrolled out onto the soil of the no-longer farms.
You could speed now from one place to another
and not see the slums, the factories in broken-eyed ruin.

Everywhere ruin—did nobody see it arriving?
—C.K. Williams, "Newark Black"

We are happy with the fake, and happy with the real, but the
near real—the too near real—unnerves us.
—Jonathan Safran Foer, "Too Near Real"

INTRODUCTION

How Blackly Lovely: Noir in New Jersey

During the past several decades, "crime"—as historical fact, as literary subject, as theme and variation—seems to have acquired a mythopoetic status in our American culture. To write about crime is to focus upon American life *in extremis*: as if distilled, pure. The complex and overlapping worlds of criminal behavior and law enforcement, highly publicized criminal trials, the dissolving of the putative barrier between "business" and "crime"—a subculture of intense interest in the phenomenon of serial killers and a new awareness of "victims' rights"—these have become significant culture issues; as in a novel by Balzac or Dostoyevsky, in which a dense swath of society is minutely examined, the anatomizing of both high-profile crimes and more ordinary, even quotidian crimes has become a way of exposing the American soul. The considerable success of Akashic Books' ambitious Noir Series is both a testament to this American preoccupation with crime as a way of decoding American life and a symptom of the preoccupation.

Noir isn't invariably about crime, nor is the subject of crime invariably a *noir* subject, but the two are closely bound together, as in this collection of original, highly inventive, and disturbing *noir* stories, poetry, and art set in the "Garden State"—a title meant to be taken literally (for New Jersey *is* beautifully rural, hilly, and even pastoral—once you are off the Turnpike and out of range of those powerfully pungent smells of industry), though many inhabitants of the state would guess that it's meant as a cruel irony.

Noir isn't subject matter so much as a sensibility, a tone, an atmosphere. *Noir* is both metaphor and the actual—raw, ravishing—thing. *Noir* is the essence of mystery: that which cannot be "solved." Most of all, *noir* is a place—"a certain slant of light"—in which a betrayal will occur.

Noir is the consequence of an individual's expectations, hopes, or intentions confronted by the betrayal of another, often an intimate. *Noir* is usually—though not inevitably—sexual betrayal: death is a secondary matter, set beside the terrible betrayal of trust.

Quintessential *noir* centers around a man—(yes, the genre has been male-oriented, by tradition)—whose desire for a beautiful woman has blinded him to her true, manipulative, evil self: the (beautiful) female as evil, like the primeval Eve. (Unbeautiful women can be evil too, though men are not so likely to be seduced by them, hence betrayed.) But the *noir* betrayal can range farther and deeper and can encompass, in more ambitious works of art, a fundamental betrayal of the spirit—innocence devastated by the experience of social injustice or political corruption.

Which is why works of enduring significance—Aeschylus's *Orestia*, Shakespeare's *Macbeth* and *King Lear*, Dostoyevsky's *Crime and Punishment* and *The Brothers Karamazov*, to name just a few—owe their genesis not simply to crimes but to unspeakable, hideous, taboo crimes: "sins" against humanity.

Noir as the primary human condition: the betrayal of one's kind.

Our indigenous and most glamorous American *noir* is likely to be identified with the Los Angeles of James M. Cain (*The Postman Always Rings Twice, Double Indemnity*), Raymond Chandler (*The Big Sleep, Farewell, My Lovely*), Dashiell Hammett (*The Maltese Falcon, Red Harvest*)—that is, the Los Angeles of the 1930s and '40s. These are "classic" *noir* works of fiction in which the *femme fatale* is a locus of evil, as she is the prime mover of plot: without the primeval Eve, there is no mystery, therefore no story. But they are classic *noir* works in which the (male) voice of the private detective, and his distinct, post-Hemingway sensibility, are raised to the level of art, not merely pulp entertainment. The private detective as a variant of a crusading knight—the "incorruptible" (male) consciousness seeking to make sense of a labyrinth of lies, double crosses, betrayals, murders. Though in life private detectives are virtually never involved with homicides or crimes of great significance, in *noir* literature and film the private detective is a successful competitor with the police homicide detective, and is not bound by the officer's putative code of behavior.

The private detective is both cynical and, oddly, innocent—open to being deceived, at least temporarily. That the private detective is open to being betrayed makes him our alter ego in the struggle of good-and-evil—the struggle of good to *know* evil, to *name and conquer it.*

These classic *noir* titles, made into equally classic films, have exerted a powerful influence upon American successors well into the twenty-first century—James Ellroy, Michael Connelly, Dennis Lehane, Tom Cook, Patricia Cornwell, and Laura Lippman, among numerous others. These are "crime" writers but the focus of their concern is moral: the knowing, naming, and conquering of evil. Where *noir* falls beyond the compass of the questing detective as in, for instance, the sequence of graphically violent, neo-biblical allegories of the West written by Cormac McCarthy (from *Blood Meridian* to *No Country for Old Men* and *The Road*), there is only the knowing and naming of evil—there is no conquering of evil. The human hope is for mere survival.

Noir has flourished in films, particularly in the wake of the influence of displaced European filmmakers (like Fritz Lang) after World War II and the Holocaust—giving to even conventional Hollywood films like Henry Hathaway's *Niagara* (1953), with its final, eerie, starkly German Expressionist scene of the killing of the unfaithful Rose (Marilyn Monroe in her breakthrough screen role) by her vengeful husband (Joseph Cotten as a traumatized and "impotent" war veteran), a mythopoetic gravity. Classic *noir* films—from Tod Browning's *Freaks* (1932) to Alfred Hitchcock's *Vertigo* (1958)—are too many to list; outstanding neo-*noir* films include Roman Polanski's *Chinatown* (1974), Martin Scorsese's *Taxi Driver* (1976), Curtis Hanson's *L.A. Confidential* (1997), and the more recent, innovative *Memento* (2001) by Christopher Nolan. In television, there have been relatively few *noir* standouts—the Kafkaesque *The Fugitive* (1963–67), the highly stylized *Miami Vice* (1984–89) with its pounding, erotic pre-MTV music track, and the more gritty police procedurals *Hill Street Blues* (1981–87), *NYPD Blue* (1993–2005), and *Homicide: Life on the Street* (1993–99). Of the two television series generally named as the greatest achievements in the history of the medium, both are brilliantly original *noir* dramas—*The Sopranos* (1999–2007) and *The Wire* (2002–08). Famously set in New Jersey, suggested in the opening credits as an appendage—that is, a "suburb"—of the more powerful crime families of New York City, *The Sopranos* is based upon creator David Chase's inspired adaptation of New Jersey Mafioso history including the careers of the Newark "godfather" Ruggiero Boiardo (1890–1984) and Abner Zwillman, "The Al Capone of New Jersey" (1904–59). (Zwillman was the most famous Jewish crime boss of his era; as C.K. Williams notes in "Newark Black": *Our gangster hero, Longie Zwillman, who had a black car.*) It was Chase's brilliantly original interpretation of the Mafioso legend—the operatic *gravitas* of Francis Ford Coppolla's *Godfather* epic rendered in diminished, often domestic images—that made *The Sopranos* like no other crime saga in film or TV history. So thoroughly has the iconic thickened figure of Tony Soprano saturated American popular culture in the early years of the twenty-first century, it's as if the image of "New Jersey" itself has been transmogrified into a set—a backdrop for the ongoing drama of organized crime in collusion with a corrupt political leadership. In place of the archetypal elder godfather Vito Corleone of *The Godfather*, played with dignity by Marlon Brando, is the distinctly less elevated but very New Jersey Tony Soprano, played by James Gandolfini.

(Among Jersey settings memorably used in *The Sopranos* is the teasingly protracted, mordantly funny sequence titled "The Pine Barrens," in which Paulie Walnuts and Christopher Moltisanti try gamely to kill a Rasputin-like member of the Russian mob in the wilderness of South Jersey from which they are barely rescued after becoming hopelessly lost. The subtext of the episode seems to be that "organized crime" is an urban phenomenon: lost in the wilderness, if only the relatively tame wilderness of the Pine Barrens, the blustering Mafioso are helpless as children.)

More recently, Martin Scorsese's critically acclaimed *Boardwalk Empire* (2010–11), set in Prohibition-era Atlantic City, draws upon *Boardwalk Empire: The Birth, High Times, and Corruption of Atlantic City* by the New Jersey judge and historian Nelson Johnson; the HBO series is a fictionalization of the flamboyant life and career of the entrepreneurial Enoch "Nucky" Thompson, a Prohibition bootlegger who hosted what is said to have been the first national organized crime syndicate meeting, in 1929, with Al Capone and other mob bosses, photographed companionably together on the Atlantic City boardwalk.

The Sopranos and *Boardwalk Empire* are *noir* romances. *Boardwalk Empire* in particular is rich in 1920s period detail—costumes, automobiles, hairstyles, vernacular speech; unlike Tony Soprano with his loose-fitting sport shirts and careless grooming, Nucky Thompson is the gangster-politician as dandy and visionary. Though frequently and graphically violent, *The Sopranos* and *Boardwalk Empire* are populated with characters who are domestic and familial; their most intense concerns are with human relations, not "business"—or not exclusively "business." (It's a measure of the romance of *The Sopranos* that the mob boss Tony Soprano is so unfailingly solicitous of his wife Carmella—even when they argue, Tony doesn't beat her. And his immense patience for his excruciatingly self-absorbed children is equally impressive.) Like the serio-comic mystery series by Janet Evanovich, featuring an unlikely female bounty hunter in Trenton, New Jersey, and particularly popular with women readers, these HBO dramas appeal to an audience for whom the *noir* quest—the knowing, naming, and conquering of evil—is linked to colorful storytelling. Not even Martin Scorsese would wish to cross the line into the annals of real-life, unorganized New Jersey crime at its most extreme: the infamous rape and murder of seven-year-old Megan Kanka, for instance, in Hamilton, New Jersey, in 1994, by the serial sex offender Jesse Timmendequas (subsequently incarcerated in New Jersey State Prison); the five or more murders committed by the psychopath Richard Biegenwald, of Monmouth County, between 1958 and 1983 (Biegenwald died in New Jersey State Prison in 2008); the slaughter of his family in Westfield, in 1971, by the accountant John List (who died in prison custody in 2008 at the age of eighty-two). *Noir* is a highly selective art—and such brute ugliness isn't redeemable by art.

In this volume, no work of fiction or poetry directly evokes such crude, hellish crimes, but the surreal-nightmare family snapshots of Gerald Slota's art at the start of each section comes closest to evoking the "pure products of America" (to use William Carlos Williams's striking phrase) from which these terrible crimes and criminals might spring.

New Jersey!—"The Garden State"—our fifth smallest state, with only Hawaii, Connecticut, Delaware, and Rhode Island below it in land mass, yet it's the state containing the "most murderous" American city (Camden) and the state generally conceded to be, square mile per square mile, the most densely politically corrupt. (Louisiana has been, by tradition, the most corrupt of all U.S. states, but in recent years Illinois has been closing the lead.) Atlantic City, Jersey City, Hackensack, Hoboken, Secaucus, Newark, Camden (three recent Camden mayors have been jailed for corruption)—in these cities as in others corruption isn't aberrant but rather a way of (political) life. (Why? The answer seems to be that New Jersey is a maze of overlapping and competing municipalities—556, to California's 480—that bring with it rich op-portunities for political entrenchment, deal-making, and outright thievery.)

New Jersey is among the wealthiest of states, with a per capita income that was the highest in the United States in 2000; judged by the desolation of its inner cities, it is simultaneously one of the poorest. New Jersey is a microcosm of the profoundly unequal dis-tribution of wealth in the United States generally—within an hour one can drive from the wealthy exurbia of Far Hills and Saddle River to the dismal poverty of inner-city Newark; from the man-sions of Princeton to the desperate poverty of inner-city Camden. Within an hour's radius of Princeton University, the most heavily endowed (per student) university in the United States, with an endowment in excess of $25 billion, are inner-city schools in ever-desperate need of funds. Sitting between the great cities of New York and Philadelphia, New Jersey has been by tradition a heavily "organized" Mafia state, as it was at one time a northern outpost of the Ku Klux Klan, with a concentration of members in Tren-ton, Camden, Monmouth County, and South Jersey. (Officially, the Jersey Klan was disbanded in 1944, but a writer friend of mine, now living in Princeton, recalls her Jewish father being harassed by the Klan in the 1960s, when a cross was burned on the front lawn of his family home in Long Branch, on the Jersey shore.)

New Jersey has had a rich history of sensational crimes. Still unsolved are the Hall-Mills murders of 1922: Reverend Edward Hall was a charismatic Episcopal priest in New Brunswick, found dead with his married mistress Eleanor Mills, a singer in the church choir; Hall's wife and two brothers were tried for the murders but acquitted, in a trial that attracted rabid national media interest. Then there is the Lindberg kidnapping-murder of 1932—*The big-gest story since the Resurrection*, as H.L. Mencken dryly remarked. After a manhunt and a badly botched police investigation, the illegal German immigrant and ex-convict Bruno Richard Haupt-mann was tried, convicted, and executed for having kidnapped and murdered the twenty-month-old Lindberg baby, taken from his crib in the East Amwell country house of the Lindbergs, near Hopewell. (Though Hauptmann was found guilty, the case remains controversial among aficionados of high-profile crime.) In more recent years the "devoutly religious, family annihilator" John List accrued a high degree of notoriety by eluding police for eighteen years after murdering his mother, wife, and three children in 1971; and the charismatic Cherry Hill rabbi Fred Neulander was a tabloid sensation for having commissioned a hit on his wife Carol in 1994. (Neulander was found guilty of conspiring to murder his wife, following the testimony of the hired assassin.) But most New Jersey crime falls far below the radar of the tabloids, as most New Jersey citizens will never merit the hysterical attention accorded a resident celebrity like Charles Lindberg.

Of the contributors to *New Jersey Noir*, only Barry N. Malzberg and Bill Pronzini take on a "sensational" subject—the assassination of teamster president Jimmy Hoffa, who disappeared from public view in July 1975 and was declared officially dead seven years later. In Malzberg and Pronzini's first-person confession, "Meadowlands Spike," we learn that—possibly!—the late, not-much-lamented teamster boss has found a resting place in just the right corner of the Garden State.

Based upon an event out of New Jersey history, though much transformed by Bradford Morrow's gothic imagination, "The Enigma of Grover's Mill" evokes the notorious 1938 Hallowe'en broadcast by the young Orson Welles of H.G. Wells's terrifying *The War of the Worlds,* which Wells set in a fictitious "Grover's Mill, New Jersey" invaded by Martians—unfortunately, residents of Grover's Mill, New Jersey and vicinity, who heard the broadcast without realizing that it was fiction, panicked and tried to flee. Morrow makes of this serio-comic situation a suspenseful, mysterious, and finally poignant story of an orphaned young man coming of age in the generation following the Martian invasion. (If you visit Grover's Mill, which is not far from Princeton, you may want to take photographs of the ruin of a water tower allegedly shot to pieces by terrified local residents, mistaking it for a large Martian.)

Sexual/erotic allure, seduction, and betrayal, the very essence of *noir*, is depicted by Jonathan Santlofer with such finesse, in "Lola," that this cautionary tale set in a partly gentrified Hoboken will take the reader by surprise—as it takes the narrator by surprise. An eerie, unsettling variant on the theme is Sheila Kohler's "Wunderlich," which unfolds like one of the crueler Grimm's fairy tales, set in the quintessence of seemingly imperturbable Jersey suburbia, Montclair. The mysterious circumstances of a yet more complex betrayal are investigated in the painfully realistic Asbury Park of "Excavation" by Edmund White and Michael Carroll: significantly, the dreaded epiphany comes on a Hallowe'en night amid campy goth celebrants like a demented chorus in the final act of a tragedy.

Richard Burgin's sparely narrated quasi-minimalist evocation of a doomed relationship, "Atlantis," takes its lovers inevitably to Atlantic City to meet their fates; what is surprising is that, for all its grittiness, revealed with Burgin's characteristic blend of irony and sincerity, "Atlantis" is still a love story. Newark, synonymous in New Jersey with urban decay, financial collapse, and physical peril, is vividly rendered in two very different stories—S.J. Rozan's suspenseful "New Day Newark" (set in a ghetto neighborhood) with its unexpected ending, and S.A. Solomon's suspenseful "Live for Today" (set mostly in the county morgue). Though each story has a female protagonist at peril in her Newark environment, and each story is written by a woman, no two stories could be more unlike.

Betrayal that isn't sexual or erotic but related to more purely masculine *noir* activities like drug-dealing, theft, and murder is explored with exacting verisimilitude in Jeffrey Ford's surreal-seeming "Glass Eels" (Greenwich) with its stunning conclusion, as in Robert Arellano's "Kettle Run" (Cherry Hill) with its achingly convincing portrayal of teenaged and older "losers." Jersey City, a place of ethnic diversity as well as long-entrenched political corruption, is an ideal setting for Hirsh Sawhney's low-keyed pitch-perfect portrait of a middle-aged Indian American at the margins of an Indian community, "A Bag for Nicholas." (Nicholas is a Caucasian drug-user of the "local bourgeoisie" for whom Sawhney's sympathetic protagonist Shez seems to have ruined his life.)

The bleak and treacherous Camden of news headlines is the setting for Lou Manfredo's deftly written story of a young police officer whose moral courage is put to a crucial test in "Soul Anatomy"—as the historic Camden, in which our great American poet Walt Whitman lived, is the setting for Gerald Stern's elegiac poem "Broken Glass." (Again, no two excursions into a troubled New Jersey city could be more unlike.) Paul Muldoon's cleverly satirical poem "Noir, NJ" is set, nominally, in Paramus: the conventions/clichés of *noir* speed past us in the poet's tongue-in-cheek rhythms and rhymes, homage to the *noir* of pulp fiction and Hollywood B-films. By contrast, C.K. Williams's "Newark Black" is a passionate recollection of the poet's boyhood in the Newark of 1940–1954, an incantation of *blackness* in its myriad guises:

> *Black slush, after the blizzard had passed*
> *and the diesel buses and trucks were fuming again,*
> *but you still remembered how blackly lovely*
> *the branches of trees looked in new snow.*

Robert Pinsky's "Long Branch Underground" is a sequence of three-line stanzas evoking a lost boyhood at the Jersey shore—*Wheel of the tides, wheel of the surf, hot nights.* It's an elegy for *Carousel waltzes and polkas . . . The manic neon chicken in spasms dashing / Into the neon basket, and rising again.* Here is a *noir* world eerily depopulated, as if everyone has died.

Similarly lyric, dramatically compressed, and delivering a whiplash of a final line, Alicia Ostriker's "August: Feeding Frenzy" evokes the horrific image of life devouring life—in which "New

Jersey" is a microcosm of the vast pitiless Darwinian world that lies beyond our human conceptions even of *noir*—in the very presence of childhood innocence.

The mysteriously shunned (male, forty-six-year-old professor) protagonist of Jonathan Safran Foer's "Too Near Real" lives a numbed half-life simultaneously in Princeton and in Google's 3-D map in the aftermath of a scandal—(sexual harassment? resulting in the death of a female student?)—and the breakup of his marriage. In a moral paralysis, he travels widely—that is, inwardly, in "virtual" space—returning inevitably to his home where he seems to have discovered (*I went up to myself. It was me, but wasn't me. It was my body, but not me. I tilted the world*) the evidence of his own death, by suicide. And my own story, "Run Kiss Daddy," turns out to be, surprisingly, the only one in this highly diverse collection to be set in the beautiful western edge of the state along the Delaware River: a story in which "nothing happens"—in the aftermath of something very brutal that has happened in the past, of which the (male, divorced, wounded) protagonist dares not speak, for fear of ruining the precarious happiness of his new life.

In such ways, the most civilized and "decent" among us find that we are complicit with the most brutal murderers. We enter into literally unspeakable alliances—of which we dare not speak except through the obliquities and indirections of fiction, poetry, and visual art of the sort gathered here in *New Jersey Noir*.

Joyce Carol Oates
Princeton, New Jersey
July 2011

PART I

INNER-CITY NEW JERSEY

LIVE FOR TODAY

BY S.A. SOLOMON

University Heights (Newark)

E
n route to her job at the morgue, Jinx walked on JFK Boulevard to the PATH station at Journal Square. It was hot for June, the evening cloud cover an airless ceiling pressing on the street. A grimy storefront diorama displayed mannequins behind plate glass, girls with bald heads and painted-on lashes, clad in cheap, thin dresses. They stood frail against the hard gray light. Commuters hustled by, indifferent to the girls' orphaned gazes.

At the station, a man with a crew cut, his florid face glistening in the heat, watched her stride by in her work pants. He spit on the tracks.

"Walk like a woman," he said hoarsely.

The train arrived. She wedged into the car. Sweat trickled down the backs of her thighs. The train labored past boarded-up factories, fossils of a former manufacturing town, brick shells tagged with graffiti (*LIVE FOR TODAY*) that had migrated from the gentrifying precincts of Jersey City. A trash curd drifted by with the Passaic River, awakened by the recent heavy rains. The Pulaski Skyway reared up like a roller coaster against a steel sky. The kid next to her pointed it out to his younger friend, drawling, "Welcome to Newark, son. Try not to get shot."

She emerged to a garbage truck rounding the corner, gears grinding a hard-used complaint, its foul breath trapped in the day's heat. The Market Street bus trailed it past dollar stores and a recently vacated video rental/laundromat/dry cleaner (*Your One Stop Shop*), shut down for supplying certain regular customers with special-order baggies in the pockets of their indifferently pressed shirts. She hurried into the institutional building housing the morgue on Norfolk, but clocked in late.

Downstairs in the autopsy room with its overflow drains set into a tiled floor, Manny was waiting. His skin looked ashen in the watery light. As usual, he was stoned. The first job of the evening (*Manner of death: Accident. Cause of death: Acute drug intoxication*), a young white woman, lay on the gurney, flame-red hair curling all the way down to the circled A (for anarchy) tattooed atop her livid buttocks.

Manny's bloodshot eyes rolled in their sockets as he slid the body off the transport. The girl's doughy bottom succumbed to gravity and she spilled heavily into his arms.

Manny crooned at her, "*Qué linda.*"

"Give her here, Romeo."

"No, she's mine, see the way she looks at me?" He scrolled her eyelid with a practiced thumb. A hazel eye flashed at them.

"Cut it out, pig."

"Listen, you're already behind on yesterday's homicides. The way you moon over them, someone would think you're a little . . ." He stuck out his tongue, liverish in the morgue light, and twirled his finger over his head. "I mean if they didn't know already."

He propped the body on the prep table.

"Besides, the cooler's out again—we called for repairs but you gotta work faster, get me?"

It did smell riper than the usual ambient odor of decay, bearable (though a civilian might observe a preference for the stronger varieties of perfume and aftershave among the morgue workers, your musks and essential oils) until it reached the no-go level, tripping the gag reflex. Jinx bit her fingers in irritation, shredded cuticles inflamed from the latex gloves they wore to work with clients. *Clients* was how she referred to them, anyhow. It was respectful. She pinched her thumb and forefinger together and squinted in Manny's direction.

"What's up with that?" He wrinkled his forehead, usually smooth like a baby's blissful brow.

"It's the universal symbol for pot-smoking loser."

"Oh," he said in a mock hurt voice. "What you saying, you gonna narc on me? Damn, they should require it for this job."

But he knew her history and knew she wouldn't snitch.

"All right," he relented, "you can have her—but be ready for me at six a.m. sharp. I'm making my deliveries." He tapped her lightly on the back and she flinched. "Twitchy, huh? You need something to relax you?"

"Some of us are over that shit," she snapped.

"Some of us still got fingers left." He inspected her ragged hands. "You better double bag those, girl. You don't know what she tracked in, just because she's Anglo . . ."

She knew what he meant: white junkies like this one were pegged as middle-class, slumming bourgie kids, dumpster divers who observed the niceties of the needle exchange. It wasn't so much of a panic if a glove finger popped and bodily fluids leaked in (an occupational risk because of the soup of potential pathogens, hep C, and HIV, among other nasties).

"Who you talking to, Manny? Once a junkie, always a junkie. I know they're all fools."

He shrugged. "All right, *blanca*." He heaved the girl onto Jinx's table, nose wrinkling as a marshy gas escaped the body. "Whoo, she's all yours. Don't do anything I wouldn't do."

He rode the gurney through swinging doors into the fluorescent hallway.

As a morgue technician, her job was to prepare bodies for autopsy by the medical examiner and afterward clean and prep them for release to the funeral home, or, if there was no family (as was often the case in the county morgue), a pauper's burial. She also performed clerical tasks associated with the issuance of death certificates and the collection and tabulation of medical information related to the conduct of autopsies, and photographed and fingerprinted decedents upon admittance for verification of identity.

What Manny meant by "be ready for me" was for the report (with corroborating photos) to read: *White female, appears 25 years of age, measures 67 inches, weighs 150 pounds, hazel eyes, short red hair.*

What he wanted was a baggie filled with those luxurious waves of hair. If anyone (there was occasionally someone, family or a friend) noticed, well, what girl didn't cut off all of her daddy's pride at least once? It was a rite of passage. Manny had been in the hair trade for as long as she'd been here: shearing likely candidates and selling their crowning glory to wholesalers, who weren't so choosy about where they got it. Downstream, the chain of custody was even more lax. She'd seen the signs downtown: *We sell human hair.* She wondered what the customers for wigs and hair extensions would say if they knew their source.

Probably nothing. Like Manny always says: "All's fair in love and hair."

But lately Jinx had been resisting, making it harder for Manny to ply his wares. It wasn't scruples on her part, exactly, but something closer to possessiveness.

Manny, in high entrepreneurial mode, had already vacuumed, disrobing the body, sucking up any loose personal effects EMS had overlooked. She snapped on powdery gloves and the requisite face mask. The girl was surprisingly clean, except for the acrid drops of urine dewing her reddish pubic hair. Most of them had to be hosed down, were caked with the release that accompanied the terminal event.

Others, like the teenage male she had prepped last night (*Manner of death: Homicide. Cause of death: Gunshot wound, perforated heart. Box #53. Decedent's race: Black or African American*), were smeared with blood and lymph, as coated on departure as they were at birth. She could have fit a fist into the exit wound on his chest. She imagined being sucked down into it, drifting through his exploded ventricles. They would become intimate; he would share his secrets, his final thoughts.

The antiseptic stung her bitten fingers as she wiped down the redhead's freckled body. Kind of fat for a user; maybe a first timer. Lousy beginner's luck. She'd heard there was a bad batch on the street (once a junkie, always). She spotted a pinhole in the glove finger. Irritated at her carelessness, especially after Manny's lecture, she pulled at the glove to peel it off and her index finger burst through the split rubber, indenting a marbled thigh. At contact, a thrill coursed through her like she'd only ever known on the small end of a syringe.

Jinx shuffled backward, landing heavily on the one office chair they rolled from station to station to do the paperwork (the county had a terminal budget problem). She crashed into the cooler which lodged the morgue's transient populace. Her fingers flew to her mouth but, remembering, she spit them out. It's not fair, is it?—but life isn't fair—fighting the hunger so hard for so long and now here it is, back again to taunt her, like a sense memory. What's the message now: better off dead?

Maybe Manny's secondhand smoke had finally gotten to her. But weed never carried this hit, such extreme bliss she couldn't possibly contain it, not if she wanted to stay alive. Truth be told, that was a coin toss, weighed against the delirious acceleration to the roller-coaster emotion of childhood—the real deal, the hard stuff, not the mediated compromise that passed for it in adulthood—and the return of tears switched off somewhere in her teens.

There was the young girl, a Latina (*Decedent of Hispanic origin? Check yes, Box #52*) NPD phoned in last week from a domestic violence shelter, her wrists slashed. (*Manner of death: Suicide. Mechanism of death: Exsanguination. Other significant conditions contributing to death: Facial contusions, subdural hematoma. Box #36. If female: check if pregnant at time of death.*)

She had glanced at the report (*Age last birthday: 15*) and realized the girl's D.O.B. coincided with her actual or presumed date of death. She'd touched the plump hand with its girlish fingernail decals, and was tapped into a current of sorrow, of homesickness, of utter aloneness so intense it was hypoglycemic: the sweats, the shaking, the blurry vision.

Last Friday she was working rapidly, mask tight over nostrils, on the remains of an old man destined for potter's field, discovered in a trash-filled alley (*Manner of death: Could not be determined*). Eyes watering, she'd abruptly snapped out of a half dream where she stood on a ship's deck, watching the shore recede in a flutter of handkerchiefs. *God willing, when you get there, you'll make good and send for us?* The family had given him all their savings. *I will, Mama, Poppa, you'll see.*

She eyed the clock on the wall, its black hands standing at 12 disorienting her as if she were back in high school craving the bell. Midnight already. She wasn't hungry, but forced herself to rise. She had to eat something. She'd learned the hard way that the body's natural signals—hunger, thirst, tiredness—were quickly confounded with cravings in an addict's haywire nervous system.

In the cafeteria, Ruby was sitting with Manny, leaning in close in the way she had that made every exchange seem conspiratorial. Jinx saw her lipsticked orange mouth twist as she approached. Manny was saying, "Jinx got a beauty on the slab, red hair to die for."

"But it's one of her babies—you know how she gets, like a bitch with her pups." Ruby smirked. "Whatsa matter, Jinx, you look like you saw a corpse," she said, laughing with a smoker's musical wheeze, a cloud of Tabu emanating from her. "Lighten up, sourpuss. Business is business, that's all, and you make it hard to do."

Jinx thought that Ruby could do with a wig herself. Her hair was in the terminal stages of bleaching, twig dry, burnt-yellow—a suicide blond.

They used to get along fine. Ruby had been her defender at the beginning, when she started working here. The other techs had sniped that she had no sense of humor, was as dull as dishwater. She supposed they were right: to this day she failed to see the joke in humiliating the newly dead with plastic pumpkins and witch hats for the annual (unofficial, after-hours) Halloween party. There was a family that time, and the county had paid a hefty sum to settle the matter. The ringleaders were fired and the others had it out for Jinx, convinced she was the rat. Ruby had tartly reminded them that it was in their job description to demonstrate a mature and respectful approach to the decedents and told them to shut their traps. They complied: you didn't mess with Ruby if you wanted to keep your job. She'd worked here forever and had the M.E.'s ear.

Anyway, that was how Jinx came by her nickname.

She ignored Ruby, wrinkling her nose at Manny's plate. "Mystery meat?"

"Quit it, Jinx," Manny shrieked, "you know I'm a vegan! It's seitan."

"Satan is right," Ruby cackled.

Jinx unwrapped her lunch, turkey roll on whole wheat bread and an orange. She ate the same thing every night. She applied this approach to her wardrobe (desert boots, Dickies, long-sleeved Ts) and apartment decor (early Sears). It was one less meaningless decision to sap her energy from the struggle.

Ruby skewered the sandwich with a curved, butterscotch-lacquered nail. She worked upstairs in processing; those tips would never survive a night in the trenches. Jinx, flushing, forced down an urge to slap her. She pushed at Ruby's fleshy forearm, feeling it tense. She glanced up without thinking, met the woman's inquisitive eyes, and looked down. Once, new on the job and reluctant to return to an empty apartment, she'd joined the crew for a few drinks, waking to find Ruby in her late-afternoon bed, preening like a ruffian alley cat. It was an episode she didn't want to repeat. She concentrated on her sandwich.

Manny, studying job postings on the employee bulletin board, said suddenly, "I don't even know if it's worth it anymore. Synthetic hair is getting too much like the real thing. I'm thinking about taking the F.T. training." Forensic technicians were a cut above them in the medical examiner ranks and were on call to investigate suspicious deaths.

"They work like dogs, Manny," Jinx said.

"Yeah, but they make great overtime," Ruby pointed out.

"Not to mention the other perks," he said.

Other perks? Jinx imagined Manny presiding in stoner's time over her frail charges, their innards barely cooled to a ceasefire, body cavities yawning for harvest, the extracted organs, tissue, flesh, and bones packed into coolers, destined for the lucrative black market. Her throat spasmed and a bitter reflux filled her mouth.

Manny said, "They can work from home; they don't have to clock in every day. They get pagers. And a van."

"Haw!" Ruby exclaimed, setting off a coughing fit. They waited. She wiped her mouth. "When it's running."

"I gotta go." Jinx stood up.

"Yeah," Ruby smirked, "me too. I got all that F.T. overtime to write up. You be good, sweet cheeks. You too, Satan." She swayed away on pumps with worn heels.

"You okay?" Manny asked her, around the gluten chunk he was chewing.

"I just need to lie down for a minute."

"Don't worry, I'll cover those gang hits from last night," he offered.

"Thanks."

The women's lounge was an industrial orange. The flickering light triggered a visual halo that meant the onset of a migraine. Her scalp tingled and burned. She closed her eyes, tried to practice the relaxation techniques they talked about in rehab. You picked a happy memory and reinhabited it, shutting out everything else. The pleasant associations were supposed to trigger the good brain chemicals, the ones the drugs had sucked out. She pictured napping in a hammock under the sun, birds singing, feeling utterly at peace. She wondered if invented memories counted and the image vanished.

As in her recurrent childhood riddle, she tried to picture being dead: floating disembodied over the earth hurtling along without her, but she is no longer she and so cannot be thinking this, or anything at all; she is dead, absent, the world with its hurt and clamor gone ahead without her. Yes. By the time her clients reached her, they were quiet, they were satiated. Those who came to her came from tragedy or neglect: the murdered, the unlucky, the abandoned—but they were past all that now, weren't they? If they found their way to her, they were reportable cases: sudden or unexpected deaths, unnatural deaths, deaths of public health interest (anthrax, tuberculosis), deaths from suspected criminal violence or neglect, car wrecks, suicides, overdoses, poisonings, deaths occurring in police custody, in jails, shelters, or other public institutions. She was their last witness: the one whose words would be the final proof of their existence. She owed it to them to be accurate.

She was familiar with abandonment. Her parents, for instance, who had disappeared while driving home from a sales convention on Miami Beach. Her father had been a rep for a hosiery company, her mom a retired "dancer" (which Jinx learned only later meant stripper) he'd met and fallen for in Atlantic City. They loved the road and took the kids along in her dad's old Cadillac that he'd bought from his boss, with its pillowy headrests and plush upholstery, whenever they could.

When her parents left on their last trip, she was nine, and her brother Hal, six. They were staying with their aunt and uncle because it was a school week and anyway her mom said this trip was for grown-ups. The wives and girlfriends shopped on Lincoln Road during the sales meetings and when the men were done with business the couples hit the nightspots at the hotels on Collins Avenue. The day of their parents' expected return came and went with no word from them. Aunt Rae said with forced cheer that the trip was taking a little longer than expected but their mom and dad would be back soon and meanwhile it would be fun! They could go to the shore, never mind that it was a school day. She muttered then, *Why don't they call?* and Hal started to cry and their aunt said sharply, *Janice, you're a big girl now, set a good example, don't upset your brother.* At least when the police showed up the charade was over. The Florida Highway Patrol thought they'd been carjacked at the I-95 rest stop just north of St. Augustine by an escaped convict from the state pen in Raiford. Back in their New Jersey town, curious neighbors stood on the sidewalk and spouted off for the news cameras. Then the excitement died down and there was just the waiting.

At least she'd waited, her overnight bag packed with clean socks and underwear, a toothbrush, pajamas. In school, each time a hall monitor came into the classroom, she thought she'd be called to the office where they would be waiting: Roy in his blue windbreaker and aviator sunglasses, Charlene in her favorite flowered driving scarf. As she grew older, as her body changed, they did not. She, approaching her mother's age, would be her best friend; they would share their secrets. It took her a long time to admit to herself that they weren't coming back. In her mind's eye they were still at that rest stop where they were last seen, giggling like teenagers over Orange Juliuses.

She had convinced herself that it was a test: if no one was waiting, how would they know to return? Sometimes she wondered if they had really existed or if she'd invented them. Absent a body, where was the proof of a life? Some paperwork, the memory others had of you. Both were easily manipulated.

Hal was grown now, a lawyer, married with two kids. He was weary of Janice's soap opera, as he called it. Life is pretty simple when you don't have many choices, he would explain to her as if she were the younger sister. You have two: you can make it hard on yourself or make it easy. You decide. Hal's wife, who was in charge of medical records at the county hospital, had found Jinx this job.

She couldn't fault them, but still managed to sabotage their good turns. And Hal was always there to bail her out, like the time he got her a job as a secretary at his law firm in Newark. Her first week she was inadvertently interrupted in a bathroom stall, finishing off a fix. It was a Friday night, after all: payday. She could still see the shock mixed with fear on the face of the pretty little law clerk who'd walked in on her. There had been a moment of complete recognition—it was this fear that kept people respectable, that maintained the thin line between order and chaos. When you lost that, there was nothing left to lose. She'd felt sorrier for the girl, still clinging to her illusions, than for herself.

Later, though, she felt remorse, when she heard Hal in his mild voice saying he'd found a clinic for her and would foot the bill. "Try to make it easy on yourself this time, okay, Janice?" She saw the little boy screaming in the supermarket parking lot one hot, airless August day, "We do so have a mommy and daddy," waving frantically at their aunt and uncle, now their legal guardians, as they walked to the car with the week's groceries. "Shut up, Jan, you don't know what you're talking about, you're so stupid," his words breaking into hungry gulps of air, nostrils whinnying with the effort. Aunt Rae, alarmed at the shouting, had turned and looked accusingly at her, rushed over with Hal's atomizer, and, smoothing away hair plastered with sweat on his forehead, helped him breathe.

Jinx raised herself heavily from the couch, its plastic cover detaching reluctantly from her clammy skin. Her head ached. She caught a glimpse of herself in the mirror, wan face, dark circles under her eyes, her own hair dull as dishwater blond, cropped short. Downstairs, the client waited on her work table. Jinx decided to finish her quickly and give Manny the goods. She'd let the others do what they had to do to get by, stop being the pathetic champion of the dead.

Don't think too much—it's not what they pay you for. Snap on fresh gloves. Dispatch digitals and prints. Dress her in a gown of institutional cotton, shorn of her mortal glory. So young for it all to be over, disembodied. But she is at peace now, whatever drove her to the nod behind her, the hunger past.

Request one last favor before she departs on this, her last earthly journey: *Tell me my destiny, I'll tell you yours.* The Amazing Jinx who after close study could read the hieroglyphics of the body: its scars, bruises, lumps, ground-down teeth, stretch marks, wrinkles. They played dumb, these dead; they struggled to keep their secrets. But their champion, their confessor, shepherd of the poor wrecked vessels, will show you lives lived with their attendant pain and occasional distraction, step right up for the sinking in of flesh and the gaseous stink forecasting your corruption, watch in dread while memory, your only weapon, fails you.

With a gloved hand, she stroked the girl's red tresses, pulling a metal comb through the unruly mass. Static electricity jolted the hair, attracting it to her gloves where it clung as if living. She took up the scissors with one hand and gathered the hair in the other, pulling it for the cut. The girl's chin lifted as she sheared the coppery coil and Jinx saw it then, the puncture in the skin over the jugular. It was the vein of last resort: only the hardcore mainlined there. The blood had stopped running to her hand where the hair bound it. Without thinking, she freed it and pulled out the forensic technician's preliminary epitaph from its plastic folder. (*Manner of death: Accident. Cause of death: Acute drug intoxication.*) She turned back to the girl, inspecting the usual points of entry, but saw none of the telltale marks on her arms or legs. A careless auditor of souls, the forensic tech, overworked, jaded, shuttling from one wretched ending to the next. This was no accidental overdose: it was homicide.

Jinx took the dead girl's hands in her own and leaned down as if to comfort her. She swore she felt a flutter of air, heard a whisper:

He wrapped my hair in his fist yanked my mouth to his crotch

"act like a woman cunt" when he finished he stuck a needle in
me have a nice ride he said I am going now I promised my mom
I wouldn't be late she always said I'll be late to my own—

She fumbled for the report. She could still catch the assistant
M.E. on duty—they could do a DNA swab, find the fucker who
did this to her before he could do somebody else. And it would be
Jinx who cracked the case—who saw that there was a case, that
the redhead wasn't just another junkie but someone's daughter
done horribly wrong.

Voices echoing down the hallway woke her from her reverie,
the click of pumps and a whiff of Tabu signaling that Ruby was
escorting identifying next of kin to the small waiting room. They
would have questions, might object to the autopsy, would be told
that their consent was not required, but that the procedure would
not delay the funeral arrangements or prevent an open-casket
viewing. The digital photo of the redhead with her flowing tresses
would be up on the computer for the grieving family, unless they
insisted on seeing their loved one beforehand. Which they apparently had, as Manny, hustling in to warn her, found her stuffing
hair into a Ziploc bag, most of it spilling onto the floor in a spray of
red like a salon massacre.

Later—after it was all over, out of work again (Ruby's shrug
tinged with unmistakable morning-after malice telling Jinx that
she couldn't expect her to save her ass this time, could she, sweet
cheeks?), a wheel click away from the drop and anticipating relief
(*LIVE FOR TODAY* inked like a tattoo on a glassine envelope)—
she walked to the train, the dawn rain running down her face passing for tears.

SOUL ANATOMY

BY LOU MANFREDO

Whitman Park (Camden)

I n certain places there exists a permeating pointlessness to life, with an aura of despair so acute that its inhabitants come to be unafraid of or, at the very least, indifferent to the inevitability of death. Camden City is just such a place.

Camden is a torn-down, ravished ghost of a city, blighted by poverty and corruption, violence, drugs, and disease. Its residents wallow amidst the decay which lies like a sickened, dying animal prostrate in the sun's heat.

Within this city, in stark and ironic contrast, the modern glass and steel complex of Cooper University Hospital rises awash in bright, artificial light, a towering monument to mainstream mankind's fierce desire to live. The hospital exists on sprawling acres of urban renewal, restored row houses lining its borders, a false oasis of promise in a true desert of desperation.

Frank Cash, senior partner of the distinguished Haddonfield law firm of Cash, Collings and Haver, slowly turned his shiny new BMW into the hospital's enclosed parking garage. He stopped just short of the barrier arm as the dashboard digital flickered: 4:01 a.m.

As the driver's window lowered silently, a cold dampness from the dark November morning intruded into the car's warm interior. Cash shuddered slightly against it, reaching a hand to the automated ticket machine and pressing a manicured finger against the glowing green button. He frowned unconsciously at the cheerful computer-generated male voice which accompanied the dispensed parking stub.

"Welcome to the Cooper University Hospital parking facility."

Tucking the stub into his pocket, Cash swung the car left and accelerated quickly up the smooth concrete ramp of the nearly deserted garage. It occurred to him that perhaps it would have been more prudent to use the family minivan as opposed to his 750. He noted a small cluster of parked vehicles at level two, centered around the elevator bank. He parked quickly and strode to an elevator.

Ten minutes later he stood facing a window in a small consultation area located within the emergency room. He gazed out across Haddon Avenue and eyed a squat building in the near distance. Emblazoned across the top, the words *Camden Police Department* gave fair warning to anyone in and around the hospital to behave themselves. Cooper had been as effectively isolated from the surrounding city as possible, Interstate 676 and parkland to the east, police headquarters to the north, renovated housing used as residences for hospital staff and medical offices to the south and west.

It had been a rather profitable project, Cash mused as he scanned the scene, absentmindedly scraping a bit of soot from the sill before him, sleep stinging his eyes. Quite profitable.

As he waited, Cash's thoughts returned to the events of last evening: the quiet dinner with family in his sprawling Victorian home in Moorestown, some reading, the late-night news, sleep, and then the phone call.

"Hello?" he had whispered into the mouthpiece, glancing to his sleeping wife as she gently stirred beside him.

"Mr. Cash?" a tentative voice had begun. "It's Ken, sir, Ken Barrows."

Jesus Christ, Cash had thought, what could the most junior member of the firm possibly want at this hour? "What the hell, Barrows, it's almost three-thirty in the morning."

"Yes sir, I realize that. It's just that . . . well, I'm on call tonight. For the FOP, you know, the police union. It's my week to be on call."

Cash frowned into the mouthpiece, again glancing to his wife. She seemed resettled, her nightly sleeping pill working its wonder.

"And?" Cash asked harshly.

Barrows paused for a moment, perhaps suddenly rethinking the wisdom of the call. "There's been a shooting, sir. A fatal police shooting. One person is dead, but no police were injured. The union rep called me from the scene a few minutes ago. He wants me down there."

Cash's frown turned to a scowl. "Of course he does, Barrows. That's the purpose of having a lawyer on call twenty-four-seven. It's mandatory when you represent the unions. But why in God's name did you feel it necessary to—"

"I thought you'd want to know, sir," Barrows interrupted, a new confidence in his tone. "You see, the shooting was in Camden City. It was a white officer, the dead man is black. And the officer involved, the one who shot the perpetrator, was . . . it was that new officer." He paused here for effect. Barrows, despite his youth, was a good lawyer. "It was Anthony Miles." Another slight pause. "I thought it best you knew, sir. Of course, I can handle it if you'd like . . . but I thought you should know."

Now Cash sat upright, indifferent to whether or not the movement would further disturb his wife. "Oh," he said, his mind shifting sharply from disgruntled employer to defensive lawyer. "Oh," he repeated.

After a brief silence, he spoke again. "Call the union rep at the scene. Tell him to put Miles into a radio car and get him over to Cooper a.s.a.p. I'll call ahead and get hold of whoever is in charge of the emergency room. I want Miles sedated. Tell the union rep to convince the kid that he's stressed out and needs to see a doctor. Once the doctors get a drug into him, the law says he can't be interviewed. It'll buy us some time. I can be at the hospital in less than thirty minutes."

"Yes sir, I'll call the rep. Shall I meet you there?"

Cash considered it. "No. Just make sure the rep gets Miles

to the ER immediately. I'll grease the wheels. I don't want some intern refusing to sedate."

"Yes sir," Barrows said, his confidence even stronger now.

"You were right to call, Ken. It shows good presence of mind."

"Thank you, sir. I thought you should know."

Cash slipped out of bed, shaving and dressing quickly. He left a note for his wife and drove to Route 38, leaving the lush, manicured splendor of Moorestown for a twenty-minute drive to the desolate wasteland of Camden City. As the BMW cut rapidly through misty darkness, Cash thought about police officer Anthony Miles.

Miles had gone directly to the Camden Police Department after graduating the County Police Academy. Like all rookies, he had been assigned to routine patrol duty with a senior training officer. In most such cases, no one in any remotely influential position would have cause to notice or care.

But Miles was different. Miles was the son of Curtis Miles, United States Attorney to the State of New Jersey. The *Republican* United States Attorney.

And Camden was ground zero for the Democratic machine that had maintained a strong and lucrative hold on New Jersey politics for more than two decades. Frank Cash, himself the son of a former county chairman, had lined his pockets and filled the coffers of his law firm with countless contracts, retainers, and fees financed with state and county tax dollars. Indeed, his firm's representation of every police union in South Jersey was merely one such plum.

So when Cash sat down to lunch some months earlier with the current county chairman, the implications had not been lost on him.

Officer Miles, the chairman had suggested, was no ordinary rookie. His father was an ambitious, driven man who had chosen a pragmatic approach to what he hoped would be an unlimited political future: he would dedicate himself to fighting corruption in New Jersey—particularly Democratic corruption.

"Like shooting fish in a barrel," the chairman said between forkfuls of shrimp. "If he's serious about it."

"Is he?" Cash asked.

The chairman laid down his fork, then patted his lips gently with a linen napkin.

"Yes, he is—it's his ticket to the governor's office."

Cash considered it. "What's our exposure?"

The chairman shrugged. "Any is too much. This young cop has his own political juice, courtesy of his old man. If becoming a cop was all he really wanted, his father could have gotten him assigned to bikini patrol in some shore town or crabgrass stakeout in our neck of the woods. Why would he want to go to Camden?"

"Maybe," Cash offered with little conviction, "he just wants to be a *real* cop."

"Yeah," the chairman said, reaching once more for his fork. "And I'm Harry-fuckin'-Truman." He leaned in across the table, speaking more softly. Cash had to strain his ears to make out the words. "Camden has about twenty-three hundred violent crimes per hundred thou population, compared to the national average of about four hundred fifty. It's been named the most dangerous city in the entire country time after time. The state had to take over the entire police department and school system because they're so fucked up. Tell me, why would the son of Curtis Miles, the guy who wants to be governor, maybe president someday, want to work in Camden? The kid's a Rider University graduate, for Christ's sake." The chairman sat back. "He's a fuckin' plant for his old man. You have any idea what motivated and hostile eyes can find in that environment?"

Cash sipped his wine before responding. "So you figure his father for a white knight sending his kid in to help?"

The chairman laughed. "White knight my ass. He's no better than anybody else. He's already greased some wheels for his son. The kid isn't on the job six months, and he's assigned to HIDTA already. The *worst* fuckin' place for him, far as we're concerned.

No, Curtis Miles is no white knight. He's just so ambitious he's willing to throw his own son into the fire to help get him what he needs to nail Democrats."

Cash shook his head. "We've chosen a nasty business for ourselves."

"Yes. And that kid working High Intensity Drug Trafficking Areas can turn things even nastier."

"Why are you telling me all this?"

The chairman shrugged. "You're the union lawyer. Sooner or later, this kid will most likely wind up in your lap. I want you to understand what you'll be dealing with. I haven't survived in this shit all these years without learning to anticipate."

Cash drained his wine glass and reached for the bottle. "I understand."

Now, forty minutes after leaving his bed, Frank Cash stared out the hospital window into the Camden night and sighed. He remembered long-ago advice from his politician father. *There are winners and losers. Be a winner. It makes life bearable.*

He turned as the door to the small consultation room opened. It was the union representative, Peter Negron.

"Hello, Pete."

The man entered the room and closed the door softly behind him. "Hello, Mr. Cash. I didn't figure you'd come down personally."

"Yes, well, I have. Has Miles been sedated?"

"Yeah, the chief resident saw him soon as we got here. They jacked the kid up on Xanax. Five minutes later, two spooks from the county prosecutor's office showed up. I told 'em the kid was medicated and couldn't talk to them . . . They left, said they'd see him tomorrow. They seemed pissed off."

Cash grunted. "They'll get over it. We needed to buy some time so I can get a handle on this."

Negron nodded. "Okay. I was with Miles when the shooting

went down. We were workin' HIDTA citywide, me and Miles and Sanchez."

"Where'd it happen?"

"Line Street, between South 6th and Roberts."

"Tell me what happened."

When Negron finished, Cash ran a hand through his hair thoughtfully. "Sounds pretty clean," he said. Then pointedly added, "*If* that's how it went down."

Negron smiled and raised his right hand. "I swear on my eyes, counselor, I ain't dumb enough to lie to the lawyer. 'Specially for this kid."

With their eyes locked, Cash nodded. "Go get him. Bring him to me."

Negron turned and left.

When Miles entered the room, Cash was immediately stricken by his youthful appearance. Although twenty-two, he looked seventeen. His black hair was long, unkempt. It spilled over the collar of the faded navy peacoat he wore. Dried vomit stained the front panel of the coat, its sour odor touching at Cash's nostrils. Dark blood was splattered across the left cuff and forearm. The young man's eyes were hollow and listless. A stubble of light whiskers covered his chin and cheeks, giving him a dirty, unpleasant look. While the clothing and grooming fit well with Miles's antinarcotic assignment, he seemed a little too comfortable in the outfit. Cash found a mild disliking begin to dawn.

"Have a seat, Miles," he said, and watched as the cop slid a chair back from the small, round table. Cash sat opposite him, folding his hands on the smooth plastic tabletop. How much bad news, he wondered, had been discussed in this very same room?

"All right," he said as Miles's eyes lifted to meet his own. "My name is Frank Cash. My law firm represents members of the local chapter of your union, the Fraternal Order of Police. I'm here to help you deal with all this."

Cash saw Miles's gaze fall away, dropping to the tabletop, his body shaking with a sudden chill. His appearance seemed to suddenly morph into that of a frightened boy caught in some youthful transgression and summoned to his father's study. Cash found his initial suspicions and dislike begin to waver. In all his fifty-one years, he had never taken a life, not even that of a small animal or rodent. And here was this boy, barely out of school, who had violently sent a man to hell in what surely must have been a horrifying, desperate moment.

"All right," Cash repeated, gentler this time, softer. "State, county, and city headhunters will be hounding you tomorrow, son. I need you to tell me what happened, *everything*, every detail. Get it straight in your head. Let's see where I can help. Just start from the beginning and go slowly. Tell me everything, even if it doesn't sound very good. It'll sound worse said cold tomorrow, believe me."

Miles raised his eyes. "Negron said he told you everything already."

Cash nodded. "Yes. He told me what *he* did and what he *thinks* he saw. I need *you* to tell me what you did. What you saw."

Miles's eyes filled with tears. "Yes. I understand."

The young policeman shifted himself in his seat, fixed an unblinking stare at the darkened window behind Cash, and began to tell his story.

"We were on patrol, the three of us, me in the front recorder seat, Negron driving, Sanchez in back behind me. It musta been about two in the morning. We were cruising known drug locales; just eyeballing. Cold, crappy night like this, most of the deals were going down indoors. Anyway, we wind up on Line Street, heading east, just rolling past the broken-down houses along there."

"Where is Line Street?" Cash asked.

Miles shrugged. "'Bout six, seven blocks south of here, just east of Broadway."

"What neighborhood is that?"

Another shrug. "I don't know. Whitman Park, I guess."

"Go on."

"So we're just rolling along, real slow—maybe ten, fifteen tops. The street is narrow, a few parked cars here and there, some just abandoned. So we cross South 6th Street heading toward Roberts. Northwest corner of Line and 6th is an empty lot where some condemned buildings got demoed. There's a fence around it, chainlink. Even though we're kinda looking around as we roll, none of us saw this old lady till she was right in front of us, like she just appeared out of the dark, you know? Negron almost ran her over. Well, she makes us for cops and starts banging on the hood of the car and screaming at us."

"Was she black? Hispanic, Caucasian, what?"

Miles glanced briefly at Cash. "Hispanic." He paused for a moment before continuing. "Anyway, she's all excited, so Sanchez gets out of the backseat and approaches her. He tins her and starts talking in Spanish, and she starts bawling and pointing to the only house on the north side of Line Street that's still standing. It was the house she had come out of."

"Had you seen her come out of it?"

"No, like one second the street was empty, the next second there she was, in front of the car." Cash noticed the trembling begin to intensify, apparently overcoming the dosage of Xanax the cop had received. When Miles spoke again, there was a rise of pitch in his voice. "So anyway, I get out of the car and Sanchez winks at me and makes a face, like he's saying, *Look at this old bitch, do you believe this?*"

"How old would you say she was?"

Miles shifted in his seat and leaned forward slightly, still directing his words at the black rectangle of the window. "Old. Pushing sixty. I don't know."

Cash smiled slightly. "Go on."

"So when I reach them, she starts speaking English, telling us there's a black guy up on the second floor of the house, been acting crazy all night, people coming and going and she was trying to sleep and told him something and he cursed her and tried to hit her, and she got scared and ran out and saw us. So by now, Negron is standing there too, and he asks her if she called the cops. She says no, there's no phone in the house, no water, no electricity, nothing. We can see it's boarded up, abandoned, and we figure her for a squatter. She tells us the black guy deals H, sometimes crack, the building is his base, everybody is afraid of him and all this kind of shit. So Sanchez starts writing it down, you know, to sort of appease her a little. We figure maybe she's stoned, you know, old and stoned and half nuts. So then Negron says he feels like a little action, let's check it out. Well, I'm a little bored myself, it was a slow tour and I figure, what the hell. So Sanchez stays at the car with the old lady to call in our ten-twenty. Me and Negron start walking toward the house."

"Describe the house."

"Two-story brick, like all of them around there. Most of the windows boarded up. There was a narrow, covered front porch with side steps leading up to it. The front door was missing, it was just a dark open hole. The east side of the house was just like the west, another empty lot."

"All right. Go on."

"Well, me and Negron get to the house and I walk around the porch to the side steps. Just as I reach them, I hear Negron cursing. He stepped in dog shit. At least he *hoped* it was dog shit. The place really stinks—piss, garbage, shit, everything. The nearest street-light is burned out, it's dark as hell . . ."

Now Miles's body seemed to tighten on itself, the trembling turning sharply into a steady shake. He tried desperately to moisten his mouth before speaking again.

"So, I'm laughing at Negron, he's wiping his shoe on the edge of the porch. I start up the steps."

"How many steps?"

"Four, maybe five."

"Where's your gun at this point?"

"Well, I have two guns on me. My Glock is in a belt holster

under my coat, and a .38 revolver is in the right coat pocket."

"Both regulation sidearms?"

"Yeah."

"Is your coat open or buttoned up?"

"Open. You know, it was warm inside the car, so it's open."

Cash glanced at the now tightly closed coat, the warmth of the room unable to reach Miles's chill. "Go on."

"The old lady told us this guy didn't have a weapon, none that she saw, anyway. We figured it for a dispute between two homeless squatters, we'd check it out and then leave. So while Negron is still scraping shit off his shoe, I go up maybe two, three steps and I hear something coming from inside the doorway."

"What did you hear?"

Miles's shoulders twitched and his right hand jerked out of his lap, fisting. "A sharp double metallic click. Like a weapon being locked and loaded. Negron heard it too. He said, *Fuck!* and I saw him duck in front of the porch and go for his gun. I just stood there, frozen."

Cash sat back in his seat, eyeing the young, trembling cop. "Go on," he said softly.

"All of a sudden this guy, this enormous fuckin' guy, is right there, right in the doorway, maybe eight, nine feet away from me. A huge, crazy-looking guy, and he's got a fuckin' rifle in his hands. A *rifle!*"

The words were pouring out now, and Cash held his questions. Let him spit it out, get it all out and over with. The details, actual or invented, could wait.

"I almost peed myself. I mean, this guy looked like a real maniac, sweating, cursing to himself, stepping out onto the porch and swinging that rifle back and forth." Miles spasmed slightly. He took a deep breath, held it briefly, then continued. "So I say, *Hey*, you know, like a fuckin' idiot, and the guy zeroes in on me, he don't hesitate for a second. I'm telling you he was *crazy*, and he starts yelling at me, something about his old lady, about his kid, something like that, and he's pointing the rifle at me and I know he's gonna kill me, and I've got my left hand on the banister, you know, I was climbing the stairs, and so I push myself backward. I don't know what the fuck I'm doing, just throwing myself down the stairs. Then I hear this tremendous explosion and there's a giant flash of light and I'm rolling down the stairs into the dirt, and Jesus Christ, I swear I did pee myself. I mean, I felt it, you know, the warm piss in my pants. I thought it was blood, I thought I was shot. Mr. Cash, I swear to God, I don't remember taking it out, but my .38 was in my hands and I'm pointing it at the guy and he's swinging his aim over toward Negron who's down behind the front of the porch yellin' something about us being cops and the guy starts screamin' he's gonna kill us and he swings the rifle back at me, right at my fuckin' chest, and he jacks another round into the chamber and my gun goes off and the guy just blinks like bullets can't hurt him, and so I figure I missed. Then he fires again and I think I'm hit again, I'm going to die, and I start firing over and over. The last shot I see his shirt, he's wearing a T-shirt, and I swear to God I see the shirt tear. It's like slow motion. The shirt gets pushed in, like somebody poked him with a pencil or something, and then it pops out, out of the hole in his chest, and it's torn, you know, the shirt is torn and it's red with blood, and it just popped in, then out of his chest. Blood sprayed out of the hole— some of it hit me. It was like slow motion. Then he falls down, sits down actually. Negron goes rushing past me. The guy drops the rifle and it slides down the steps and Negron, he's all red and excited and he sticks his Glock in the guy's face and says, *You son of a bitch*, and the guy just plops onto his back and his head hits the porch, and that's it. That was it."

Cash let a few moments elapse before asking, "Would you like some water or something? Coffee? Maybe the doctor can give you something more to relax you."

"No sir. No." Tears welled in Miles's eyes, and he wiped them quickly away. He sighed and looked down at the floor, his right leg shaking, anger and shame weighing heavily on him. The tears welled again, and Cash rose and turned to face the window, his back to the young man. Uneasy moments passed before he sat down again and spoke.

"What happened next?"

Miles shook his head clear. His voice was low, flat. "Sanchez came up and started running his hand over me. You know, I was down on the ground, the guy had fired right at me, so Sanchez figured I was hit. He kept saying, *Holy Christ, are you okay, are you okay?* I stood up. Sanchez took the gun out of my hand and put it in my pocket. We just stood there looking at each other. Then Negron said, *Come on,* and he ran into the house. There coulda been a second perp, we had to clear the place, so me and Sanchez followed him."

"Did you look at the body?"

"No."

"Go on."

"The old lady told us the guy's room was on the second floor. We went up. It was very dark. Then we saw an old kerosene lamp in what we figured was the guy's room, that was the only light. Negron and Sanchez went in. That's where they found the heroin on a small table against the wall. I just sorta wandered into the bathroom. And for the first time in my life, my mind was a total blank. I wasn't even thinking, *Hey, you're not thinking about anything.* It was just completely blank, empty. I had a pencil flash in my pocket. I took it out and turned it on. That's when I saw myself in the old mirror, in the bathroom, you know, and I started . . . I started crying. But it was crazy, like I was crying for no reason, because my mind was blank, totally blank. I was just looking at my reflection, then I started shaking like a leaf and threw up in the sink. Just like that, I puked, and I felt so embarrassed. Negron came into the bathroom, he had his light on too. I don't know what he was saying, I felt so ashamed, and then he just went away and I was alone. I shut the door. I wanted to wash out the sink, clean myself up,

but there was no running water. I didn't want to leave the bathroom. I was *embarrassed*." Miles shook his head slightly. "Then it
dawned on me, what the hell, I did my job, I've got no reason to
be ashamed. Then, all of a sudden, I got real hostile . . . like I was
thinking, *Fuck everybody, fuck them*. It was stupid, I guess."

Cash didn't comment. Instead, he asked, "What happened
next?"

"Sanchez came in, didn't knock or anything, just opened the
door and walked in. He said he was going to seal the building
and call for the detectives. I think that's when he told me they
had found some crack too, I don't remember for sure. Anyway, I
walked out of the bathroom. There were uniformed cops everywhere. Sanchez had put out a *Shots fired—ten-thirteen*. I wandered
off, went downstairs. Some neighborhood people were standing
outside the house, a little crowd of them. I guess the radio cars
woke 'em up. It was very weird, this deserted street all of a sudden
with this crowd . . . They looked like . . . like zombies or something.
Like it was Hallowe'en. They were talking and looking at the dead
body and having a good time. I think some of them made me for
the cop who shot the guy. I got some dirty looks, you know, and
some mumbles. Most of them didn't seem to care much, though.
One old guy wanted to shake my hand, told me there were a few
others around needed killing."

"Where was the woman who started the whole thing?" Cash
asked.

"Some uniform was holding her in a black-and-white, waiting
for the detectives. Anyway, I went to look at the body. You know
. . ." He shrugged and let his voice trail off.

"You said the people were looking at the *dead* body. How'd you
know it was dead?"

This seemed to stun Miles. "I just figured. I don't know, he
looked dead."

"You said before you hadn't yet looked at the body, so how'd
you know it looked dead?"

Miles did not respond. Instead he seemed puzzled, confused.

Cash said softly, "Listen, Anthony, I'm only asking you what others will ask. And you have to provide the right answers. Just off the top of my head, you had better polish up your demeanor and change some terminology about certain things when you're speaking to the investigators. And you need to make eye contact with them, not stare out the window like somebody reciting Hamlet's soliloquy. You can't say you responded to the call because Negron wanted 'action' or because you were 'bored.' You can't say you didn't know what you were doing when you threw yourself down the stairs, you can't say you don't know how your weapon got into your hand. You can't say you felt hostile or pissed off. Look, I'm not trying to put words in your mouth, Anthony, but you need a tighter version, a neat, professional version. You took the call because the woman made an official complaint, you defensively threw yourself out of the way of the first shot, you drew your weapon, and after Negron's shouted identification as police officers and the perpetrator's second shot, you fired that weapon. Your gun just didn't 'go off,' you fired in defense of your life and the life of your partners. Now I'll ask you again, how'd you know the man was dead before you looked at the body?"

Miles was sweating heavily at this point and at last opened his coat. He shifted in his seat and looked into the lawyer's eyes. "I knew he was dead because . . . because Negron had examined the body shortly after the shots were fired, and he told me that the perpetrator appeared to be dead."

"All right," Cash said with a curt nod of his head. "And after they sealed the house, what then? Did you speak to anyone? What did you do?"

"Sanchez approached me. He told me not to talk to anybody, not even another cop, until after Negron got ahold of the union lawyer. Then he slapped me on the arm and walked away; he was trying to disperse the crowd. In the meantime, more cops poured into the area. Negron was keeping guys away, you know, so they wouldn't mess up the scene. I just sorta got lost in the crowd."

"Is that when you looked at the body?"

Miles squirmed slightly in his seat. "Yeah. I walked over and there he was, just where he fell. His eyes were open."

"What did you think when you looked at the body? Did you think, *This guy almost killed me*, something like that?"

Miles hesitated. "Look, Mr. Cash, I didn't think anything like that. And what does it matter what I thought? Thoughts don't mean much. I had . . . I had crazy thoughts, but they weren't anything like you might think."

Cash smiled a thin, tired smile. "You're right, Anthony, most thoughts don't mean much. But tell me anyway. I need to get the whole picture in order to best protect you."

Miles looked pale. He was trembling more noticeably now and clasping his hands together in an attempt to steady them. He suddenly removed his peacoat, folding and dropping it neatly to the floor. He peered up at Cash. "All right," he said. "You want to hear it, I'll tell you. But like I said, it was a little crazy. I don't really understand it, but here it is. I went over and looked at the body. It seemed sort of . . . sort of fake, you know? Like a mannequin or a pile of laundry. It was like . . . like a machine that somebody unplugged. And then, all of a sudden, I started thinking about . . . about college. When I took an anatomy class, senior year. The professor I had was great, he made it very interesting, you know? We learned about the human body, the bones and muscles, the glands, the brain, the blood and heart, all functioning together, forming a human being. You know, it doesn't matter how smart you are, if you're rich or poor or whether you're good or evil, *everybody's* got the same stuff inside, like a computer or something. Your values, your personality, that's all secondary. What's important is your body, your *anatomy*. That's what I thought about when I looked at the guy. My anatomy elective."

Cash said nothing when Miles fell silent. Over the years he had interviewed enough people to know when to be silent and when to speak. He knew Miles would continue. Cash didn't care about body parts, he cared about the facts surrounding the shooting. And he was willing to let Miles digress for a while if that's what it took to gather those facts.

"Anyway," Miles continued as though there had been no break in his narrative, "I just kept on thinking about anatomy and my professor. The human body was like God to him, he worshipped it. Like even though he spent years studying and teaching, he was still fascinated by it. Some of the students didn't give a damn, but I did. I found it all so amazing. I remember discussing it one day with some blonde who sat next to me in class. She said it was boring, she only took the course because it fit into her schedule and was offered as a pass-fail. I tried to explain why it was so fascinating, but she was completely turned off by it. Then she said something that had never occurred to me. And it all came flooding back into my head while I was looking down at the bloody hole in that guy's chest."

Cash found himself frowning. "And what was that?"

Now Miles raised his eyes to meet Cash's. "She said, *This guy,* meaning the professor, the one I figured was so cool, *This guy is a real cold bastard. He talks about people like they're meat. To him, there's no difference between anybody—just between dead and not dead.* That's what she said. At first it kind of pissed me off. But then after I thought about it, I began to see her point. And I had it filed away in my head all these years that she was right, you know? Like people really are more than just blood and veins and body parts. But when I looked at that body tonight, I realized the only difference between it and me was that it was dead and I wasn't. The *only* difference. Its systems were shut down, mine weren't. Its heart was stopped, mine was beating." Miles shrugged. "See? Crazy, right?"

"Yes, well . . . people have odd thoughts at times like that." Cash wanted more relevant information. "What about the perpetrator, Anthony? How many times had you shot him?"

"Well, there was the chest. There was also a side wound, the right side, by the ribs. And one of the bullets hit him in the hand. The EMT found that one. The detectives checked my gun. I had fired all six rounds."

Cash reached across the table and patted Miles's shoulder. "This sounds like a very clean shooting, son. If Sanchez goes along and the crime scene unit confirms those two rifle shots, you'll waltz through the mandatory grand jury inquest. You did what you were forced to do. You need to realize that, calm down a little."

Miles looked up at Cash, his sad eyes hooded. "Mr. Cash," he asked softly, "have you ever wept?"

The question surprised the older man. "Sure, son, everyone cries. Don't think because you're a man or a police officer that you're not allowed to cry."

Miles shook his head sharply and leaned forward in his seat. His tone implored Cash for understanding. "Not cry. I'm talking about *weeping*. When I looked at that guy, I sat down on the porch next to him and I wept. I mean, really *wept*. In my whole life I never did that; sure, I've cried—from pain, frustration, anger, sorrow, but I never wept. Not until tonight."

Cash straightened in his seat. Jesus, he thought, the kid was really taking this hard. All this crap about weeping and crying, as if there were some difference. "Look, son, it's tough, we all cry, and no cop who saw you will ever mention it. They know it could be them next time."

Miles reacted sharply, almost rising from his seat. "No, damnit," he said in a suddenly strong, clear voice. "It's not the macho thing, it's not about *crying*, it's about *weeping*! You don't understand. I didn't care about that guy, or his family, or his friends, nobody. I only cared about his *body*, his blood and his brain, his chemistry, his parts, his fuckin' anatomy. All that incredible machinery, broken, dead. I wept for *that*. Don't you understand? Nobody ever thinks about that or cares. But that's all there is, Mr. Cash, that's all there is to care about."

Cash leaned back in his seat. "Listen, Anthony, you're tired, you're upset. You're not making a hell of a lot of sense here, and tomorrow no one will appreciate that kind of talk. It doesn't sound . . . just doesn't sound right, do you understand?"

Miles shook his head and abruptly stood up. He was still trembling. He stepped around the table to the window. "I don't care how it sounds, it's true. Just look out there." He gestured at the window. Cash turned somewhat nervously, as much to keep his eye on Miles as to glance out the window. "Look out at Camden. Tell me, what value does a person have if he's a rapist, a murderer, a junkie? Or a liar or a cheat, or a mean bastard or skinflint for that matter? How many people out there fit that description, or part of that description? If some terrorist blew it all to hell, what would be said? All those poor people, those poor human beings, murdered. But they'd be talking . . . about something else, something totally different from what I'm saying. They wouldn't care about the *bodies*, the machinery. *That's* why I wept for that guy, because I destroyed his body. If his soul even existed, it wasn't worth a damn to him, me, or anybody else. Humans are pompous fools, they award themselves souls so they can look at a cow or a monkey and say, *I'm better than that, I'm a human being.* So what, Mr. Cash? How can anyone really give a goddamn?"

Cash rose from his chair and moved closer to Miles. He faced the window, speaking to his own reflection in the darkened glass. "Anthony, you killed a man tonight. When you took this job, you must have asked yourself at least one time, *Am I willing to chance being killed? Am I willing to chance killing someone?* Well, tonight it came to pass, son, and you did what had to be done. If you're going to get all philosophical about it, you'll only cause yourself a lot of grief. You wouldn't be so damn philosophical if you were lying in the morgue right now, or up in the OR with a bullet lodged in your spine. You killed a man; I don't give a damn if you think you killed his soul, his body, or his goddamned asshole. He's dead and you're not. So when you're interviewed tomorrow, you forget about all this bullshit and you talk facts; you talk distance in feet and inches, you talk lighting and visibility, and you talk police procedure. You talk it because that's what they want to hear. That's what they *need* to hear. If you have a problem with something, talk to a priest. If you can't handle it, go see a psychiatrist. This is a police shooting and we talk facts, not bullshit. Do you understand me, Anthony?" Cash turned and peered at the young officer. "Do you understand me?" he said into the bloodshot eyes glaring back at him.

"Yes, I understand. It's *you* who doesn't understand. You prove my point. Answer the questions, fill out the forms, toe tag the corpse, and shovel it under. Then on Sunday talk soul and spirit." Miles paused and returned to his chair. He sat down heavily and spoke softly: "I'm sorry. Maybe I don't know what I'm saying. Maybe you're right. Maybe any damn thing. It's dawn and I feel like I came to work a week ago. I'm exhausted. Can I go home now?"

Cash turned back to the window. "Where are your guns?"

"The detectives took them. They gave me a receipt." Miles produced the wrinkled paper and placed it on the table.

Cash glanced at it. "All right, put it away, hold onto it. You know procedure. You'll be reassigned to a desk job until you're cleared on the shooting. Tomorrow we'll talk again and cross the T's and dot the I's. Then you'll sit for your official interview. I'll be there personally to monitor things."

Miles stood up and began to leave the room.

"One more thing," Cash said to the man's back. "Stay home. Let Negron take you straight home and stay there. Don't speak to anyone about the shooting, not even Negron. I'll call you tomorrow."

Miles placed a hand on the doorknob and started out. Before leaving, he turned slowly and spoke softly: "Mr. Cash, I know what everybody thinks. I know what *you* think. Tonight, any other cop would have been assigned some lawyer right out of school. But because of my father, you showed up personally. And I'm sure you know how grateful he'll be for that."

Cash wore a neutral expression. "Yes," he said.

"I need you to understand something, though. I want everybody to understand something. The last thing in the world my father wanted was for me to become a cop. He tried his best to change my mind, and when he couldn't he tried to talk me out of working for Camden PD. But he couldn't do that, either. There are some good people in Camden, Mr. Cash. They're trying to make a life for themselves."

For the first time since entering the room, a small, tired smile touched Miles's face as he continued.

"I just wanted to help them do it. That's all I ever wanted. The other cops, they hardly talk to me. Negron and Sanchez have me for a partner because they pissed off the duty sergeant. But they've got me all wrong."

He turned back to the door, speaking as he left the room.

"I was just trying to help."

When Miles was gone, Cash turned to the window behind him, his cold, gray eyes studying the early-morning light as it began to nudge against the slowly dying night sky.

He stood there alone for quite some time. He wondered why Negron, from his position of cover behind the porch, had not fired.

He wondered why Sanchez had not fired.

And as the Camden sky grew brighter, he wondered about organs and brains, nerves and enzymes, anatomy and souls.

NEW DAY NEWARK

BY S.J. ROZAN

Central Ward (Newark)

A new day was coming to Newark.

The boy had actually got himself elected mayor.

Miss Crawford was satisfied with this. She knew him now for some years, not just seen him on the TV, mind you, but she knew him. Not because she was his people. His people were from Harrington Park, and Miss Crawford had watched him sideways like lots of folks at the old Brick Towers back when he was a councilman and he first moved in. The boy himself went to Yale and Stanford and places like that, and besides he had those green-blue eyes. Wasn't no other politician she could remember ever set foot in Brick Towers, and this baby-face councilman was going to live there? Something had to be up, no question. But the councilman was always polite, he learned her name right fast, and if something was going on she never knew what it was. He walked up the stairs like the rest of them when the elevator was out and one time she saw him bringing groceries for old Mrs. Green next door to him. Miss Crawford herself, she lived on the second floor, so it wasn't no thing, but she couldn't help noticing that since he moved in, it wasn't like the elevator went out less often but it got fixed when it did. The lightbulbs in the halls got replaced when they burned out too, not six months later.

So when the boy announced for mayor, that first time, she thought, Well all right. None of that with the elevator and the lightbulbs happened all the years that other boy was mayor, did it? Strictly, that one wasn't no boy, excepting that Miss Crawford was so far past her threescore and ten that she could call anyone a boy she liked to, thank you very much. That other one, he was a grown man with expensive suits and a gap in his teeth and he should have known better. Oh, he spoke beautiful. If he'd took to preaching instead of politics he'd have had any pulpit he wanted and Miss Crawford just knew he could've sold the Lord to the Devil himself. That was the trouble with him right there. In the boy's first campaign the gap-toothed mayor kept telling everybody who'd listen, *Newark's not for sale*, but he was the one buying and selling. He was everyone's friend and everyone's favorite uncle, he threw ice-cream socials and all, and he got big glass buildings built downtown. But here in the Central Ward, were the schools safe? Did anyone think to fix the sidewalk cracks, where poor Leteesha Monroe broke her leg? Did the police run off the drug dealers from the playgrounds? Course not. They stopped their patrol cars and called the dealers over, but sure as God made little apples, that was to get their share of the take. Miss Crawford might be eighty-eight, she might be five feet tall and weigh less than a sack of flour, but she knew what time it was. Maybe the boy would be as bad when he got elected, but he couldn't be no worse. And the elevator was running. So she voted for him, and he lost, but then he won the next time, which was now.

So it was a new day in Newark.

Now, that didn't mean the old day was gone away. Things took time, Miss Crawford knew that. Those gangs peddling their poison had cleared out from the schoolyards, and that impressed Miss Crawford. The new mayor promised that and he delivered it. But those same no-account punks sneered from the streetcorners now, and the police cars still rolled up and rolled away. That would be the hardest part of the new mayor's job, to Miss Crawford's mind: straightening out the police. He could hire all the new chiefs he liked, and the new chiefs could take up the rotten apples when they found them, and she'd seen that start to go on already. It was just, there were so many of them. Which wasn't no way saying

Newark didn't have police you could trust. It surely did, and more every day.

That nice girl who moved in upstairs from Miss Crawford in January, she was a new officer, just out of the academy. She was from Weequahic Park over in the South Ward, but the police assigned her to the 4th precinct and so she moved here. "Like the mayor," she told Miss Crawford in her kitchen as they got acquainted, very neighborly. She poured Miss Crawford coffee and said, "You know, when he was a councilman he represented the Central Ward so he wanted to live here. In the old Brick Towers, you remember that place? He inspired me."

Well, there you go, Miss Crawford thought. Do right and you never know how far it'll spread. She told the girl officer—Patrol Officer Joyce was her name, Aleksandra Joyce—about how she used to live in Brick Towers too, with the councilman before he was mayor, about him carrying groceries and walking the stairs.

Officer Joyce's face gleamed. "I knew he was like that, I knew it. And I thought the old mayor taking down Brick Towers right after that first election, that was just spite."

"Oh, child, it surely was."

"Well, I'm glad anyway," the girl had said impulsively. "If there was still Brick Towers, you would never have moved here, Miss Crawford, and then we wouldn't be friends."

That made Miss Crawford feel all warm, and she sat in Officer Joyce's kitchen more times than that. The girl needed friends too, you could tell that when she talked. She shrugged it off, acting all tough police, but Miss Crawford didn't get to be this old for nothing.

"It's always like this for new officers, I guess," the girl told her. "Especially women."

"Life's hard on women everywhere," said Miss Crawford.

"You got that right."

Another time: "It's like a club. The older cops, they've been in this club a long time, and they don't necessarily welcome new members."

Miss Crawford had nodded at that, and just said, "These things take time." Officer Joyce smiled, but Miss Crawford felt troubled in her mind. Here was a good girl and an honest officer, trying to do right, and the same old, same old was holding her back. Right here on these blocks of the Central Ward, Robbie down at the grocery still had police taking coffee and donuts in the morning, bags of potato chips and pretzels too, then just waving goodbye as they strolled past the register. The Shaw twins at the garage still changed the oil in officers' private cars for nothing, and shopkeepers all up and down the streets still handed over contributions to the Widows and Orphans Fund. In cash.

All that was down at least some to the people who lived here, as much as the bad police, and Miss Crawford went and scolded Robbie or one of the Shaw boys from time to time, but what were they going to do? Chances were already poor they'd get police protection if they needed it, but they'd be poorer if they didn't play along, and everyone knew it.

Yes, things took time, Miss Crawford thought as she trundled her grocery cart along, but sometimes, like now, she wished the time had already come. She walked the long way home, because over around the other side of this block, that was like the Wild West over there. Drug dealer there by the name of C-4—wasn't even no name, but she guessed it was supposed to be tough—he let his crew do anything they wanted. She wasn't scared of him, but she wasn't stupid neither, and more than one time C-4's crew was out there shooting rats in the empty lot. Bullets bounced around, didn't they? Miss Crawford would rather take a dozen extra steps home than get shot by crossing where some punk thought he saw a creature uglier than him. Every now and again, somebody went and called the police. Didn't help. Even if they were good police and not rotten ones, by the time they got there all the guns were hidden, or at least lying on the ground. Being caught with a gun, that was one crime it was hard to talk your way out of in Newark. Which didn't mean the gangbangers had no guns, of course they did, every last useless one of them. It only meant they paid some attention to not getting caught.

Now, over here on this side of the block, that drug dealer Bigmouth, right there on that corner with the knit cap down over his forehead, Miss Crawford could ignore him like he deserved. She knew that boy when he was a baby, she watched him grow up on these streets. Rashawn was his name, though Miss Crawford couldn't remember the last time she heard anyone use it. His momma, she wasn't no good, with her men and her liquor, and all her babies had to drag themselves up because she wasn't helping. That didn't give Bigmouth an excuse, neither a reason, for being the way he was. It gave Miss Crawford something, though. Whenever she started to get afraid of him, she remembered him running down the street in his diapers. Then she could just walk on by.

Bigmouth anyway, he thought she was too poor to bother with and too feeble to bother him. She knew it, and it suited her, but he didn't feel the same way about Leteesha Monroe's oldest boy and that did not suit Miss Crawford at all. That was a promising child right there, a boy who could write poetry and nice stories, he played basketball and he could sing too. He'd be in middle school next year and he could go on to college and be somebody, if the somebody he wanted to be wasn't more and more like Bigmouth every day. The car and the bling and the gun, that was what the Monroe boy saw, that was what all the children saw. Wasn't easy to tell them to work hard and stay in school when it *was* easy for them to stand on street corners, just a year or two older than Leteesha Monroe's boy, and get paid by trash like Bigmouth to steer rich white children from the suburbs to his door. Runners and snitches, Bigmouth used them as too, because everybody knows little pitchers got big ears, but everybody forgets. And to call him with the cell phone to tell him when the honest cops were coming, because who those were, and who they weren't, was another thing everybody knew.

All this was a big problem for the new mayor, but he had lots of problems. It was a bigger problem for Leteesha Monroe, and she had lots of problems too, the poor girl working two jobs, just trying to do right by her children. Miss Crawford, her and her Teddy hadn't never had no children, which she was sad about when she was of that age but it was behind her now. She just helped everyone else raise theirs. Her whole life she was a teacher's aide, right here in the Central Ward, and she watched people's babies even sometimes now, as far as her old bones would let her. Helping Leteesha Monroe, that's what was on her mind as she pushed her cart, which was why she almost ran Bigmouth down.

Him and his cap and his pants so low she swore she didn't know what kept them on his fat behind, they took up the whole sidewalk. Bigmouth had his hands stuck on his hips and he was smiling out across the street like he was some farmer and all this was his green pastures. He stood sideways to her and he didn't see her and he sure didn't move. Sometime, Miss Crawford might have just walked around him onto the grass; but last night it rained and the grass was muddy, and she had her cart with its wobbly wheel, and she'd been giving a thought to Leteesha Monroe. So him taking up the sidewalk set her anger off, and she stomped her foot and told him, "Boy, you move aside!"

His face got all surprised, like he didn't know where the sound came from, then he looked down and saw her. Out popped that nasty grin. "Well, lookee here, Miz Busybody."

"You didn't buy that sidewalk, boy, so you best let people use it."

"Why should I buy it when I already own it?" He smiled across the street; some of his crew were sitting on a stoop over there, watching and snickering.

"You don't neither. The peoples of Newark owns it, and I'm one of them, so let me pass."

"Maybe I will, and maybe I won't."

"Maybe you better."

"Or you gonna do what, skinny-ass bitch? Call a cop?"

"I might, for real. Not one of your friend cops. One of the new cops."

"New cops? Lady, what's wrong with you? You believe all what you hear from that carpetbag mayor?"

Miss Crawford snorted. "You got enough schooling to know what *carpetbag* means, child?"

Bigmouth laughed. "It means he ain't really black. He don't give a shit about these blocks and he sure ain't about to run on over here and help you out."

"Now you listen here, you drug-dealing no-account. You move aside right now, or you go ahead and knock down a lady." Miss Crawford waited a second, then she took a step and plowed her cart right on. Bigmouth sneered but he stepped away like she knew he would. His boys might love to see him swagger, but it wouldn't help his gangsta reputation none for them to watch him throw an eighty-eight-year-old woman on her rear end.

Miss Crawford went on home and unpacked her groceries. She stacked them neatly in their cabinets and she scratched behind the cat's ears when he jumped up on the table. Facing down Bigmouth didn't amount to nothing and she would've forgotten all about it, except that across the street, three doors down from Bigmouth's crew, someone else was hanging out too, and watching. And it was Leteesha Monroe's oldest boy.

Bigmouth was wrong about the new mayor. He surely was black, for one thing, and for the other, he did care about these blocks. Especially these blocks. But he was new, and he had lots of problems, and what was it Miss Crawford herself had been saying to Robbie just now as he bagged up her groceries? *It's a new day in Newark,* she told him, *and what's wrong can be righted if we step up and right it ourselves.*

Two days later the sun was out and the breeze was warm and come afternoon Miss Crawford felt like a walk. She wasn't in need of groceries but she went that way nonetheless, along the side of the street where Bigmouth's crew hung out. She passed them with her head high and without a word, and then stopped three doors down. Like the other day, there was Leteesha Monroe's oldest boy.

"What you doing here, child?" Miss Crawford demanded. "You got no homework waiting for you?"

"Done it." The boy fidgeted uncomfortably.

"And your momma got no chores?"

"Done 'em."

Miss Crawford looked him up and down. "Well, I got chores. You come help me with my cabinets where I can't reach, and I'll pay you. That suit you?"

He shrugged, still a good enough boy to know his duty. "I guess."

She nodded. "Later today, right before suppertime. And boy? No point in your hanging around here day and night. Those punks, they don't need you and they don't want you. And you too good for them, you surely are."

He didn't meet her eye. Miss Crawford marched on to the grocery and passed the time with Robbie. She bought three cans of cat food, because sooner or later the animal was going to eat her out of what she already had, wasn't he? Then she headed back along the other side of the street, and blessed if Bigmouth wasn't standing on the exact same piece of broken sidewalk as always.

"Rashawn, move yourself aside."

Bigmouth stared with that mean grin. "*Rashawn?* Old lady, who you talking to?"

"Oh, get out my way. I need to get home. Every time I come by here, you get all up in my face."

"Listen, old bitch, I got a question for you. You in such a damn hurry to get home, how come you even come by here? You live over there, be much faster the other way. *You* just like getting all up in *my* face?"

"Don't like nothing about your face, boy. But that other boy, can't deny I like him less."

"Who?" Bigmouth scowled. "C-4?"

She snorted. "C-4. Pure foolishness is all that is. You, at least I know the name your momma give you. Far as him, he's just one evil child. Don't like the way you strut around these blocks like a rooster, Rashawn, but I be sorrier if he turn out to be right."

"Right? What you mean, who's right?"

"That boy. When he say he's gonna take these blocks from you."

Bigmouth frowned down at her. "He say that?"

She squinted at him. "You ain't pretending to me you never heard that? I'm just a old lady, live with a cat. If I heard it, I know everybody did. You planning on hiding your head in the sand? Go right ahead, boy, but just remember when you do that, what sticks out." She looked at him again, then walked on home.

The Monroe boy came over right before suppertime. He put the cat food and soup and all the flour and sugar in the cabinets where she wanted them. The flour and sugar, she had out because she'd been baking raisin cookies, and along with five dollars, which was fair, she gave him some of the cookies and a glass of milk. She had some herself too, and while they ate them she asked him about school and basketball. She told him how good the church choir sounded and she said she could hear him especially, which she wasn't sure was true but it made him smile. Besides that smile, all she got was one-word answers, nods, and shrugs, because that was how boys acted at that age, but she heard enough to be satisfied he was still going all those places they talked about and that's why she was asking.

"All right," she finally said, packing more cookies in a sack and handing them to him, "you take these for your brothers and your sister. Tell your momma Miss Crawford sends my best."

The next afternoon was sunny again. Miss Crawford went out. She took a breath in the bright sunshine and walked around the block the other direction.

The boy standing in her way on this side wasn't C-4 himself. Miss Crawford supposed that meant he was off somewhere doing his drug-dealer business, which was the only time Bigmouth cleared off his square of sidewalk too. This boy here, she didn't know what his momma called him but on these blocks his name was Late Nite. He stepped aside after the tiniest little look at her, like she wasn't worth his worry. But she stopped in front of him and tilted her head up—he was a tall one—and she said, "Yo, son. You work for that ugly boy, call himself all letters and numbers?"

Late Nite drew his eyebrows together. "Say what?"

"C-4," she said impatiently. "Came over here to talk to him."

"He's busy." Late Nite looked like something was funny.

"Don't you mock me, boy. He hiding out already?"

The snicker stopped. "What?"

"I say, is he hiding out? 'Cause that ain't gonna help him Friday."

"Friday? What's that?"

"It's the day at the end of the week. The day Bigmouth and his crew from over there—" she jerked her chin "—say he gonna come over and clean his clock."

"What clock? What you talking about, *clock*?"

Miss Crawford regarded the young man. "I don't like that Bigmouth none," she finally said, "but Lord Almighty, at least his crew ain't stupid. Maybe I was wrong. Never you mind." She turned to leave.

"Wait, old lady. Just wait. What the hell you saying?" He stepped around in front of her.

"Watch your tongue, boy. Don't no one curse at me."

Late Nite rolled his eyes. "Yeah, yo, sorry. But lady, what you saying?"

"Not sure I should tell you now. Like I say, maybe I was wrong."

He made a fist, though he didn't raise it to her. "If you got something you think C-4 oughta know . . ."

Miss Crawford took a quick step back, eyeing the clenched

hand. She didn't take her eyes from it as she swallowed and said, "Why I'm here, I was studying on it, and I decided, if one boy gonna be running both blocks, might better be C-4 than Bigmouth."

"Running both blocks? Who say?"

"Bigmouth. Starting Friday. High noon, he be here, like this was some stupid movie. That's what started me thinking. C-4, he mean and ugly, but he run a business. He don't be playing no games over here. If we gotta choose between a clown and a hard case, maybe best we have a hard case. I imagine, C-4 make a deal, probably he stick to it."

"That's for sure." The young man waved it aside. "You telling me Bigmouth and his crew coming here Friday, to get up in C-4's grille?"

"How many times I gotta say it before it sink through your thick skull? Bigmouth, he's thinking this the time to do it, because of the amnesty."

"Amnesty? What the—what do that mean?"

She gave a sigh. "The police amnesty, you natural fool. All them cops C-4 be paying to watch his backside, they getting amnesty this week if they sign a paper says they ain't gonna protect you all anymore. The mayor, he wanted them to have to tell all about you too, but that got negotiated. You know that word?"

"Course I know that word," Late Nite snapped. "You mean—"

"Yes, young man, I mean you on your own now. You tell C-4, he see any of 'em coming for their payoff, he better run, because from now on they gonna be ratting on anybody tries to offer them money. That was part of the negotiation." She looked to see was he following her, then added, "Of course, Bigmouth, he on his own too."

He stared at her. "Old lady, how come you telling me this?"

"'Cause you say C-4 too busy to talk to me."

"That ain't what I mean. I—"

"Oh, I know what you mean, boy. I come over here because next week or the week after, new cops is gonna be asking to be paid off by you punks. Things don't never change. But like I say, C-4 a better bet than Bigmouth for the peoples round here." The young man said nothing to that. Miss Crawford waited and then she said, "If C-4 got some smart boys, you ain't one of 'em, so I'm gonna help you out. Was I C-4, not that I'd ever want to be such a devil, but was I, I'd be heading over Bigmouth's way early Friday morning, while all his boys be getting ready for the showdown and his pet police be keeping their hands off. That's called a ambush, maybe C-4 knows that word. But go on, you do as you please. Whatever happen, folks around here be better off, one of 'em goes down." Miss Crawford stared Late Nite in the eyes again, and then she walked away, thinking, was that amnesty real, it might just be a good idea.

That day before supper Miss Crawford had the Monroe boy come over again. He rearranged the pictures on the wall in her bedroom and carried the broken kitchen chair down to the trash. She gave him a slice of apple pie and asked him what he'd heard about the trouble on the block.

"Trouble?" The boy looked up sharply. "Don't know about no trouble."

"Well, you know more than I do, so that's a relief. Maybe it won't come to be."

"Whatever, Bigmouth got it covered." The child was straight-up bragging.

"Hope you're right, boy. I don't like Rashawn none, but the devil you know is always better than the devil you don't."

"What devil's that?"

So she told the child about C-4, over around the other side of the block. "He say he coming over here Friday at noon to take these blocks from Bigmouth."

The Monroe boy stared, then finished his pie in two big bites, and gulped his milk. Miss Crawford packed up the rest of the pie for him to take to his momma, and watched him from her kitchen window as he hurried down the street. She hoped he'd hold that pie careful until he finally got it home.

Miss Crawford heard Officer Aleksandra Joyce come home after her shift the next afternoon, and she popped her head out the door and asked her in. Miss Crawford had coffee ready and a plate of cinnamon cookies just out from the oven.

"You look tired, child," she observed as Officer Joyce took off her big belt, with the gun and the flashlight and who knew what all, and laid it on the chair beside her. "Hard work bringing law and order to Newark, I suppose."

"That it is," Officer Joyce agreed. "Worth it if it gives folks like you peace enough to make cookies like these, though."

"Why, thank you," Miss Crawford said. "Have another, please do. Those police, they still giving you a hard time?"

Officer Joyce shrugged. "I'm still new."

"Plus," said Miss Crawford, "I expect some of them got other ideas about policing than the ideas you got."

The young woman sighed. "They sure do, Miss Crawford. The mayor, I know he's working on it. Like you told me, things take time." She smiled wearily.

"Well," Miss Crawford took herself another cookie, "maybe if more police like you was in the middle of things, it would all get better. So the question is, how we going to get you in the middle of things?"

"That's one of the reasons I moved to the neighborhood. So I could know what's going on. Know more and more people."

"And what about things? What about if you know things?"

"Like what things?"

"Like, supposing you was to know about a thing that was going to happen. A bad thing, and you was in time to put a stop to it so no one got hurt."

"Miss Crawford?" Officer Joyce put down her mug. "You know a thing like that?"

"If I tell you something," Miss Crawford asked the young woman direct, "do you know people in the police you could tell, who ain't in the pocket of no drug dealers nor no gangbangers?"

"I do," Officer Joyce said promptly. "My captain was brought in by the chief that was brought in by the mayor."

"You saying you trust him?"

"Yes."

"That's very good." Miss Crawford nodded, satisfied. "Yes, I believe that's very good."

Though she wasn't one for excitement, come Friday morning Miss Crawford was just a little bit wistful that she wasn't a fly on the wall in that basement hole Bigmouth called his headquarters. She wasn't positive what the NPD had planned, but it involved special officers, not the usual ones on these blocks, who were still deep in the pockets of the drug dealers and everybody knew it but no one could prove it. Miss Crawford did go out and sit on the stoop across the street early in the morning, so she saw C-4 and his boys coming around the corner. She was interested to see that the officers who swept them up were in plainclothes, so C-4 and his boys wouldn't scatter nor throw their guns away, while the ones who pounded on the headquarters door just after so they could grab Bigmouth and his crew getting set to head over to C-4's territory, they were in uniforms. One of them in uniform was Officer Joyce, which gratified Miss Crawford. She was also gratified that the whole operation was so cleverly planned that no shots were fired at all. Though still, it was a good thing it had happened in the morning, while the children were at school. No use having them in danger, hanging out on the stoops and all. There was no need for them to see it, they'd hear all about it by suppertime, C-4 and Bigmouth and all their boys in jail.

Miss Crawford went home and turned on the radio while she baked a sweet potato pie. She listened to WBGO because of the old-school jazz they played, which she and her Teddy had always enjoyed, and then the news came on. It told about the alleged gang members arrested, most of them in possession of weapons, just that very morning. The police suspected these young men of dealing drugs, though they couldn't prove that yet. All very well, thought Miss Crawford as the radio went back to music, but those guns every one of them were carrying was the real problem for those boys, and that problem was very bad. Being caught with a gun like that was a sentence for sure. How long it was going to be, well, that depended on if you had anything to say that the police wanted to hear. Those boys would be racing to sell each other out, starting already.

The timer dinged and Miss Crawford took the pie out of the oven and set it to cool. Then she settled herself in front of the TV with the cat on her lap. The new mayor was going to be making a speech, about how the people of Newark were taking the city back. Miss Crawford wanted to hear it.

NEWARK BLACK: 1940–1954

BY C.K. WILLIAMS
Vailsburg (Newark)

Black coal with a thunderous shush
plunging into the clearly evil-inhabited coal bin.
The black furnace into whose maw
you could feed paper to watch it curl to black char.

The hats women wore with black, mysterious veils,
even your mother. The "mascara" she'd apply
more meticulously than she did anything else.
With her black lashes she was almost somebody else.

The incomprehensible marks on blackboards at school
you conquered without knowing quite how.
The black ink in the inkwell. The metal pens
with blots that diabolically slid from their nibs.

Black slush, after the blizzard had passed
and the diesel buses and trucks were fuming again,
but you still remembered how blackly lovely
the branches of trees looked in new snow.

The gunk on the chain of your bike.
The black stuff always under your nails.
Where did it come from, how to get it out?
Even between your toes sometimes there was black.

The filthy tires hung on hooks in the garage-store
we had to pass through to get to our *shul*.
Black Book of Europe, first proof of the war on Jews—
illicit volume, as forbidden to Jewish children as porn.

Black people the states in the South began to send up,
keeping what they needed for cheap labor and maids
and exporting the rest: a stream of discarded humans,
with the manufacturing plants just then closing down.

The photo of black children in the '20s, frolicking
on the bench of the Lincoln statue by the courthouse.
I took the bus once to go sit in its lap, *his* lap:
how kind he looked, how surprisingly hard his bronze lap.

The other statue, *Captive's Choice*, in a park:
the girl kidnapped by Indians who forgets she's white,
then, "saved," gives up Indian husband and children.
Who decided it should have been that, and there?

The first black kids in our school, fine with me,
because Clarence Murphy, sixteen in fourth grade,
stopped beating me up because I'd killed Christ
and raged instead with even more venom at them.

I was afraid of Clarence but not of black people,
except that day on the bus: the sweat-stench of men
who'd worked hard and not had time yet to change.
Though I already knew it was shameful, I fled.

"Blackballs" to keep Jews, Italians, and Irish,
then naturally blacks, out of the country clubs
in Maplewood and Montclair. The unfunny jokes
about signs on their gates: *No Dogs, Niggers, or Jews*.

Our gangster hero, Longie Zwillman, who had a black car;
so did our mayors—bought off, we were told by "interests."
Irish, Italian, finally at last a black mayor:
all the bought-off ones with their Cadillacs of corruption.

Thick soot on the bricks of the mills by the tracks,
smoke billowing, then extinguished forever.
Rivers with rainbows of oil on their surface,
their beds eternally black venomous chemical sludge.

Miles of black turnpike and parkway pavement
scrolled out onto the soil of the no-longer farms.
You could speed now from one place to another
and not see the slums, the factories in broken-eyed ruin.

Everywhere ruin—did nobody see it arriving?
Urban flight, urban decay, shopping centers and malls,
the department stores downtown shuttered,
then small businesses, theaters, and the rest.

The finally unrecognizable city, done in by us all.
Only the ever benevolent Lincoln, unblackened
by time or pollution, emblem of promise and hope,
patiently waited, patiently waits.

PART II

Romance & Nostalgia

LOLA

BY JONATHAN SANTLOFER

Hoboken

I met Lola on the PATH, the train that goes under the Hudson River, a thought I tried to deny twice a day when I rode it back and forth to Hoboken, the idea of the tunnel suddenly sprouting a leak, water shattering subway windows, pouring in, drowning me, always on the edge of my mind, which is why I focused on everything else.

Lola was sitting across from me, head buried in a paperback, one of those romance novels with a girl in the arms of a brawny he-man. Her black-red nails tap-tap-tapping the back cover had me hypnotized until she looked up, blue eyes lined with kohl, dark arching brows as if she were about to ask a question though she wasn't looking at me, just reacting to the sound of the subway doors opening and closing, but it was enough, a moment, a connection. She went back to her book and I noticed the gold band on her finger, which was disappointing, not like I was thinking we'd get married or anything, but I'd have preferred she was single, which makes things easier.

She was a little younger than me, maybe thirty though I'm no good at ages, no good at numbers of any kind, which is why they never let me do the measuring at the place where I build made-to-order stretchers for successful artists, which I don't mind, I like making them—I've always been good with my hands, and it's quiet work, just me and two other guys, and I take pride in it, sanding the edges and making sure the corners are perfectly square because there's nothing worse than a lopsided painting—though sometimes I get a little resentful that I spend my days building stretchers for other artists, but that's life, right?

That first night, Lola was wearing gold sandals, toenails painted the same black-red, and she had really nice feet, nice legs too, bare because it was a hot day though the PATH was frigid. Every once in a while she rubbed her hand up and down her legs like she was trying to warm them, which was even more hypnotizing than her book tapping.

She had a good figure too, her top loose but made of some slinky fabric that outlined her breasts, and her skirt was short enough to see her thighs, which were thin but muscular. I thought about asking her to model for me, a line I'd once used that had worked—women are so easily flattered—but I didn't think she'd go for it, being married and all, and I couldn't come up with anything else, I hadn't prepared and I'm not really good with girls even though some say I'm very good looking.

When the train stopped at Hoboken I knew she'd get off—I didn't see her as the kind who'd live in Jersey City, and no way Newark. I waited for her to go past me, we were only a few inches apart and I could smell her perfume, something flowery but not too sweet, and I breathed it in trying to hold onto it, and then someone in front of her stopped short and she backed into me, her perfume in my nose and her hair tickling my cheek for just a second, and she said, "Oh, sorry," and I saw it in slow motion, her red lips yawning the words, OOOHHHHH SSSSOOOORRRRYYYY, and I never wanted the moment to end. So I followed her.

It was still light out, a mist coming off the Hudson River like a veil in front of the Manhattan skyline. She headed away from the water toward the main drag, Washington Street, which had become gentrified over the past years. Hoboken was sort of a dump, famous as the birthplace of Frank Sinatra and not much else, when I first moved there after graduate school because I couldn't afford Manhattan rents, not if I wanted a studio, which I did, and I have a pretty good one, my own building in fact, a small brick one next door to Pablo's Towing Station on the furthest-back street in town, still not developed, a dark lonely stretch, which suits me, and practically no one knows I live in the building because I've done nothing to distinguish it, left the rusted steel door the way it was the day I moved in, and I've yet to clean the broken glass or ever-accumulating beer cans from the two-by-four plot of ground out front, so the place looks deserted unless you happen to see the lights go on and off, but there's really no one around to see that either.

She went into a liquor store, the yuppie one, not the wino one, and I watched her through the glass choosing two bottles of red wine and quickly turned away when she came out, then followed her again, leaving just enough distance between us.

She lived in a renovated brownstone on a quiet side street, a really nice one, so I figured she had money.

After she went inside I waited a few minutes then checked the mailbox. There was a letter addressed to Mr. & Mrs. Moretti, and a postcard, which is how I learned her name, Lola.

Lola. Lola. Lola. Lola. Lola.

I folded it into my pocket, went across the street and stood under the awning of a beauty salon that was closed, and waited until it got dark and a light went on in an upstairs window, and I watched Lola slowly peel her top off, and even after the light went out her image burned in my mind and I stayed up the whole night making one drawing after another of her, naked, framed by the window, smudging the charcoal with my fingers to capture the soft swell of her breasts.

The next day I stayed home from work and made paintings based on the drawings. I stopped just before six p.m., changed out of my paint clothes, put on a clean shirt, walked over to the PATH, and sure enough there she was.

This time she went into a little gourmet shop and I followed, brushed past her in the condiment aisle, keeping my head down inhaling her perfume, and on the way out I accidentally-on-purpose banged into her and she dropped her bag and I said I was sorry and helped her pick everything up and offered to carry her bag home but she just smiled and said, "No biggie," and this time I didn't have to follow her because I knew exactly where she was going, so I waited, then went and stood under the awning, and when it got dark she did the same thing—undressed in front of the window, a little slower this time—and I thought I'd go crazy and was even thankful when the light went out so I could go home and make more drawings.

The next day I followed her from the PATH, and the day after I just waited under the awning until she came home. I didn't want to rush it, didn't want it over too soon. I brought my camera with the telephoto lens and took some pictures of her in her window, half naked, and used them for more paintings, which were starting to fill my studio.

It was later in the week that I finally saw the husband, pin-striped suit, gold-tassel loafers, a lot older than I expected, a lot older than Lola too, at least fifty, maybe more, balding, overweight, a surprise and no question in my mind that she'd married him for money, disappointing as I'd grown to think more highly of her, but still, I forgave her.

Over the next few weeks I got their routine down. Lola almost always came home by six; the husband not until eight, and some nights not at all, so maybe he traveled or stayed in the city if he worked late, my guess Wall Street, which was very convenient to Hoboken. One evening, I went over to where the ferries come in from Wall Street, and there he was with a scowl on his face like he was pissed off about something, like he didn't have a gorgeous wife and tons of money, which annoyed me because some people don't know how lucky they are.

A few times I followed Lola into the city. I was curious to see what she did all day. It turned out she just took long walks along Fifth Avenue or in Central Park or went shopping in fancy stores like Saks or went to art galleries or museums, which made me like her even more; but I got to thinking she was lonely and how happy we'd be together and how she could be my full-time muse and I'd put her on a pedestal and she'd never be lonely again.

One night, a truck delivered a painting, a big one covered in bubble wrap, and when it got dark I went right up to her windows and peeked in and could see it leaning against the living room wall, an abstract, which I don't like, but figured I'd win Lola over to portraiture once she saw all the ones I'd made of her.

I knew it was getting to be time because I could hardly sleep or eat and no matter how many times I jerked off thinking about Lola's lips or her black-red nails on my flesh or her muscular legs wrapped around me, it just wasn't enough. I kept thinking, *Do it now,* but restrained myself because it seemed different this time, it seemed like love, and I never wanted it to end.

Sometimes, on the nights her husband didn't come home, if the weather was nice, Lola would eat outside at one of the restaurants near the waterfront, and I'd find a spot where I could watch her and take pictures, which I used for a series of paintings called *Lola Eating.*

I guess the thing that finally did it was the night I saw them together.

I was in my safe spot under the awning, Lola undressing in the window, and then I saw the husband tugging her toward him and he was about to switch off the lamp but she stopped him, and it was like watching a play, a horrible play, the window open—I could hear their voices though not what they said—the two of them naked, him kissing her, groping her, and if the damn light hadn't finally gone off I'd have burst in and killed him and made Lola my own.

I must have walked through all of Hoboken that night, along the waterfront where the air was hot and damp, that fishy smell coming off the river, the view of Manhattan like the Emerald City in *The Wizard of Oz,* so close you could almost touch it, but unreal. Then up to the college on the hill where a bunch of coeds were walking and laughing and I had such murderous thoughts it must have been on my face because they stopped laughing when they saw me. Then along Washington Street, all the restaurants and bars open, people chatting and smiling and having a good time as if everything in the world was okay, when *nothing* was okay. I wove up and down the side streets, sweating, that fishy smell following me, mixing with the garbage stewing in the hot night air, and when I finally got home there was a rat rooting around in the small plot of dirt in front of my place and I got a brick and smashed it, over and over and over, then dragged my rat-bloodied hands across half the Lola drawings, smudging the charcoal until it turned to brown mush because I was finished with her; it was over between us.

After that, I was happy to go to my job every day, building stretchers, and stayed late so I wouldn't run into her. I was getting over her, the loss and all, and there was this new girl, a blonde, who rode the PATH and lived in Hoboken, alone—I know because I followed her—and she might have become the one—I was getting ready—but then, I saw Lola again.

"Don't I know you?" she asked. She was standing over me wearing skinny black designer jeans, the crotch right at my face blocking my view of the blonde.

"I don't think so," I said, holding my breath, my heart beating fast.

"Sure," she said. "It was at Caterina's, you know, the gourmet place? You knocked a bag right out of my hand?"

"Oh—right—sorry about that."

"No biggie," she said and started chatting, asking if I lived in Hoboken, and I told her I did, starting to feel lightheaded because I'd been holding my breath, and after a minute, when I didn't say anything more, she went and sat down opposite me and put in her iPod earphones and crossed her legs, top one bouncing to the beat of the song in her head, her lips moving too, and when we got to Hoboken she gave me a little wave, then got off, and I purposely lagged behind—I really wanted to be finished with her—but when

I came out of the station there she was, and she smiled, and that was it, like we'd never broken up.

I started making new drawings and paintings of her and stayed home from work for a week, and when I finally felt ready to show them I showered and changed and combed my hair and went and waited by the PATH train until I saw her.

"Hi," I said.

Lola looked up sort of confused like she didn't recognize me, then smiled and said, "Oh, hi," and I just sort of fell in line with her as she walked. I'd prepared some small talk this time, stuff I'd Googled about Hoboken to impress her.

"Did you know they held the first baseball game here?"

"Really?" Her dark eyebrows arched up.

"And it's where Lipton Tea and Maxwell House Coffee were made."

"I didn't know about the tea. But the big Maxwell House sign is still there, and I like it."

"Right," I said, a little annoyed with myself that I'd forgotten about the sign.

"You're like a regular Hoboken tour guide," she said, and that's when I told her I was an artist, a painter, and she asked, "What do you paint?" a question I really hate, but said, "Portraits," and she said, "Really? Of who?" and I wanted to say, *Of you,* but said, "All sorts," and she asked, "Where do you show?" which is my other least-favorite question, but I said, "I'm between galleries," and she said, "Oh, that's too bad," and I said, "It's okay," and quickly added, "I'm having a show in Europe," and she said, "Where?" and I said, "Japan," because it was far away and I didn't think she'd be going there anytime soon, and she said, "I thought you said Europe," and I laughed and said, "Oh—it's all the same to me," and she laughed too and said, "My husband goes to Japan all the time, to Tokyo," and I said, "Why?" and she said, "For business," and I asked, "What kind of business?" and she said, "Finance," and I said, "My paintings aren't leaving for Japan for a few weeks if you'd like to see them," and she stopped and looked at me, dark eyebrows arching up again, and I said really quickly, "I don't mean to be forward, I just thought you might like art," and she said, "I do, but——" and I said, "That's great," and added my warmest smile, the one I practice in the mirror, and she said, "Well . . . maybe," and I said, "How about tonight?" and she gave me that look again, then started laughing and said, "You *are* forward," and I laughed too so she'd think I was a good sport though I was no longer sure why we were laughing, but she said, "I can't tonight," and I said, "Of course, I understand," which is what people on television say all the time, and that was that. I was disappointed but not defeated, because one thing I have is patience.

I waited a couple of days so it wouldn't feel forced, then timed it so I'd bump into her on the PATH again.

"Hi," I said. "Oh, hi," she said. And right way I started telling her about my job, which she said sounded interesting, and I dropped some names of famous artists I built stretchers for, and she'd heard of a few. But I didn't push it. I didn't want to ruin it.

Over the next week, I made sure we happened to meet but I never asked her to come see my paintings, though I'd drop a reference to them like, "I painted half the night" or "I think I finished the last painting for the Japan show," and finally she asked *me* if she could come see my work, and I said, "How's tomorrow night?" but real casual, the whole time my brain going, *Lola Lola Lola Lola,* and she said, "Where do you live?" and I told her and she said, "Really? I didn't know *anyone* lived way back there," and I said, "Oh, it's nice, and my studio's really big," and she said, "I don't know . . ." and I said, "It's right next door to Pablo's Towing Station and Pablo's got guard dogs, so it's perfectly safe, nothing to worry about," and used my practiced smile again, and she said, "Oh, it's not that . . ." and seemed to be thinking it through and finally said, "Okay, but you'll have to come get me because I'm not walking all the way back there alone at night," and I said, "Of course not, I wouldn't want you to," and she asked if we could do it on the later side because she liked to have dinner with her husband, and I tried to keep my smile in place when I said that was fine though I was afraid she'd say she wanted to bring him along, which would ruin everything, but all she said was, "How's nine?" and I said, "Perfect," and started walking away, my mind seeing Lola in all sorts of naked poses, but she called after me, "Hey, don't you want my address?" And I turned and said, "What?" And she repeated the question. And I said, "Oh, right," and laughed maybe a little too hard.

I stayed up all night arranging and rearranging all the portraits till everything was perfect, then cleaned the studio and scrubbed the little storage area behind it, which has stone walls and is dank and dark and must have been used for some kind of cold storage at one time and served my purposes really well. I even sprayed it with Febreze because I wanted it to smell fresh for Lola, and put a clean sheet on the cot, and made sure the cuffs were not rusted from the dampness. Then I showered and washed my hair and shaved and used Old Spice and put on a new white shirt I bought at the Gap just for the occasion.

The air was heavy with that fishy smell and I worried it might rain and I hadn't thought to bring an umbrella and had forgotten my gloves, so I pulled my jacket over my finger when I pressed Lola's doorbell.

A minute later she appeared, smiling, but her eyes looked red as if she'd been crying.

"You okay?" I asked.

"Fine," she said, but the minute she closed the door behind her she got upset because she'd left her keys inside.

"Isn't your husband home?" I asked.

"No," she said. "He's working late," and I thought, *My good luck!*

Lola said she had a key hidden under a mat at the back door and I followed her. The whole time she was waving a hand in front of her nose, "Oh, that Hoboken smell, it's always bad when it's going to rain," and said she'd better get an umbrella and unlocked the back door, and I said I'd wait but she insisted I come in.

When she flipped on the lights we were standing in her kitchen, which looked right out of a magazine with Mexican tiles on the floor and fancy appliances and pots and pans hanging over a huge island in the middle of the room, and when I said it was really nice she said she never cooked so it was a waste, then said there were lots of umbrellas in the front hall closet so I followed her, careful not to touch anything, past a dining room with a long table and stiff-backed upholstered chairs and the living room with that abstract painting I could just make out in the dark, and when we got to the front hallway she stopped, and turned, and kissed me, her tongue in my mouth, and I couldn't breathe I was so excited, but then she pulled away.

"Oh God," she said. "I'm sorry. I don't know what's wrong with me."

I told her it was okay, but she started crying and said she was a terrible person, that she was unhappy and didn't love her husband but couldn't leave him because he was rich and how was she going to make it on her own, and leaned against me sobbing, and I patted her hair and tried to breathe normally, thinking I couldn't do it *here*, not in her house, and then she pulled away again and said she was sorry but I had to excuse her, that she couldn't possibly come to my studio, not now, and I stood there a minute thinking how it had all been ruined, but then she kissed me again, and we stumbled into the living room, our mouths glued together, and she hiked her skirt up and practically ripped her panties off and tossed them across the room and tugged my jeans down and we sort of fell onto the floor, and when we were doing it she said, "Put your hands around my neck," and I did, and she tossed her head back and forth and I asked, "Am I hurting you?" and she said, "No, I like it," so I squeezed a little harder and felt her nails dig into my back and couldn't hold on much longer and told her, and she said, "It's okay, I'm on the pill," and when it was over she said, "You'd better go, my husband might come home," and led me through the kitchen and helped me on with my jacket and hugged me really tight like her life depended on it, which was kind of ironic I thought, and kissed me really hard again, and when I got outside I felt confused and it took a minute to gather my wits—my head was spinning—and I hadn't gone a block when a police car screeched to a halt and two cops got out and one slammed me against the cruiser and twisted my arm behind my back, while the other one fumbled my wallet out of my jeans. "What's going on?" I asked, but they didn't answer, just clamped handcuffs on my wrists, then one of the cops kneed me in the balls and I doubled over, and the other cop said, "Shut the fuck up," and the first one said, "See if the knife's on him," and I said, "*Knife?*" as the cop slipped on a rubber glove and brought a small kitchen paring knife out of my pocket, covered in blood, and there was more blood dripping down the side of my jacket onto my jeans, and I heard the other cop on his radio say, "We've got him, weapon still on him too, a real bozo. The husband's dead in the upstairs bedroom, multiple stab wounds. Wife's okay, but someone from the rape squad should meet us at the OR," and I said, "No, no, it wasn't like that—" and the cop elbowed me in the gut.

Then an ambulance pulled up and I saw her, Lola, being led out of her brownstone, leaning on an EMT guy like she could hardly walk, and sobbing, her hair a mess, lipstick smeared across her face, blouse torn, her black-red fingertips fluttering at her neck like it hurt really bad.

We locked eyes for a moment, my mind going, *Lola, Lola, Lola, how could you?*

Then another cop car arrived and the first cops gave them my address and told them to go to my place and I pictured all the portraits I'd made of Lola on the walls and the storage room all clean and neat and smelling of Febreze, and the wind picked up and blew that fishy smell off the river as a cop shoved me into the backseat of the cruiser and slammed the door.

THE ENIGMA OF GROVER'S MILL

BY BRADFORD MORROW

Grover's Mill

I t has slipped back into obscurity now, like a sun that rose out of nowhere in freakish glory before disappearing once more behind stone-gray clouds. But for a brief moment Grover's Mill was the most famous town in the country. For it was in this quiet New Jersey farmland hamlet where I was born that the Martians landed on Halloween eve, 1938, to unleash a surprise takeover of Earth with killing machines on tripod stilts.

Our family was no different than others gathered around their Philco radios, their Emersons and RCA Victors, their big Zenith consoles, listening in horror as Orson Welles's popular Mercury Theatre broadcast broke the news of the invasion from Mars. Except that my parents and my father's parents and I, forced by the Depression to live under one roof on a dead-end street off Cranbury Road, found ourselves at the epicenter of the attack. Like many in the audience, we had tuned in too late to hear any references to H.G. Wells, and didn't understand this was all meant to be a dramatic sleight-of-hand. The horror-struck voices of eyewitness field reporters, the screams and state police sirens, the devastating sounds of extraterrestrial machines hurling hellfire heat-rays—it was all so real that even in Grover's Mill we believed the world was about to end. My mother and grandmother rushed from room to room, whipping the curtains shut, turning off every light in the house, as news flashes of increasing desperation continued to stream in on our Philco gothic cathedral. Seven thousand infantry, the grim newsman reported from the scene, were wiped out by the Martians in a matter of minutes. Pandemonium reigned. Fearing for their lives, people were fleeing, we were told, in cars, trucks, trains, and on foot, up and down the Eastern seaboard. The description of gigantic three-legged metal monsters wading across the Hudson toward Manhattan, like mere men might cross a shallow stream, was terrifying. Nor will I ever forget peeking between the drapes of our front room window, my mother's trembling hand on my shoulder, as we looked for signs of these invaders from the Red Planet. The gunfire we heard outside was, in fact, very real, though it would later prove to be some panicked farmers shooting at a nearby water tower they'd mistaken for one of the Martian tripods.

As it turned out, the world didn't end on Halloween eve that year. But my father's life did, and so did mine in a way. His suicide would become a mark of solemn, mostly unspoken shame for the Mecham family. Or, that is to say, for every Mecham except me, his namesake son Wyatt, who felt only black despair. Not that I didn't understand their shame. Because who would want to admit that an otherwise sane, sober, solid man such as my dad—a decorated World War I veteran, forced by injuries and the stock market crash into early retirement—chose to sneak out the back door, leaving behind his family to the obscenity of alien violence, only to drown himself in Grover's Mill Pond with boxes of nails crammed into the pockets of his trousers and coat?

I was not quite eight when my dad died, but I have keen memories of him, memories as sharp as paper cuts. The pipe-tobacco perfume of his mustache when he tucked me into bed and kissed me goodnight. Watching him at the workbench in my grandfather's basement wood shop, where he taught me the craft of cabinetry—I write this sitting on a Windsor chair he turned on his own lathe. Nor did the prosthetic leg, which he himself fabricated after losing his real one to a grenade blast, slow him down when we used to walk into town on some errand or another.

Above all, we loved haunting the pond together, fishing from the same bank where he had once seen Woodrow Wilson casting for bass with Walter Grover, whose family our town is named after. When the fish weren't biting, we'd take a walk around its edges, him gimping along with me close beside, drawing strength from the many beautiful hemlocks, huge willow oaks, and mockernut hickory trees that grew along the shore. Sometimes we'd stop and pick flowers together, a damaged soldier and his fond son, to bring home a bouquet of wild herbs for my mother, a clutch of asters or tawny day lilies. It seems to me even now that Grover's Mill Pond was so much a part of my father that when he felt the world was coming to an end, his only recourse was to go embrace its watery soul, become one with it. And like him, I grew up understanding that the pond—at thirty-seven acres really a small lake—lay at the heart of my personal universe from as far back as my conception on its very shores.

In hindsight, I realize that although after his discharge from the army my father was awarded a sack of medals, he was too deeply scarred by what he had witnessed on the fields of France to be consoled by some shiny coins dangling from pretty ribbons. Soft visions of mustard gas, of men with bayonets lurching at mirror images of themselves, of tank treads churning fallen soldiers into foxhole mud—these visited him often in shrieking nightmares that woke the whole household when I was growing up. So when Halloween eve came around, I guess my poor father had seen enough war that he couldn't face the big one, the unwinnable one, the one against the Martians.

The police found his wooden leg on a grassy beach where he presumably entered the water. At least he'd had the wherewithal to realize that keeping it on would have worked against his purpose that night. I still own it, my most cherished heirloom. And while I've heard it said drowning is the least painful way to die, the lungs filling with water just as if it were simply wet, heavy air, who would really know? In my father's case, it was the only conceivably meaningful death, so there's a dash of solace in that. And I'll take a dash of solace over a dash of salt on an open wound any day.

* * *

My mother would wind up in the pond too. After Orson Welles had his little joke on America, and Grover's Mill in particular, and my family in point of fact, my mother Mildred changed, spiraled downward. Her dark hazel eyes behind those horn-rim glasses she always wore grew misty and vacant as Christmas approached. She would be in the middle of doing something, baking bread, say, and the cawing of crows in a tree would distract her so that she'd head outside to see what the fuss was about, only to return an hour later having no memory of why she'd lit the oven and what this batter was doing in a bowl on the kitchen counter. Our bedrooms were separated only by a door, and I could hear her talking to herself at all hours of the night. I cupped my ear to that door but never understood the meaning of anything she mumbled. *Native ear long nursery, peach. Tat sing, dat-tut-tat. Why the fall flow jigger?* Part of me wondered if she wasn't trying to communicate with the Martians.

What I did begin to understand, and quickly, is that I was in the midst of losing her as surely as I'd lost my father. She spent a lot of chilly evenings out in Van Nest Park studying the skies for saucers even though she, like the rest of the country, had been as-sured by the authorities, not to mention a contrite Welles himself, that the invasion was a hoax. I suppose my mother might have been looking for vindication for her husband's death, or else hop-ing against all odds that some real Martians would take her away to join him. I recall thinking, as I hid behind a big rhododendron bush one evening watching her pace back and forth across the long grass, glancing up then shaking her head and staring at the ground, that she was becoming alien herself—or, at least, alienated. On the other hand, to be fair, let me confess here that she and I both did believe we saw suspicious lights that infamous night, like moving and beaconing stars in the ghastly sky.

She started drinking. I imagine it didn't take much gin-mill hooch to send her, a thin, nervous woman, off the edge. Drunk, she began saying things at the dinner table that upset my grand-mother. Things like how she wished she'd never met my father and how she'd give anything to get away from Grover's Mill. How she hated its bleak bone-cold winters and sauna-muggy summers. How she couldn't stand being this tantalizingly close to Manhattan but not having a plug nickel to go bathe in those bright big-city lights.

Once when my grandmother thought I wasn't listening, she confided to a visiting neighbor lady, "Mildred's gone and turned into Grover's very own *Mill Dread*. If it weren't for the boy, I'd set her out on her ear, for all that she's my own poor son's widow." I cringed at her soft, confident chuckle and crept away to stalk the pond's edge.

My grandfather took a kinder approach. He was no less a carpenter than my father had been. Indeed, father had taught son. Because my mother said she'd give anything to spend the upcoming springtime days rowing out to the middle of Grover's Mill Pond to watch the skies for activity, maybe take a picnic with her son, he indulgently refurbished my father's childhood rowboat for us to use. It was so beautiful, that boat. I could never get enough of leaning my head over its side and watching reflected sunlight dancing off the water, making its varnished belly glisten with different ever-changing shapes! And I must admit it made me feel proud to take my father's place at the oars, even if I risked being seen by some of the whispering kids at school who already deemed my parents lunatics. After winter faded away, we kept it tied up at the nearby dock of a friend of my grandfather's and went out on the water often.

For a time, my mom did seem to improve. Less midnight babble. Less astronomical observation. Her hooch still flowed like the Passaic, but not so much that she couldn't start doing a bit of bookkeeping at Grandpa's hardware store while I helped with the shelving of paint cans, drill bits, saws, glue pots, and yes, even boxes of nails after school. Rowing and fresh spring-into-summer air brought a bit of healthy glow back to her cheeks. Life seemed on the upswing.

It was an afternoon in late September—the first autumn colors blushing in the red maples and sweetbay magnolias, the rushes and deer-tongue grass swaying in breezes—that hinted of cooler days to come, that we rowed out for what would prove to be the last time. We'd made liverwurst and onion sandwiches together back at the house, her favorite. Some peanut-buttered celery stalks, along with dill pickles and potato chips, were packed in the small wicker basket with a couple of bottles of cream soda. This was to be a real feast. Also, it was an important moment for me, since I'd finally got up the nerve to tell her—now that she seemed enough recovered from my father's suicide to act more or less normal—that our mother-son outings were going to have to wind down, maybe even stop. Some kids at school had seen us out here together on Grover's Mill Pond enough times that I was now officially getting razzed as a mama's boy. Time had come for both of us to grow up.

What happened next happened so fast I can scarcely picture it, quick as when a lightbulb blows out and the room goes instantly dark. We'd been talking about heaven knows what, a V of geese migrating south, how the pickles from Miller's are crisper than the ones from Malory's. Then I blurted it out. My concern about being seen out on the pond too often with my mommy, and how I was catching unholy flak for it at school. She pulled a hidden flask from her jacket pocket, unscrewed its cap, took a deep drink from it, and lit into me. Something about cowardice, something about me being my father's son, something about how alone she was in the world and that I couldn't possibly understand her pain. In the sorry wink of an eye, she was back to being her old unhappy self, wagging that silver flask in my face as she made her points.

My grabbing at it, slapping it away, was pure instinct. When it flew out of her hand and splashed in the greenish water, she just as unthinkingly stood up in the unsteady boat, snatched one of the oars, and tried to fish her flask back. I shouted at her to stop, that she was going to fall overboard, but before she could even turn her head to respond, the boat tipped over, throwing us and our wicker-basket banquet into the pond.

Our immediate impulse was to save each other. That much I recall with total clarity. But since I was the only one of us who could swim well enough to possibly get to shore with heavy, water-logged clothes acting as a full-body drag anchor, I flailed her over to the capsized rowboat and shouted at her to hang on until I came back with help.

"I'm gonna drown, just like him," she gurgled, water running out of her mouth. Her face was as white as paint primer.

"No you're not!" I shouted. "Just stay put, you hear me?"

Wriggling out of my coat and frantically toeing my shoes off, I swam like mad, frozen with fear as well as the water's chill. With every kick and doggy paddle stroke I made, the possibility that my mother was about to die in the same pond as my dad became more and more real. Half-drowned myself, I lurched into some sedge, covered in mud, slime, and a slick of slimy decomposing leaves that had fallen on the pond. By the time I managed to summon help, and some men hurried out to where the capsized rowboat serenely drifted, my mother had vanished into the murk. The frog-men, one of whom I recognized as having been on the same team that retrieved my drowned father not a year before, had her up to the surface in no time. But it was all too late. Her narrow pale face was already bloated, her lips gone purple.

So began a time in the house off Cranbury Road that degen-erated from bad to awful. My grandmother and I hardly knew what to do with each other when alone in the same room. I think she blamed her son's suicide on my mother, my mother's death on me somehow, and also blamed me for having been the reason my parents were forced to get married in the first place. Much as I couldn't admit to personal responsibility in that matter—after all, I had no say in their out-of-wedlock lovemaking under spicy-smelling sweet pepper bushes on the pond's bank—I understood how she could see me as a living symbol of her precious Wyatt's downfall. As for my grandfather, he was truly heartbroken, and shouldered much of the blame himself.

"If I hadn't got it in my head to fix up that boat . . ." he would mutter, then his words would trail off.

Grandmother Iris, who got more brittle and cranky by the day, could only agree with him. After my mother was buried in the cemetery next to my father, I was left by default in her care. Ours was a house of grief. But whereas my grandfather grieved for my mother and me, I got the sense that Grandmother grieved mostly for herself and the burden that I now had become. In school, we read about the ancient mariner and the albatross. I'd become an albatross, if no longer taunted for being a mama's boy. The crowd of punks who'd made that accusation now shunned me for a different reason. I was, they decided, an angel of death. Someone to be avoided like the plague. I had neither the will nor way to contradict them. At home in bed, listening to the ticking clock in my parents' empty bedroom, I found myself wondering if they weren't right.

People die in threes. So goes the old saying. Though several years had passed since my parents' drownings, one intentional, the other not, death once more came lurking to round out the number. My grandpa had taken ill with a case of walking pneumonia at Thanksgiving and was hospitalized in nearby Princeton by early December. The snow was particularly heavy that year. Wind drifted shapely piles around the house and frost clung to the windows in fernlike patterns. Since my grandmother hated driving in bad weather, a man named Franklin, who responded to an ad she placed in the local paper, drove us to the hospital every other day to visit. I couldn't help but notice that around Franklin my grandmother seemed to lighten up a little, which was a relief to me, since I could only imagine how, deep down, she must have faulted me for her husband's illness. Franklin sometimes stayed for dinner after we returned from Princeton, recounting the places in the world he claimed to have visited—exotic locales like Morocco and Brazil and Fiji. What he was doing in these far-flung countries and how he could afford all his globe-hopping was unclear to me, but what did I care. Pretending politeness, I listened, at least in the beginning, even though I figured it was all a pack of lies. If from the very beginning I didn't trust his stories and overconfident manner, his presence meant my grandmother and I weren't left alone at a painfully silent table. For that I was grateful.

As with my mother, my grandfather seemed to be improving daily, only to abruptly take a downward turn and die of complications between Christmas and New Year's. My grandmother's heartbreak over this, I must admit, startled me. She wept the most genuine tears I'd ever seen well from her steely eyes. For a time, I wondered if she wasn't going to end up in the hospital herself, so bereft was she. Neighbors dropped by with tuna casserole, cold fried chicken, and potato salad, which I lived on for breakfast, lunch, and dinner, noticing that she ate nary a morsel.

Franklin helped make arrangements with the crematorium and drove us over to the funeral home so we could pay our last respects before Grandfather was fed to the furnace. Though she abhorred her husband's final wish not to be laid to rest in the ground, where he would rot like old maggoty timber, my grandmother honored his instruction. We caravanned with several dozen of his friends and longtime customers to the dam-end of the pond, where the ice was still unfrozen. On a gusty, blue-sky day in the dead of winter, the minister delivered yet another eulogy before my grandfather's ashes, gray as pumice, were scattered on the equally gray water. I couldn't help but think, as I burrowed my freezing face into my wool muffler, that at twenty-five dollars per eulogy, our family kept the minister so busy he might as well have been put on hardware store's payroll.

Gallows humor, not very funny. But I didn't have much to

laugh about, anyway. The wind made a swirling snow-devil out at the far edge of the pond, where some kids were ice-skating, blissfully unaware of why a bunch of people in overcoats were huddled down at our end. We trudged along after the service, climbed in our cars, and slowly drove home.

Life at school didn't improve. The opposite. I should have been grateful that the punks had given up teasing me, but instead I felt ignored. What was worse, I was now pitied by many of my imbecile classmates. How I hated the sympathetic stares I got from students I hardly knew. Walking the hallway between classes became an ordeal both embarrassing and infuriating. My only recourse was to feign sickness as a way of getting out of school for stretches of time, at least until winter subsided. And when the weather warmed, I simply began ditching classes and hanging out by myself down at the pond. The school's student counselor dropped by one evening and spoke about my absences and failing grades with my grandmother and Franklin, who was by that evening, as he was most every evening now. I eavesdropped from an adjacent room and was relieved and angered by my grandmother's response which was, in essence, "The boy's suffered a series of bad blows and ought to be allowed to work through his mourning as need be." I was relieved because this meant I was, as I understood, freed from adults lording over me, telling me what to do. Angered because I knew, even then, I didn't have the first idea how to mourn, and was essentially abandoned to my own devices from that moment on.

At what point did I begin to suspect Franklin was trying to seduce my grandmother? I was young enough at the time—fifteen at the end of World War II—that anyone beyond their teens was an oldster to me, yet in retrospect I realize Franklin must have only been in his mid-forties. Though my grandmother was a decade or more his senior, she was still a handsome woman in her hawkish way. But no, I thought, shoving away this disgusting thought as one might a snapping rabid dog. Don't be ridiculous. Franklin, fraud though he might be, was acting charitably toward a sonless widow and a luckless orphan stuck under the same roof, wasn't he?

I wasn't overly surprised when he moved into the house that spring as a boarder. My grandmother explained she could use the extra money to help pay down the mortgage, but I knew she could have gone on just fine without, living off the healthy proceeds of the sale of the hardware store. I had grim mixed feelings about the way things were developing. On one hand, as I say, I welcomed the buffer Franklin constituted between my grandmother and me. On the other, it took my breath away, angered and confused me, how proprietary he became. Not just toward my grandmother but the whole household, myself included. His authority was established with an almost businesslike swiftness, as if he were born to the task. Impressive, too, was the ease with which he pushed back whenever I got it in my head to challenge him, even over the slightest thing.

When I commented, testing his patience one evening during dinner, that Franklin was more a last than a first name, he laughed softly, picked a fleck of tobacco that came loose from his hand-rolled cigarette with his thumb and pinky finger, and said, "I've heard that one before. Benjamin Franklin and all."

"Well, why don't you let people just call you Frank? Wouldn't that be easier?"

"Would you want to call our recently deceased president Frank Delano Roosevelt?"

"Why not? It's less of a mouthful," I countered. "Anyway, you're not the president."

He regarded me with a slow sidelong glance. "I like you, Wyatt. And respect you enough not to call you Wy. Franklin comes from the Middle English word for freeman—*Frankeleyn*. Frank means something else altogether. The Franks were a German tribe, named after a kind of spear they used back in the early times. When they moved from Germany to Gaul, that's how France got its name. I hate the Germans and can't stand Frenchmen. But I like the idea of being a freeman. So, Franklin it is," he said, and took another drag off his cigarette.

Increasingly, he enjoyed making smart little speeches like this while my grandmother now and then glanced over at me and nodded, as if to say, *You might learn something if you keep your trap shut and listen.*

I didn't hate him, not yet, but I couldn't figure Franklin out, either. He seemed never to have worked a day in his life, and it was unclear to me where he came from, what his background was, if he had family, how he knew so much, and how he managed always to have enough money to pay his room and board. The first person I ever heard use the word *enigma* was Franklin. And though he was talking about something else, politics or religion, say, when I asked him what it meant and he answered, "Anything that's baffling," I knew I'd never forget that word because it perfectly defined Franklin himself.

For instance, how could anybody dislike my grandfather's sweet old dog, Claude? I inherited him after my grandfather passed away. For a while, Claude became my best friend in the world. I could tell that he missed his master as much as I did, but he slipped into the habit of sleeping on the rug by my bed at night and accompanying me on my walks around the pond. A mangy mutt with a messy coat of blacks and browns and what looked like a smile perennially on his face, Claude—so named because he was prone to knocking things over, digging up the yard, a real *clod*, in other words—was a comfort to me, a pal in those months of grieving the loss of my one remaining male relative. As much affection as I directed toward Claude, Franklin showed him a hostile impatience.

"That dog should be kept outdoors," he told my grandmother at breakfast one day, after Claude had an overnight accident on the front room rug.

"It's my fault," I argued. "I should have taken him out for a walk before I went to bed. He couldn't help it."

Franklin's condescending smile was directed toward my grandmother, as he continued, "He's pretty old not to be house-trained. By which I mean Claude, not Wyatt, of course. With your permission, I can build a dog house for him."

"I don't know," my grandmother hesitated. "There's a foot of snow out there. I'm afraid he might freeze."

"Dogs are used to weather. He'll be fine."

Seeing that my grandmother was actually weighing Franklin's inhumane proposal, I slapped my hand on the table, making the silverware jump, and shouted, "No way is Claude going to be thrown out in the cold! He'll die out there. Grandma, I promise it won't happen again. He's a good boy."

When, a month later, Claude disappeared, never to be found, I knew Franklin was somehow behind it. I had no proof, however, and because we three had been all but snowbound together, the weather that winter being the worst anybody could remember, I couldn't figure when or how he would have managed to spirit Claude away without me or my grandmother noticing. At the same time, there were no telltale tracks in the snow. It was as if Claude had simply floated away, transported into the sky on flurries.

The spring following my grandfather's funeral, Franklin busied himself fixing rain gutters that had been damaged during a wet, heavy April blizzard, the last of that wretched season. He worked on repairing the front porch, wearing a jacket that had been my father's and a porkpie hat I recognized as my grandpa's. A closet-shopping regular part of the family, he'd become, not that I had much say in the matter. I knew if I confronted my grandmother about the indecency of Franklin wearing these clothes, I'd get a sharp rebuke in response. Instead, resentment started to build in me like steam in a pressure cooker. I sensed he could tell, and that he got a perverse kick out of it.

One day he found me down at the pond fishing. Clearly, he'd been looking for me, because he said, "There you are."

I didn't look up from my line lying like a skinny snake on the water. "There I am," I said.

My grandmother had recently accused me of being more and more disconnected from those around me, and I didn't bother to argue with her. I was even more disconnected than she knew. Had been in a couple of fights after school, on days I was forced to attend, and simply let the other guy win, if only to avoid having to talk about it later. I figured if I'd somehow pulled off a victory, I would have to accept congratulations from kids I hated or else deal with demands for a rematch. I wanted nothing to do with any of that malarkey. Instead, I filched some cover-up powder from my mother's cosmetics kit to camouflage my black eye and bruises, though I wondered if it was possible, actually, to filch anything from my mom now that she was dead and gone.

"Catching anything?"

I squinted up at him, said, "Caught a pretty good size stick an hour ago."

"Threw it back, I guess," he quipped, sitting next to me.

There was nothing to say so I left his line unanswered, just like my own line out in the water.

"Wyatt?" he went on, his voice pleasant as punch. "Iris wants me to paint the house."

Iris? My grandmother, Mrs. Mecham, you mean? I said nothing.

"And I was wondering if you'd like to help me. It'd go a lot faster with two of us working on it together. You game?"

I shrugged, uncomfortable with him sitting so close beside me. "I don't care."

"Great," he said, standing after grabbing me by the back of the neck and amiably shaking me side to side, like we were old buddies. I wrenched away, staring at the clouds on the pond. "We start first thing in the morning."

It would seem that Franklin had, maybe at my grandmother's behest, removed quite a stash of paint and primer, brushes and sandpaper, drop cloths and ladders, from the hardware store before its new owners took possession. He made me help him lug all this possibly stolen stuff from the cellar after breakfast.

As with most everything, Franklin possessed a remarkable knowledge about how to paint a house. We scraped away the old curling and chipped surface of each course of clapboard first, then sanded, primed, and brushed on two coats of yellow oil paint—a pale jaundiced yellow that was my grandmother's preference—with white trim. Work went along steadily and in a few weeks the job was done.

Me, I was sick of the place by the time we finished, but Franklin and his Iris walked around it in the morning, afternoon, and then again before sunset admiring its every angle. Whereas they couldn't have been more pleased with the outcome, I felt horrified and ashamed. We'd somehow robbed the house of its history and personality by making it look so different. It didn't dawn on me until after we'd folded the drop cloths, cleaned the brushes with turpentine, and put everything back in the cellar, that what we had done was paint my parents and grandfather out of the picture. I realized too late that I preferred it the way it was before, comfortably the worse for wear, a pleasant dirty white instead of this cat-piss hue.

Even more than this, what came out of the experience for me had nothing to do with the project itself, but with a growing curiosity about and deepening distaste for the project manager. The same way you can look an animal in the eye and know if it's sick or healthy, I studied Franklin over the course of those days together and began to form a strong opinion as to his character. I didn't let on as I observed him. I did as I was told, faking as respectful an obedience as I could.

When he said, "Climb up the ladder and see if you can't get a little more trim gloss on that eave," I climbed up the ladder and brushed more trim gloss on the eave. When he said, "Lunch break, Wyatt," I came down from wherever I was on the side of the house and sat in the violet shade with him and ate a ham sandwich, listening to him pontificate about how smelly the canals are in Venice in the summer, and how warm the mink hats they wear in St. Petersburg are as the snow drifts down over Palace Square, and how in Varanasi, also known as Benares, one of the oldest cities in the world, says he, Indian seekers—*would-be freemen*, he called them—bathe themselves in the chocolate brown waters of the Ganges to find their way toward heaven, or some such. He was consumed by his stories and his own voice, while I watched a troop of black ants at my feet carry tiny morsels of ham and rye away toward some unknown underground destination.

As I listened and watched, my eyes narrowing to gain better focus, I began to believe, with the certainty of one who knows firsthand that death follows life, that there was something deeply disturbed about Franklin. Something unnatural, off. Was he just delusional, a suave but big fat outrageous liar? Just a user and a taker? Or was he on the lam, untrustworthy, hiding here in Grover's Mill from someone or something? Was he dangerous? Was he possibly *evil*?

"Did you wash yourself in the Ganges too, then?" I asked, just to see what he would say, not really caring whether he did or didn't.

"I'm not a Hindu," he answered. "No point."

"So what'd you learn, seeing those poor sons of guns dunk themselves in muddy water?"

Franklin sighed, looked away. "That human beings may be the lowest class of species in the universe. But let's change the subject. Your grandmother—"

"Iris, you mean?"

"—wouldn't appreciate me telling you such negative things, Wyatt. Besides, you're young. The world's mostly ahead for you. You'll have your own experiences and form your own conclusions about everything when you grow up."

"I don't need to get one day older to form my own conclusions," I said, hoping to provoke some telling response.

"No, really?" turning his slitted eyes on me.

I don't know why I felt the strongest urge to hit him in the face with one of my already clenched fists, but knew I'd be over-powered in a flash, so I said with as bitter and worldly a tone as I could muster, "Look, Frank—I mean, Franklin. I already know the world stinks. I don't need to go to Venice or any of your other fancy-ass places to figure that out. I'm not stupid any more than you're a Hindu."

Franklin thought about that, or pretended to, for a minute. Then said, mock cheerful, "Lunch break's over, Einstein. Time to get back to painting."

Life pressed on over the next months. Franklin arranged for the three of us to go to Radio City Music Hall to see a show featuring the Rockettes, and while my grandmother was thrilled, I couldn't help but feel guilty about our grand adventure—he bought dinner at a ritzy restaurant, my first encounter with creamed herring—knowing it was something my mom would have given anything, but anything to do.

Being by now a total outcast, a shunned goat, at school, and not caring what others said about me, I started spending after-noons up at the cemetery, hanging out near my parents' side-by-side graves, before heading down to do my daily walk around Grover's Mill Pond. The role of mama's boy, or daddy's, was one at this point I relished rather than rejected, wishing the bullies could fairly taunt me with such labels again. What would I give if I could still fish the pond with my father, or row out to the middle for another picnic with my boozy mother. Answer is anything. But I didn't have anything to give, nothing anyway that would bring them back. And so, I found myself hanging around as much at the cemetery as at the drowning pond, the ash-carpeted pond, because in both places I noticed my heart calmed and my chance at happiness improved. Or, not *happiness*—less miserableness.

The keeper of the graveyard, a pasty middle-aged fellow with gimlet teeth, unwashed hair, and a kindly sad look in his eye, asked me one Tuesday, when there was no funeral to oversee or vandals to chase away, what I was doing there so often.

"Why you asking?" I asked him back. "Am I breaking a rule or something?"

"No," he said, shoving his hands into trouser pockets, shy, I thought, about talking to the living as opposed to the dead. "Just seems like a young fella like you ought to be having fun with your friends somewhere, instead of haunting an old boneyard like this."

I shrugged.

Then he asked an unexpected question: "Well, seeing as you're here so much, how'd you like to pick up a little extra walk-around money?"

So it was I was hired to mow the lawn, sweep leaves and other leavings off the oblong marble markers, pick up trash—I couldn't believe all the junk, candy wrappers, discarded funeral programs, even a used condom—left behind by sloppy mourners and cemetery-goers. Ralph paid me in cash, and other than giving me my assignment for the day, didn't pull a Franklin on me by expecting me to listen to dumb speeches or answer a bunch of questions, so we got along pretty well. He had a daughter about my age named Mollie, who tagged along with him to work sometimes, and because she seemed to share my outcast ways, we sat against one of the mausoleums and chatted during breaks or after work. Like me, Mollie had lost her mother. Not to death, but because she ran off with another man.

"She might as well be dead and drowned as your mom," Mollie said, shaking her head as she looked at me with unblinking, pretty brown eyes, dark as wet bark. "Don't hate me for saying so, but I sorta wish she *had* drowned. Least that way I could feel sorry for her."

"Yeah. I know," I said.

Because I didn't have any costly hobbies, and didn't care about going to the movies or buying burgers and malted milks—I would have treated Mollie, but she had no more interest than I did in these things—the money started adding up. I kept it hidden in the lining of a seersucker jacket I rarely wore, which was safely hung in the far back of my closet. My grandmother occasionally asked me what I'd been up to all day, and was perfectly satisfied with the hodgepodge of white lies I concocted for her benefit. As often as not, I even told her the partial truth—"I helped mow somebody's lawn"—to which she would respond, "Good way to get some exercise," and the matter would drop. While I was pretty sure Franklin knew I was lying half the time, he let it ride. So long as I kept *our* lawn mowed.

It was about this time, when Franklin announced his intention of painting and wallpapering the interior of the house, a project my grandmother embraced wholeheartedly, that I began to develop an idea of my own. My idea began small, like a baby worm inside an apple. But as the days rolled by, it slowly formed itself at the core of my raw existence. Here I'd been earning money for no reason, but now I needed money if I was going to run away and start a new life somewhere else. I didn't know any other place besides Grover's Mill, but my home wasn't home anymore, it was being leached away from me. Now at least I had a plan, a reason to get out of bed in the morning. And if I wavered, a particularly disturbing encounter with Franklin solidified my goal.

This occurred when we were nearly finished with stripping off the old wallpaper in the dining room, a stately leaf-and-floral pattern with Greek vases that I used to get lost in staring at when I was a kid, which was to be replaced by a more up-to-date geometric design. To me it was just more of the same business of erasing the past, but I had no will to get all hot under the collar over it. The two of them had gone into New York to pick the new paper in a showroom there, so it was a moot point.

Helping Franklin with this work during the mornings before heading off to my chores in the cemetery, where I could hang around with Mollie, left me little time for my loitering by the pond, and school was just a fading memory. I'd basically dropped out, without anybody making much of a fuss about it. I assured my grandmother I would finish high school later, after taking time off to regroup. Meantime, working both jobs—and let me say here, if I might, that I was a hard worker, despite any attitude issues I had regarding Franklin—left me a worn-out rag at the end of the day. It was everything I could do to get some supper into my belly, do the dishes, slip past Iris and Franklin as they listened to some variety program on the radio, and head upstairs to bed. A fast masturbation into one of my socks, and I was quickly in dreamland.

One night, I'd gone down the hall to take a pee. After I lay down again, for whatever reason, I was having a hard time getting back to sleep. I tossed and turned, punched my pillow, adjusted my blanket, then had finally started to drift off when I heard someone turn the knob on my door and softly glide into the room. Far too startled, not to mention frightened, to speak or scream or even move, I lay there listening, and waited. Some long minutes passed, my heart up in my throat, and I did hear shuffling, very soft, across the rug, and the delicate, awful sound of breathing. I could swear I heard the intruder reach down and lift something up from the floor and—I can't say for sure because my ears were so full of the shush of my pounding heart—inhale. The next sound was not as indistinct. A floorboard creaked, only somewhat muffled by the braided rug. The silence that followed was, as the cliché goes, deafening—and it went on for such an excruciatingly long stretch of time that I began to wonder if I hadn't dreamed the intrusion. I continued my vigil with a corpselike stillness, and after a time I heard the faintest thud—not a thud, more like a *poof* of air—followed by another unnatural silence, and then the expertly turned handle again, though oddly no footfalls from my bedside back to the door. Mortified, I didn't move a muscle, barely breathed, hoping against hope that there would be no further activity. As the room began to lighten, the sun not yet risen outside but the sky pinkening the sheers in my window, I recovered my wits and began trying to sort out what in the world I'd experienced.

Franklin, who considered himself a bit of a chef, was making Irish oatmeal and Belgian waffles in the kitchen that morning, whistling, as I walked in and poured myself a glass of milk.

"Where's my grandmother?" I asked.

"When I came down, she wasn't up yet so I checked in on her and she's a tad under the weather this morning. Would you mind taking that up to her?" pointing at a tray set out with a soft-boiled egg, unbuttered toast, orange juice. The unnecessary touch of flowers in a cream pitcher nauseated me, I must confess.

"Breakfast in bed," I said, and proceeded to do as he told me.

Not that I suspected for a moment my grandmother had been the person who visited my bedroom during the night, but seeing her in bed, white as if she'd been soaked in bleach, feeble from flu, confirmed it hadn't been her. I placed the tray on her bedside table, asked if there was anything else I could do.

"No, Wyatt. I just need to sleep, is all. I'll try to eat some of that later."

Back downstairs in the kitchen, I certainly wasn't going to give Franklin the pleasure of hearing me ask if he happened to notice any burglars in the house last night. Best, I knew, just to leave him thinking I was dumb as a brick. One thing that continued to bother me as the day wore on was how my intruder, surely Franklin, managed to exit the room without making a single hint of sound. He'd deftly stolen into the room. Stood over me silent as death for a long time. But then it was as if he'd simply floated to the door when he made his escape. How did he do that? I took to leaning one of my schoolbooks—which I secretly read on evenings when I had enough energy—against the inside of my bedroom door before going to bed. This way, I figured I'd know if he had snuck in again in the middle of the night. I kept my father's wooden leg beside me under my blanket too, with which I planned to bash in his skull if the chance arose. But every morning I saw that the book was still there, so I gathered he had lost interest or decided it wasn't worth the risk.

As work in the rooms continued, the wariness and hostility I felt toward Franklin only grew, despite his apparent decision not to trespass further on my privacy while I was sleeping. Grandmother's health improved, in no small measure because of Franklin's doting, but rather than making me glad this only irked me. One could reasonably argue I had no right to feel competitive with him, but any natural instinct—granted, piddling—I had about being a good grandson was crowded off the stage by Franklin. He was like a land-going octopus with tentacles wrapped around nearly every part of my life. When she was sick, confined to her room, my grandmother had instructed me to do whatever Franklin said—that until she was back up and out of bed, he was head of the house. The only problem was, this edict remained in effect even now that she was back to her old, cold self. I found myself living with a strange new father now, one with whom I didn't share a drop of blood in my veins and toward whom never a kind thought ran through my mind. Had my real father been alive to see what was happening here, or so I fantasized, he'd have beaten Franklin to within an inch of his life and then dragged him—one leg powering the way—down to the pond to finish the job. Sweet dream, but just a dream.

The only time I felt free from the so-called freeman these days was when I was with Mollie. Much the same way the rich like hobnobbing with other rich people, loners are drawn to loners. Mollie and I were living proof of this. One might think that with his wife having run off on him, her father Ralph would have been extra strict about letting Mollie out of his sight. But from the first he seemed to trust and like me, so my wandering off from the cemetery to the pond with his daughter, our spending every spare hour we had in each other's company, didn't bother him. I felt like we had his silent blessing, and while he was rough-edged, unshaven, and stained by melancholy, I thought of him sometimes as a surrogate father, though I never told him such. Besides Ralph, nobody knew a thing about me and Mollie, because nobody cared. It was the only part of my life I inhabited with perfect independence, and as such it was my greatest joy.

Once, lying in the tall grass with Mollie, secluded from everyone and everything but a red-tailed hawk circling high overhead, she asked me, "How come you hate that man living in your house so much?"

"I never said I hated him," and kissed her again, hoping that would be the end of it. Franklin was the last person I wanted to talk about here with Mollie.

When she pulled her lips away to breathe, she said, gently, "But you don't need to say it in words, Wyatt. Whenever he comes up, the look in your eyes says it all."

Mollie wasn't someone I wanted to lie to, so I told her, "Look, he just gives me the creeps, all right? He treats me like I'm his slave or something, and my grandmother goes along with it all. I just need to get out of there, the sooner the better."

"What's he done to give you the creeps? You don't seem to be afraid of anything, from what I know."

I told her about the night in my bedroom, and how every time Franklin was near me he got too close. I told her how even the way he smoked his cigarettes had a wickedness to it, how his endless stories seemed like a madman's fictions, and that every favor he'd done for us seemed to have strings attached. "It's like he's a virus, taking over our lives and making us sick. I feel like I'm living in his house now, instead of the other way around."

The idea I'd been harboring, and the mounting hatred that fueled it, took a giant leap in a more dangerous direction when my sixteenth birthday rolled around. Franklin got it in his head that this was too important a milestone in my life not to celebrate in grand style. I'd have preferred to eat pizza out of a box, but he would have none of that.

"We're throwing you a party," he announced a couple of weeks before the big day, knowing it was the last thing I wanted. "Oh, yes. Cake, candles, champagne, the works."

"I don't care if he is turning sixteen, Wyatt's still too young for champagne," my grandmother objected, if meekly.

"Bosh," was Franklin's response, not even bothering to look in her direction. He had her, by this time, utterly under his sway. She said nothing further.

When the question arose as to whom we might invite to this proposed party in the newly refurbished dining room, Franklin had a ready answer that floored me.

"Well, of course we'll ask over some of the neighbors who've known you for years. The McDermott clan, the Riordans. I guess there's nobody at school, but maybe the minister and his wife might like a nice slice of homemade cake and a glass of spiked punch," he said, ticking these off on his finger tips. "Oh, and you'll want to invite that girlfriend of yours, Mollie."

Grandmother Iris jolted wide awake suddenly, and said, "Why, I didn't know you had a girlfriend, Wyatt."

My arms crossed, astounded, fuming, I stared at Franklin who calmly returned my gaze with one of shameless triumph.

"That's because I don't," I snapped.

"Well, however you want to label her," Franklin said, waving off my denial as if it were a casement fly, "I'm sure she'd love to come. Bring her father Ralph along too, if you think he owns a bar of soap to clean himself up with first. He can make himself useful by helping me chaperone you two lovebirds." These last bits about soap and lovebirds, meant for me alone, Franklin said under his breath.

Iris confirmed she'd missed it by adding something trite like, "By all means, let's invite the lucky young lady and her father. Wyatt, shame on you for keeping this a secret from your poor grandmother."

Looking back over the years, having had plenty of time to

think about it, I've come to believe this was the moment when Franklin sealed both our fates. I couldn't have known it for a fact just then, as I excused myself, rose from the dinner table, and fled the house to walk to the pond in growing twilight. But what I did know, with blinding clarity, was that I had not been hallucinating on several recent instances at the cemetery when I thought I'd seen somebody, or something, lurking in the grove of oak trees near the McKearin family plot, or prowling in the weeping branches of the huge willow that hunched over the Wylers near a brook whose waters emptied into Grover's Mill Pond. And this somebody or something was clearly spying on me, hoping not to be seen.

I hadn't wanted to admit it to myself, in part because a reasonable voice inside assured me it was a madness not unlike my mother's, but in that moment I also knew for certain that on one particular occasion, when I saw Franklin's shadow cast on the fresh-mowed graveyard lawn, it had not two legs but three. I might have dismissed this out of hand had not Mollie seen the shadow that afternoon too, and agreed that the person hiding behind the big Dutch elm did seem to have three legs.

"Optical delusion," she later judged it, making a little pun to try to leaven things.

I wasn't so sure.

Down by the pond that evening, after Franklin had revealed himself as a menace, a true nemesis of mine, I tramped slowly around the pond—my pond, on which I'd always been able to rely. Bile pumped through my heart as I tried to breathe in and out to calm myself, but the stagnant air only stung my throat. Franklin had done everything he could to usurp the roles of my father, my mother, my grandfather, and now had in essence declared himself my babysitter, my watchman, my warden. What was clear to me, clear as the shimmering full moon that floated on the face of the water, was that if I simply used Ralph's wages as I'd intended—to run away, whether with Mollie beside me or not—Franklin would track me down. He seemed to know every inch of the world like the back of his bullying hand. Had me convinced there was nowhere I could hide but that he'd rout me out, like the woodpeckers in Van Nest Park rout out bugs secreted in tree trunks. No, I couldn't afford to delude myself on that front. And if my hunch was right, that he was one of the invaders left behind after the Halloween eve attack half my lifetime ago—one who somehow escaped death, immune to the microbes that exterminated the others—then it would be all the easier for him to seek and find me. They have their extraterrestrial sensory powers, after all.

There are four ways a person can die. Natural causes, accidental, suicide, and murder. And while I don't like to think of myself as someone drawn to death, by that time I had firsthand knowledge—and, in these waters, firsthand experience—of all of the ways to heaven or hell but one. It fell to me, I believed deep down, to complete the cycle. What did I have to lose? Mollie would still love me, I was sure. She would understand. So much for the aphorism about death coming in threes.

My father owned a service revolver which I inherited upon his death, along with his war medals, his fob watch, and other mementos. I stored these in his locked steel box, the key to which I kept hidden along with my stash of money in the back of my closet. There were half a dozen bullets in the safe box as well, and though they were pretty old, all I needed was for one of them to work.

Needless to say, I didn't invite Mollie or her father to my birthday party. Why should I subject them to Franklin's humiliations? Instead, I left the house, which smelled admittedly wonderful with a chocolate cake baking in the oven, and met Mollie as usual in the cemetery. Knowing it was my sixteenth birthday, Ralph had given me the day off, and since Franklin was caught up with his party preparations, I knew she and I could while away our hours in private. I had already hidden the revolver, loaded and ready, wrapped in a camouflaging green T-shirt of mine under a juniper bush by the pond's edge. So my day was free and clear.

I had asked Mollie not to buy me a present. Better, I told her, to save her money. She did, however, produce a small rectangular box wrapped in shiny paper, which she presented to me with an excited smile.

"It's not much," she said.

"No, it's beautiful."

"You haven't even opened it up yet, silly."

"I mean just everything. The shiny paper, the ribbon, you."

"Stop," she said, with a blushing frown. "Open it."

Inside was a pocket-sized field manual on the trees and wild shrubs of the Northeast. I was thrilled, but said, "Hey, you promised you wouldn't spend any money."

"Don't worry, I got it cheap at the thrift shop. Besides, I know how much you love to be outdoors so I figured you might want to know what everything's called. For your next birthday, I'm thinking about a bird book, or maybe one with all the insects."

"It's the best present anybody ever gave me," I said, and we shared a long, yearning kiss.

Mollie and I spent the next hour lying side by side in a hidden clearing, marveling at the names we read together—*flowering dogwood, staghorn sumac, sourgum*—and the color illustrations beside each description. In my life I never felt so deliciously sheltered from the world, alone and yet so complete and contented, and when I set aside the book and began kissing Mollie again it was the most natural possible act for us to make love, and so we did, each of us losing our virginity that afternoon as the sun crawled down the sky.

The ache I felt when saying goodbye to her, moving just as naturally though nowhere near as blissfully into my next important inevitability of the day, was painful, to say the least.

I had no idea whether I'd ever see Mollie again. The chances were good that Franklin wouldn't be fooled by my ruse, that he'd overpower and possibly do to me exactly what I planned to do to him.

The party was supposed to begin at six. Glancing at my father's fob watch, which I'd decided to take along with me today, I
saw that it was already five-thirty. As I walked to the place where
I'd hidden the revolver, my afterglow of happiness and euphoria
began to dim just like the cloudy sky itself, moving toward sunset
and the end of the autumn day. Franklin and Iris, I imagined, were
getting pretty anxious by now. "That kid will be late to his own
funeral," I could hear my grandmother rue with a cluck of her
tongue. Franklin's comments would not be as colloquial or forgiv-
ing. I pictured him pacing from room to room, steaming mad. I
could almost hear him from here at the pond swearing I was the
most ungrateful little bastard he'd ever met in the four decades
and seven continents of his experience.

My guess that he'd angrily throw on his jacket—my father's,
that is—and march in a snit down to the pond to find me was dead
accurate. Loitering in full view, pretending to be sulking, brooding
on the shore, I waited for him to come, service revolver shoved
into my coat pocket. There was a breeze over the pond, rippling it
like a melted washboard. A flight of starlings, black tatters blown
along, swarmed above. Soon enough, here came Franklin, a determined look on his vile face, his jaw set, his hands thrust into his
trouser pockets. I saw he was wearing a colorful cravat, one of my
grandfather's.

"What's the big idea, birthday boy?"

I didn't say a word. Just wanted to let my silence draw him
closer, like he was a kite and I was reeling him in on an invisible
string.

Predictably, he just kept talking, scolding me as he neared
where I stood. "Don't you have an ounce of respect for others?
Your little harlot Mollie and the rest are probably already back
at the house waiting for Mr. Sadsack. Well, this game of yours is
going to end. I know places far away from here where delinquents
like you can be sent for rewiring. Get you a brand-new personality. Tomorrow—" and I pulled out the revolver when he was two

strides away and pulled the trigger, putting a slug right into his heart. He dropped before me without so much as a groan, eyes widening, on his knees in an attitude that looked for all the world like someone shocked into prayer, and I shot him once more, this time in his face.

Methodically following my plan, I removed my clothes and swam his limp body out toward the middle of pond, where I sank him as well the revolver. Back on shore, I dried myself off quickly with the shirt I'd used to wrap the gun, dressed, and walked back home, numb and amazed.

"Oh, there he is," Grandmother Iris cried out.

Franklin had been mostly right about the guests having already arrived, though of course he'd been mistaken about Mollie and her father. I accepted a glass of punch from the adult bowl, the one with champagne added to the cranberry juice, and did my best to engage in conversation with the neighbors.

When Iris asked, "Where's Franklin?" I answered, "How should I know?" though I could hear my voice quaking. Not from guilt, but something more akin to excitement. I couldn't believe I had summoned the courage to carry through with my idea. To say one is proud of taking a life is fundamentally unethical, morally wrong—I know, I know. But Franklin had become, for me, a saboteur, a guerrilla, an enemy combatant, and taking him out of the picture seemed more an act of domestic warfare than anything else. I held to the belief that my father would have approved.

"He went out looking for you, you know," she went on, a raspy reproach underlying her words.

My charade didn't last long. After several more trips to the punch bowl—I'd never had a drop of booze before in my life—I decided, woozily, to tell the minister what I'd done. My grandmother was by then beside herself worrying about Franklin and I thought there was no point in dragging out my little pantomime. From my perspective, I had rid myself and the world of a scourge.

A scourge that threatened not just me, but everyone alive. I had, in the end, nothing to hide.

Problem was, when I confessed that Franklin wasn't here because I'd killed him, and that he was dead in the pond along with the revolver I assassinated him with, the minister scoffed. "I'm well aware that you have your issues with Franklin, Wyatt, but I think the alcohol is speaking here, and not you."

"No, ith's true . . ." I slurred.

"I know things have been tough for you, my son. Losing your mother and father, your grandfather. All tragic indeed. But blaming bad things that happen to us on others is not the Christian way," he said, putting a large, warm, consoling hand on my swaying shoulder.

Tongue foundering from the champagne, continuing to insist I was guilty of murder, I passed out and was carried upstairs to my bedroom.

By the next morning, Franklin still having not returned, my grandmother reported him missing to the police. At first she neglected to repeat my drunken claim that I'd killed him, assuming as the minister and others within earshot had that I was expressing an immature desire rather than an absolute fact. But after a few more days, having sobered up, of my continuing to insist, adding that I was quite certain Franklin wasn't of this world, she finally broke down and reported me. In her shoes, I might well have done the same.

The officers, themselves doubtful, especially in light of the more unusual aspects of my theories about Franklin, allowed me to walk them down to the place where I had hidden my weapon and committed my crime. No one had heard gunshots the night he disappeared, fortunately or unfortunately. Nor had anyone reported seeing anything unusual on Grover's Mill Pond that evening. Joined by a detective, the cops walked through the grass and down to the gently lapping water, seeing and saying nothing until one of them knelt and picked up a spent bullet shell.

"What kind of a gun was it you said you used on the victim?" he asked, standing.

"I'm not sure, exactly," realizing I might better have kept the revolver if I wanted to convince anyone of what I'd done.

That they found no traces of blood in the grass strengthened my case about Franklin's origins, I felt. Perhaps he didn't bleed because his kind didn't have actual blood running in their veins. And yet I could have sworn I saw his face erupt in a gushing geyser of red when my bullet hit its point-blank mark. On the other hand, I reasoned, maybe theirs is thinner and evaporates like so much mist under a hot sun.

What happened next confounds me to this day. They brought in divers, yet again, and this time even dragged the pond with a special boat they commissioned for the job, having taken me into custody for my own protection, as they put it. And what did they come up with? Nothing. No body, no revolver—just the usual jettisoned tires, an old boot, a porcelain dolly missing its head, fishing tackle, and part of a rusted nineteenth-century threshing machine. My court-assigned lawyer got me freed in no time, but not before the tabloid papers had a field day with me. I still have some of the newspaper clippings. *Murdered Martian Missing in Grover's Mill. Boy, 16, Claims Revenge for Dad's Death at Martian Hands. War of the Words in Jersey Missing Mars Man Case.*

Mollie and I were kept apart by my grandmother, who now had taken a much harder line toward me, especially after the discovery of the bullet casing which, although it proved nothing to the authorities, she understood as very damning. Citing me as a troubled child, abnormally disturbed after my parents' deaths, a juvenile delinquent and high school dropout, an unruly young man given to thoughts of violence, potentially psychotic and a danger to her and society, she moved to have me committed to a state hospital for evaluation. I voluntarily agreed to this because, for one, it got me away from her and, second, made it possible for Mollie to visit me, as the facility was a relatively short bus ride away. Third, though I didn't talk with anyone about it, I felt safer sleeping in an institution designed to keep some people in and other people out, than I ever did back home in my bedroom, knowing that Franklin had somehow managed to escape my attempt to rid the world of him.

When half a year after Franklin's vanishing a large amount of money was discovered missing from my grandmother's bank account, it was clear I couldn't have taken it since I was essentially under observation day and night. The authorities traced a money transfer to a temporary account in Greece. I heard that an international dragnet of cops pursued the thief, but the trail was as cold as the far side of the moon. Mollie, whom I married while still in the hospital once we were both of legal age, tried to use Franklin's larceny to prove to me that I was mostly right, that Franklin *was* evil, a con man, the opposite of honest, direct, *frank*—but also that he was not some alien.

"Martians don't need money," she assured me, with a wistful smile.

I nodded my head in agreement, hoping to mollify Mollie, knowing it was her fondest wish that I might come to my senses and sanity based on this information. Whatever I thought I had done the night of my sixteenth birthday, I had *not* done—this is what the few who cared about me wanted me to understand. The time had come for me to seek a discharge and take my place once more in society. So I renounced as delusional any lingering thoughts I had about Franklin—believe it or not, I never knew his last name; did he even have one?—though I held privately to the hypothesis that he was probably spirited out of the pond in a rescuing spacecraft rather than somehow disappearing that afternoon with numbers to Iris's savings account, having had enough of us both.

When she died of cancer, not long after my release, Grandmother Iris willed the old house to me, there being no one else left to give it to. In her final years, I think she might have seen the light about who Franklin really was. Oh, I don't necessarily mean that she ever embraced my theory, which I cling to even now in judicious silence but sure as a spore clings to a moldy loaf of bread. Yet the fact that they never did find his body after so many days of dredging, so many man-hours of frogmen searching Grover's Mill Pond's muddy bed, surely must have left her uneasy. I would like to think that if he didn't really die from the gunshot wounds that night, and if he didn't drown when I swam his leaden body out into the pond as far as I could before I submerged him, filling his mouth and nostrils with the water meant to weigh him down like liquid concrete, if he did happen to best death a second time, then Iris might have been paid a visit by Franklin. An after-midnight visit to her bedroom, not unlike the one I experienced that time.

And if she did, and he came floating into the scene of her helpless troubled slumber, inhaling, hovering, I'd like to think that maybe she felt a panic of second thoughts about this beast she allowed into our family house off Cranbury Road. I would like to think that if in naked terror in her bed, she reached to her bedside lamp and turned on the light, she might have seen him undisguised, monstrous and gloating, for what he was.

BROKEN GLASS

BY GERALD STERN

Mickle Street (Camden)

Broken bottles brought him to Mickle Street
and pieces of glass embedded in the mud
to Whitman's wooden house across the street from
the Church of the Most Unhappy Redeemer for when
it was too quiet he broke another bottle
and he collected his glass in a paper bag
and when he was *verloren* he cut himself
though just as like he cut himself on a wall
while doing an exercise to stretch the tendons
so he could get rid of the numb and burning feeling,
or sometimes he sat on a hydrant and once on a bench
with drooping slats so when the slats gave his back
also gave and feeling came back to his foot
as it came back to Whitman when he sat
on the orange rush seats or rocked in his chair between
the visits and loved the hollyhocks that grew
in the cracks and for a nickel the whole republic
would turn to broken glass as Oscar insisted.

WUNDERLICH

BY SHEILA KOHLER
Montclair

When she is almost seventy, he comes into her life in the fall. It is unusually warm, even in the evening, as she drives her car through the sultry streets toward her spa which is named after a saint. Lately, since she is no longer teaching, she has spent a lot of time there. When she called for an appointment, the receptionist asked her, "Do you prefer a woman or a man?"

"It doesn't make any difference," she replied, thinking one pair of hands was like another.

She did not ask the price. She spends money easily. Her husband has provided some from his hard work as a doctor over the years. They have lived hard-working, modest lives, and he has invested conservatively. They bought their rambling Victorian house in Montclair when such places were cheap. Her husband spends little on himself. He does not care for luxury. He mows the lawn, while she weeds the hydrangea bushes by the blue door and cuts back the roses along the fence. He wears his clothes until they are threadbare, spends little on his lunch, and rides the train into the city to work, leaving his elegant car covered in their garage. He has never wanted to travel overseas. She has never been able to have children.

"But I do want you to be happy," he said this morning, putting his hands on her shoulders, standing on their sunny screened-in porch, where they eat breakfast in the warm weather, safely protected from stinging or biting insects. "After all, we should enjoy the time we have left. We can't take the money with us when we go. Buy yourself whatever you like."

So, feeling the pain down her left leg, she decided to try a body massage.

"I'll give you Gabriel, then. I think you'll find him excellent," the receptionist at the spa had said after a moment's reflection.

She made the appointment for an evening hour. Waiting alone in the empty rooms of her big house for her husband's return from the city, she often thinks of the lonely lives of the suburban women in the houses all around her. She and her husband had moved out here from the city, because her husband said it would be safer for their future children. The tree-lined streets seemed so empty. She had asked him, "Where are all the people?"

Finding a place to park is another matter. She drives around until she finds a small space near the stone Congregational church and walks from there in the twilight, arriving early. The spa is in a basement without windows, artificially lit. A small pool is illuminated from below, so that the water looks phosphorescent and milky. Many people drift around: hairdressers, manicurists, waiting customers in pink robes.

She is thinking of her mother who died so young when she is brought back to reality by Gabriel's approach. He comes up quietly, appearing out of nowhere in his soft, crepe-soled shoes and shiny white uniform. He bows his blond head slightly and shakes her hand firmly, with old-world politeness. "Gabriel," he greets in a mellifluous voice. He looks fresh-skinned, rosy-cheeked, and snub-nosed. Piercingly blue-eyed, he holds himself erect and seems professional. "Follow me," he says commandingly. She listens to the sound of his shoes as he walks lightly, like a dancer, along the narrow, silent corridor to an elevator. They go up several flights and walk down another dimly lit corridor. He opens the door onto a small, dark room and asks if she has any injuries or areas of the body that need special attention.

She mentions her lower back and left leg where she was once

injured skiing and sometimes has pain. He tells her to undress, cover herself with the white sheet, lie flat on her stomach, and place her face in the face cradle. Then he leaves her alone in the shadowy room.

Strange music plays softly—stringed instruments, something being plucked, perhaps even a harp and a cello or violin. Two instruments pass a melody back and forth in counterpoint.

When he comes back into the room, he puts his large hands on her shoulders and presses down gently, running his fingers softly along her spine. Then he folds back the sheet and begins to work on her, using a scented oil. She thinks of the words of Matthew's Gospel about the three kings from the East bringing frankincense, myrrh, and was it gold?

"How's the pressure?" he asks.

"Perfect," she murmurs.

He has a pleasantly light but efficient touch, and he remains silent. She wonders what he might be thinking, and why he, an unusually handsome man, has chosen this profession, working on one body after the next, the young and the old, the fat and the thin, the black and the white. Perhaps they all seem identical to him, these bodies he touches so intimately. Then she dozes off a little and loses herself for a moment. When he tells her, in his soft voice, to turn over, lifting the sheet so that she can do so without exposing her body, she is surprised that the time has gone by so quickly. He massages her sore leg carefully and says, "I hope you don't mind me saying this, but you have the body of a young woman. I see a lot of fat young ones these days."

She smiles and responds, "You have healing hands." Before she leaves the room, feeling light, almost floating, the pain gone, she gives him a good tip and tells him she will return the next week.

"Come up directly. Now you know the way," he says.

She goes back regularly, once or sometimes twice a week, making her appointments directly with him, always in the evening which she finds too long. She goes along the narrow corridor, up the elevator, and down the next one, into the small room. Lying in the dark her mind wanders freely, and she thinks how strange it is that she lives these two lives, the one with her husband filled with conventional truths, and this other, imaginary one, in the secret room, where she explores hidden feelings.

The massages seem to be having a good effect. As she steps lightly in her tight, white trousers and pale, fitted jackets, through the long, wide aisles of the fine supermarket where she shops, with its fresh fruit and vegetables and bright flowers, people come up to tell her she is beautiful, almost as though she trails the seductive odor of the massage oil which she keeps on her body, not showering sometimes for days. Men whisper words to her on the train, words she does not quite catch and has to have repeated embarrassingly. A red-faced gentleman who sits beside her repeats, "I said, nice legs!" Once a young black man says, "You look terrific!" and tells her she should write down her secrets in a book.

"I did," she replies. She has written a memoir, though without secrets of that kind.

Instead of having her straight hair dyed blond and cut short, she now has the courage to let it turn white and grow long, down her back. Her husband encourages her: "Let it go white! Don't cut it!" Uncolored, her hair falls in soft, white curls. She likes to put her fingers into it and flip it back from her face luxuriously.

Women whisper shyly to her in the ladies' room. "Oh! I love your hair!" or "What color was it? I hope mine goes light like that." Once, when she asks for a senior ticket at the station, the young woman says admiringly, "I do hope I look like you when I'm a senior."

Even her nails, which she has always bitten nervously down to the quick, grow long. She keeps them clean and white-tipped, thinking of the young Madame Bovary.

She thinks of the things that go on growing in the dark of the coffin: the nails and the hair. She wonders if it is because she spends so much time in that secret room, in the muffled light, her face in the cradle, her eyes closed, her mind elsewhere, that her hair and her nails grow so luxuriantly, that her skin seems so smooth. Is it possible that age—that universally ugly thing—can appear beautiful, that she has been left unscathed, eternal?

She was pretty as a girl with a good figure, and attractive as a young woman, but never before have people accosted her thus in the street or come up to her when she goes swimming. Her husband is not the sort to pay much attention to her looks or give compliments. He loves her blindly, whether she looks old or young. Besides, he is still a busy man, refusing to retire, leaving early in the morning and coming back late at night, caring for the sick and the suffering. He is concerned with the state of the world, the wars in Iraq and Afghanistan, and the erosion of the earth. He refused to turn on the air-conditioning in their sunny house during the sultry fall weather. Now, in winter, he opens the curtains to take advantage of the greenhouse effect and consume less heating oil. He turns off lights, avoids the dishwasher.

At first, she supposes it is because she is old that people feel free to say these things to her with impunity. Then she forgets to look into the mirror at the wrinkles, the brown spots, the blue veins in her legs, and the sag of her skin.

She spends much of her day keeping fit. She jogs regularly and takes up yoga. She practices all the difficult poses: the wheel, the splits, the bind, the headstand. She stands on one leg, like a tree, head held high, arms raised to the sky. She looks around with secret satisfaction at the younger, heavier participants who strain, sweat, and topple. She consumes only fruit, vegetables, and nuts, and so loses weight. Sometimes a voice records her actions as though she were writing the story of her life in her head.

It takes her awhile to realize that Gabriel is not charging her for the hour-long massages since she seldom checks her bills. She orders other services as well: manicures for her long nails which she now paints a blood-red. She thinks the receptionist has made a mistake but fears getting Gabriel into trouble. It even occurs to her that he has fallen in love with her, and that this is his way of letting her know.

Finally, she asks him. He confesses shyly, not looking her in the eye, that he is writing something about her and does not like to charge his "characters." "You can hardly be both a client and a character," he says with a little grin. "Don't mention the massage at the desk, please."

"Goodness! Everyone in this town seems to write! You have put me into a book?" she asks, amused and flattered, wondering what he could have written about her. She lies facedown, staring into nothingness, while he massages her neck. Her own memoir has sold quite well. People were fascinated by the changes in her life. Then he lifts the sheet, and she turns over. He is wiping his long tapering fingers on a towel, as she lies flat on her back before him in the darkened room, arms at her sides.

"Well, actually, it's only a story so far," he says and smiles, with a flash of even white teeth. She peers at him more closely and realizes his blue eyes are slightly slanting in his flat face, giving him an Asian look. His arched nostrils quiver.

"And what happens in the story?" she asks, curious now.

"I'm not quite sure yet," he says, looking at her with a glint of mischief in his eyes. "I'm relying on you to find me the middle and the end. We already have a fine beginning."

She catches a glimpse of something almost devilish in his expression and decides she will not come back again, even if the massages are therapeutic and free. She will go elsewhere or ask for a woman. She does not like the idea of being spied on, of being used for someone else's purposes. What is he writing about her? What will he expect her to do to complete his story: fall in love with him because of his soft flattery, his caressing hands, his piercing blue eyes? Throw herself at his feet with desire, or even pay him to make love to her? He is quite mistaken, quite mistaken, she thinks, annoyed.

Another strange thing has happened. After all these years, she is more in love with her husband than ever. She has always loved his thick hair, his luminous, dark eyes, his sweet voice, above all his intelligence and learning which have taught her so much. She has appreciated the way he takes care of her, carrying her suitcase to the train, dusting off her sandy feet at the beach, washing their dishes. She thinks of him as a character out of Chekhov, with little ambition but much energy and intelligence.

Now, sometimes, when she sees her husband coming in the blue door late, looking gray and drawn, or rising in the morning, forced by faintness to put his head down between his knees, she feels almost breathless herself. She knows that, at seventy, they must soon leave one another. How could she go on without him? He is not a strong man, slim, with the heart of a thoroughbred, and a delicate, appealing beauty that is almost feminine. She makes passionate love to him in their big blue bedroom, as though each time were the last.

Still, she misses the healing quality of the masseur's hands, and the mysterious odor of the oil he rubbed on her body. People don't seem to notice her as often. She has again become invisible. The pain has come back too. She tries other spas and masseuses, but they either hurt her or hardly touch her or talk too much. She decides to return to Gabriel. She will not ask him what he is writing.

She comes and goes in silence, leaving the darkened, upstairs room with only a quiet "Thank you," pressing a twenty- dollar tip into his hands with a stiff smile. She notices a gradual change in the pressure of his hands. They are increasingly forceful. Often, he presses down on the calf of her bad leg, as though deliberately to hurt her. She cries out, "That's my bad leg! Be careful!" but he does not respond. He seems less and less polite. Occasionally, when she opens her eyes and looks up at him, she seems to see a hostile snarl.

He now talks to her freely, disturbingly. "Do you want to know my surname?" he asks.

"It is not necessary. I don't really need to know," she says.

"It's Wunderlich," he says pausing for effect, lifting his hands from her leg.

"That means wonderful in German, doesn't it?"

"You are thinking of *wunderbar*," he retorts, laughing loudly at her mistake.

She feels foolish and asks, "Well, what does it mean?"

"Actually, it means strange, weird," he says, snickering nastily.

"You are German?" she asks, surprised, though she realizes she has always suspected he was a foreigner.

"Volga German origin," he replies.

She doesn't understand, thinks he has said, *Vulgar German*, which doesn't make any sense. He explains that he comes from a group of persecuted people who lived along the Volga river during the time of Catherine the Great, who were invited into Russia from Germany. Later, they had their rights revoked and their land seized. His family had immigrated to America.

She keeps her eyes shut, does not respond, and the silence resumes. But one afternoon, he comes back to the subject of his writing. He tells her he has been writing since he was very young.

Lying faceup but not looking at him as he stands at the foot of the bed, massaging her feet, she asks, "Why do *you* write?" She has written her one book and, despite its success, has had no desire to write another. Recently, when she has done readings from the memoir someone in the audience inevitably comes up to have a copy signed but instead of complimenting her on her pages, the reader leans forward to whisper in her ear that she is beautiful or comments on her wonderful white hair.

He has his hands on her sore leg now. "I suppose it makes me feel in control. I can do what I want on the page, make my characters come and go, live and love, or die," he says, making her flex her leg, turning it out from the hip, so that her knee brushes his thigh.

"I thought you said your story depended on what your characters decided to do? I thought the middle and the end were up to me," she finds herself saying in an almost pleading tone, feeling him reach up her thigh, with pressure.

He laughs loudly, and when she opens her eyes, she notices his teeth in the muffled light look long and not as white as she thought. "Well, I lied. The truth is, in the end, I am the one who decides. I allow my characters some freedom on the page, it is true. For a while they must feel free to find their own way, and sometimes they surprise me, which is amusing and makes for a good story. They provide me with the real details that make my stories believable."

"What details did I provide?" she asks suspiciously. What does he know about her? She has never told him anything, has she? What has he written about her?

He has her left hand now, the one with the wedding ring, and he snaps the fingers back, one by one. "I have described you as you are: with your thick white hair, your sciatica, your skiing accident, your dear, distant husband." He rolls the stool with an ominous rumble of wheels, to the head of the bed, sits down, and puts his hands on her shoulders. "I have read your memoir. You left home when you were fourteen, went to stay with a friend from school. Your mother was of Italian origin, an addict, the kind that uses needles—not very clean ones, in her case. She became ill and abandoned you. You became a waif. A teacher helped you for a while, for favors, it seems, if I read between the lines correctly?"

She wants to get up and leave, but he has his hands around her neck, pressing down so hard that she has difficulty breathing.

"Your husband saw you on the street and found you a bed in a hostel. He helped you get student loans, encouraged your literature studies, rewrote your papers. You found a teaching position at the state college. All these interesting facts are there, but in the end I am the one who must find a conclusion. There are certain universal requirements to stories, I'm afraid. You can't just do what you like: they require a twist at the end."

She feels a little tremor go all through her naked body as he takes her head and lifts it slightly and turns it sharply to one side. Who is this man and why does he talk so strangely? Did she put all of this in her book, and why does he want to use her story for his own ends? She must get up and leave, but instead she finds herself asking him, "What about you? Have you always been a masseur?" only to regret it immediately.

He tells her, his hands lingering painfully on her shoulders, digging into the nerves around her neck, "I have done many things to support myself. I even worked as a go-go dancer in my youth. They threw so much money at me!" He laughs in a loud vulgar way she finds distasteful.

"You danced naked?" she says, shocked at this revelation.

"Just a G-string and socks by the end, and sometimes not even that."

"Wasn't that humiliating?"

"Not at all. It made me feel powerful: money raining down on me, pushed into my socks, my G-string, by eager hands. You can't imagine how much money they gave me just to see my nakedness," he says triumphantly.

She remembers something with shame, something she has not put in her book: the teacher who helped her, took pity on her, a middle-aged married man she had seduced. He was completely bald and rather fat. She made him spend money he could ill afford on her. She remembers the feeling of power, standing in an expensive shop looking around at the elegant clothes she wanted so badly. She remembers a soft beige cashmere coat that tied around the waist, pink silk underwear with lace, even a rhinestone necklace that glittered gaudily around her smooth young neck.

She looks down at Gabriel's hands on her collarbones and notices a dark spot on the back of his left hand. She wonders if he has some sort of terminal disease.

"They wanted to see the size of my cock, you see," he chuckles, standing up at her head and reaching all the way across her body to the tops of her thighs, so that she feels his sex pressed against her shoulder. She is disgusted, aroused, and terrified. He adds, "An unusually large one, if I say so myself. A Master Cock. I can balance a beer bottle on it when it's erect. Would you like to see it?"

The strange music plays on, the monotonous melody going back and forth from the harp to the violin. The odor of the pungent oil fills the room. She hears the squelch of his crepe-soled shoes as he turns around the bed. She decides the man is quite mad, quite mad, and probably dangerous. Still, she cannot move.

He goes on, "Or perhaps you'd like a sip from such a source of life and love?"

She sweeps the sheet around her, finally has the courage to rise up from the bed, to turn her back on him, and fumble for her robe, the slippers, her handbag. She says, "I will let the authorities know about this."

He laughs. "You are making a great mistake, you know. A Great Mistake. This is your last chance. After this, I'm moving on. You won't find me again and that would be unfortunate for you."

When she rushes up to the man at the reception to report the incident, he looks at her strangely.

"Not possible," he says in a low voice, shaking his bald head at her. "None of our certified masseurs would act in this way, my dear. They have been trained. What did you say was the name?"

"I assure you he did!" she snaps, incensed. "Gabriel, his name is Gabriel Wunderlich. I want to report him to the police!"

"Wunderlich? Mr. Wonderful?" the man says with a half-grin, shaking his head slowly. Why is he calling her *my dear* in such a condescending way and looking around the crowded room with an apologetic smile as though embarrassed by her?

"No! No! That's not what it means!" she says, as though the meaning of the name were important.

"I'm afraid you must be mistaken, my dear," he responds slowly, enunciating, as though she is mentally deficient, or a foreigner.

"Yes! Yes! That's his name. He's a Volga German. Someone who came from Russia to Germany, or was it Germany to Russia?" In her distress she is confused, cannot remember.

He raises his eyebrows at her, purses his lips. "In any case, my dear, I assure you we have no one of that name here. We had a Gabriel at one point, but he left some time ago, and he was a Gabriel Hart, an Englishman, I believe. Perhaps you'd like a nice cup of soothing chamomile tea?" Clearly, he thinks she is mad.

She rushes home, shuts the curtains, takes off her clothes, and climbs into the double bed in the big blue bedroom, though it is only five in the afternoon. She lies with her face to the wall, shivering. When her husband arrives home he comes to her bedside and asks what is wrong, but she cannot speak. "Go away," she says.

She goes on lying there all the next day, refusing to eat, until her husband comes home again and finds her still in bed. He says severely, "You must get up! This is ridiculous! There is nothing wrong with you." He tells her, "Perhaps, after all, you need to go back to work. Why don't you write something?"

She is walking through the hot streets one fall evening, alone, a year since she first met Gabriel. The light is dim, the shops shut up, and the side street, where she thinks she parked her car, deserted. The solitude of the tree-lined suburban street seems worse than any forest. The echoes of her childhood loneliness chime unbearably in her head.

She is not thinking about her massages, the strange words Gabriel Wunderlich or whatever his real name was said to her in the dark room. She has tried to write about him, following her husband's suggestion, but she cannot find the end to the story.

It has been a long, tiring day. Increasingly, she finds all the sport she does tiring. After her swim, she ate a whole bar of chocolate gluttonously in the ladies' room. Then she gathered her hot white hair up into a tight bun on the top of her head. She noticed the brown spots on her cheek, the two broken nails and that none of them looked very clean. Staring at herself in the mirror, she drew back her lips and saw her long teeth, the pale gums receded. For the first time she understood the old expression, *Long in the tooth*.

Now she turns her head, aware that someone is following her in the deserted street. She hears the familiar squelch of the crepe-soled shoes and smells the secret odor of the oil in the evening air. She says the name aloud: "Wunderlich." She wants to run, but in her high-heeled shoes and tight skirt, her heart beating hard, as in a dream, she cannot advance. She glances nervously over her shoulder into the shadows of the solitary street. She must get to her car.

But when she looks back, she sees no one. All she can hear is the sound of her own words, recording her life, the end of her story, and the crepe-soled shoes, echoing in her mind.

ATLANTIS
BY RICHARD BURGIN
Atlantic City

She sat up in bed, rigid but strangely alert, as if trying to identify the sound of something underwater. When he touched her shoulder to try to make her lie down again, she turned toward the wall.

"What's wrong?" he said.

She shook her head back and forth.

"Rina, come on, what is it? You're scaring me."

"I don't feel good."

"Take a hit of that joint I made for you on the bureau. It'll help."

"How long we gonna go on like this, huh? What's your plan, Stacy? Is there one?"

"What do you mean? I don't understand."

"Course you don't understand," she said, finally facing him. "Things going along pretty much the way you want? Just stay high every minute with me in this tomb under the ground, that's below sea level, for Christ's sake."

"I'm not high every minute." He wanted to add that his place wasn't below sea level either but he wasn't 100 percent sure if it was or not.

"C'mon, can you face reality just a little? You wake up and have a Quaalude so you can take a shower. To counteract that you smoke a joint so you can have sex with me in the morning. Then to get through the day you take more Quaalude or sometimes E. Then it's back to pot so we can watch TV and go to sleep. What do you think, you're gonna die if you aren't high for a minute?"

"Okay. We'll cut back a little. I'll cut back."

"It's not just the drugs."

"What?"

"We never go anywhere. We never do anything."

"What're you saying? We go out."

"Sure. We make heroic little runs for food to the deli or sometimes we even make it to the supermarket. We have to get high to do that too. And then, of course, we go out so you can get more drugs. How come we never go to New York anymore?"

He felt a surge of anger but told himself to stay cool. He'd seen her like this before and knew that if he just stayed cool things would eventually get better.

"I thought we agreed we'd had enough of New York," he said, turning his head away, hoping to see a bit of a tree trunk perhaps, but the blinds were shut.

"I meant living there, I'd had enough. I didn't mean never visiting. I'm sick of these dealers and crack whores you go to all the time."

"It was one guy and his girlfriend. You're exaggerating."

"I'm sick of all the other Fort Lee zombies too. I'm too young to live like this, to just give up."

He was scared now. Something in her tone of voice and in her eyes frightened him. "I didn't think we were giving up," he said softly. "I thought we were just taking a little break, like a kind of vacation."

"This ain't a vacation. We're just dying is what it is."

"Come on, you don't mean that."

"I do mean it. We have to get high to go to the bathroom and nobody's washed a dish in a week."

He felt himself start to vibrate then. He didn't know if it was from the pot, his Viagra, or if it were somehow cold in his apartment (though it was close to the end of June), or maybe it was just the impact her words and tone of voice had on him as if they robbed him of his sense of warmth.

"Okay, you tell me what you want me to do," he finally said.

"Jesus Christ!" She looked at the little clock on the bed table. "It's almost three in the afternoon. My sleep patterns are completely destroyed." She put her hands over her eyes as if she were going to cry but then got out of bed decisively. "I know what I'm going to do. I'm going to take a shower and then I'm going to get some food for us, and while I'm gone you think about what we're gonna do."

"You worried about money? Is that it?" he said sharply. It was odd to talk to her that way when she was standing in front of him completely naked. She turned to face him again and he tried to stay focused on her face though he didn't want to see the look in her eyes.

"Yah, okay, I admit I'm a little concerned about what you're gonna do when your parents' money runs out," she said. "You haven't even tried to get a job since you quit your last one."

He sighed, then stopped himself abruptly. Sighing was definitely the wrong route to take with Rina. Instead he told her that he wasn't going to start dealing, if that's what she was worried about, that he'd just done it for a little while years ago. He checked her reaction but it wasn't what he'd hoped for. She was slowly shaking her head back and forth again.

"We're setting ourselves up to get in a lot of trouble," Rina said. "Your landlady gave me a funny look yesterday."

"A funny look? Big deal."

"A killer look that said, *Bitch, I'd just as soon off you as not*. I feel like any day she could call the cops on us."

"She won't do anything. She wants her money too. Who else would take her bottom floor and pay what I do?"

"You sure about that? I think it's time to go someplace else for a while is what I think. But you think about it while I'm out. You focus on it without getting high first, if you can, and when I come back you tell me what you came up with, okay?"

* * *

She had to know how he'd feel, didn't she? Hadn't he jumped out of bed right after she said it and volunteered to go shopping with her? But she insisted she wanted to go alone so he could think, in other words, worry. That was Rina in a nutshell—*Runaway Rina* he'd nicknamed her in his mind a long time ago—who'd run away from home as a teenager, and never came back first from Vineland to Atlantic City, then from A.C. to San Francisco, and finally from New York with him to Fort Lee. Come to think of it, his own mother would sometimes leave or threaten to leave him and his father too, whenever she wanted to get back at them for some perceived deficiency or slight, of which the world had no end, of course—so why take the lackings of the world out on your family? The vibrating was getting worse and he was feeling more and more cold. He pulled the blankets up on his shoulders and tried to get warm.

He thought of something else then. A woman who looked like Rina could do anything and might well be doing it right now with anybody. He pictured her breasts—smallish but with oversized nipples, when they erected. He'd never seen nipples like that before, and knew he never would again. They were once-in-a-lifetime nipples—he was only thirty-four but he already knew that. The first time he saw them erect he'd nearly come just from looking at them. How could she have done him the way she did just a few hours ago and then gotten angry enough that she'd leave him like this? There was no logic with Rina, ever, so he could never relax with her. The slightest thing could upset her and then he'd worry that she'd leave him or else screw someone else, which amounted to the same thing.

He got out of bed and took a Quaalude from the bureau. What would his father have done in this situation? He'd been with his own Rina all those years. Of course it was absurd to compare himself to his father who was so much more mature and honest and who barely even drank, much less took any drugs. His father was emotionally strong all right, in a way he never could be. He'd stayed over forty years with Stacy's mother—a woman he should have left but didn't. What hadn't he endured? The death of his parents, his brothers and sister. Career frustration, raising two difficult children, especially him. But never drank, never really complained, even after his stroke from which he finally passed. He always tried to help everyone, particularly his hypochondriacal wife. Never cheated either and even quit smoking on his own at the age of sixty-two.

His father was physically strong too. Once during a family vacation in Atlantic City when he was only seven or eight, he went in the ocean holding his father's hand because the waves were big, enormous to his child's eye and stronger than any water he'd ever felt. It was a little scary because he couldn't really swim much then and when the waves came they'd crash over his head and knock him down. But his father never stopped holding his hand. He could feel his hand underwater as if it were stronger than the surf, then feel and see it again when he emerged from below. He remembered laughing, squealing with delight, and his father laughing too, only letting go of his hand when they reached the sand in front of the boardwalk.

How exciting yet strangely innocent the boardwalk was then! Little kids ran freely up and down it laughing and yelling and carrying their cotton candy like magic wands. There was a funhouse then, around where the Taj Mahal was now, and horses still dove into the ocean from the old steel pier. One time his family went to the Miss America pageant and he picked the winner, young as he was, Miss Ohio, which made his mother marvel at him. Still, what he remembered most was jumping the waves with his father, holding his hand firmly as they crashed over him.

But this was becoming too painful to think about. What was the point of getting things you loved if you could never get them back again, if you could only lose them, as if life was nothing but an extended game of hide-and-seek? And now Rina was playing another form of hide-and-seek with him.

He decided not to wait for the Quaalude to hit and began

smoking the joint he'd left for her on the bureau. It was the right decision, he said to himself, as he finally lay back under the blankets.

When she walked into the tiny kitchen carrying the groceries he was still lying down pretending not to be high. She began putting the food away quickly and didn't answer him when he said hello.

"So did you do some thinking?" she finally said, coming into the room at last.

"Yah, I did."

She stood in front of him dressed in her tight blue jeans, staring at him, waiting.

"How'd you like to go to Atlantic City?" he said.

They were driving at least five miles under the speed limit so they wouldn't risk being stopped (not trusting the landlady, they'd decided to bring their whole stash with them) when he sensed something, a kind of tense quiet that permeated the closed-in space of the car. For a minute he debated whether to ask her what it was—always a dangerous question these days. If only she'd followed his advice and taken a hit before they left or at least had a Xanax, but she was stubborn that way. She was trying to set an example. He turned on a rock radio station he thought she'd like (he would have preferred jazz or classical), but her mood didn't change. That was her method when she wanted to talk about something—to just disappear into a cone of silence until he couldn't take it anymore.

"You're being pretty quiet," he said, deciding to play it halfway.

"I'm just wondering about things."

"What things?"

"I'm wondering why Atlantic City? Why exactly are we going there?"

"I thought you liked to go swimming, you always did before."

"I do like swimming but there are plenty of other places we could go on the shore where we could swim."

"It's the same ocean, isn't it? And Atlantic City has the boardwalk."

"So you think we have the money to stay in a hotel there?"

"I told you not to worry about money, baby. We can afford to stay there for at least a few nights."

"And I guess you don't plan to do much gambling then?"

"Not if you don't want me to," he said, silently congratulating himself, not only on his answer, but because he thought he really meant it. "So have I answered all your questions?"

"Some of them."

"Only some of them?"

"I have issues with Atlantic City too, you know."

Then he remembered that she used to work as a dancer there (before they met in New York), and she might have done some hooking too. He'd never asked her too much about that. Atlantic City was also where she went first when she ran away; he could understand her mixed feelings.

"So what do you want? You want to forget all about it and just turn around?"

"I don't see why we can't go to a quieter place to swim and cool out and be together. Some place like Ventnor or Longport, that's less tempting."

"What do you mean *tempting*? What would you be tempted to do?" he said, thinking of her dance routine again.

"*I'm* not tempted to do anything there. I was thinking of you."

"Me? Why me?"

"I don't know. I can't help thinking you're planning a meeting with some big-shot dealer there. I'm afraid you'll be tempted to make some kind of score."

He felt his heart beat but kept his cool. Could she somehow know about Ike? Ike had really seemed to care about him, especially after his father died, giving him some prime territory to deal in. A few months ago, in fact, he heard that Ike had moved to Ventnor for a little peace and quiet. This was too good to be true, yet it was true. He could visit him in Ventnor and Rina couldn't possibly object to that. He wouldn't have to set foot in Atlantic City except to visit the beach where he'd swam with his father. He could meet Ike in a clean, family-oriented place where he could even bring Rina.

"Okay, we can stay in Ventnor," he said. "That's cool."

She took his hand which in itself made it all worth it. "Thanks, sweetie," she said smiling.

"I like you, Stacy, you're a good kid. Whenever you're in Atlantic City you look me up and I'll take care of you. You look me up and I'll *set* you up, deal?"

That's what Ike had said to him the last time he saw him, a few years ago in Harrah's. There was always work from Ike and good money too. Sometimes he even gave him a girl and he'd get a free blow job as a tip. Ike was a first-class guy all around. He only dealt with the best people: first-rate dealers, hookers, and clients—all top of the line. Even when he'd moved to New York and started getting out of the business a little, Ike still kept in touch.

"Tough without your old man, huh?" he'd once said to Stacy, putting his arm around him in the Taj Mahal. "Wish my kid loved me the way you love him . . . You know, Stacy, maybe you should go back to college. That's what your old man wanted. He told me that more than once."

"Really?"

"Sure, you were always on his mind. He even told me once while we were playing bridge. Your old man was one hell of a bridge player too."

"Did you ever tell him . . . ?"

"About the work we do? Course not. You think I'm crazy? Your old man never suspected a thing. He was as innocent and pure as a child. I loved the guy like a brother. You let me set you up with something big—a one-time deal I'll give to you instead of my own son, and then you go back and get your degree. Then we'll see about your future."

Sure enough, in less than a month he'd set him up with a killer deal. "I offered a deal like this to my son Dominic, but he thinks he's such a big shot in Vegas now that he don't need this no more," Ike had said with bitterness. "Believe me, he'll live to regret it."

So Stacy took the deal, although he never finished college.

He was remembering all this while Rina was sleeping next to him in the motel room in Ventnor. He wouldn't postpone visiting Ike any longer. It was simply a question of explaining it to Rina. He was sure she'd be reasonable about it.

When he finally brought it up, they'd just come back from a swim, walking to their room with arms around each other's waists, hands sometimes tapping each other's bottoms. The ocean always had that kind of effect on him, and on her too. Once in the room they had sex quickly—not even bothering to smoke first. He felt hot and happy and it seemed a good time to tell her (even though he was straight).

"So let me understand this," she said, "we're here for what, three hours, we just finished making love, and you want to go out right now and see this old guy, who was a friend of your father's?"

"I told you about Ike, he was like a father to me after my old man died."

"I wouldn't say he was like a father to you. More like the God-father. He set you up big time in the business is what you mean, and now you want to work for him again. Isn't that what this is about? I should have known that's why you wanted to go to A.C."

"You're way off, Rina, that's not it at all."

"Oh, so you wanted to come here to make me happy, making me come back to where I was at the lowest point in my life. You can't even bear to hear what happened to me in A.C., can you? Not even to this day."

He turned away from her and looked at a sliver of the sky

barely visible through the blinds. How could a sky be both blank and blue? He hated it when she was sarcastic and bitter. "You can tell me," he said, hoping she wouldn't. "Really, you can tell me."

"Forget it," she shot back in her tough-girl voice, though when he turned back to look at her again her eyes were moist. "I'm not making that mistake again. I don't need to tell you any of that shit 'cause I know it hurts you."

"Well, I didn't bring you here to hurt you, either. You seemed like you wanted to come more than you didn't. And I wasn't even thinking about Ike when I suggested it, I swear. About your past, I guess I just blocked it out. I'm sorry."

"What were you really thinking about wanting to go to Atlantic City?" (She said the name of the place as if it were Afghanistan or North Korea.)

"Well, number one, it's an obvious place to go to for fun—not for you maybe, I understand, but in general—and second, I was thinking of my father and my family. We went to A.C. a lot when I was a kid. Those were good times for me, that's all."

He briefly considered telling her how his father used to hold his hand in the water but decided not to.

"So you never thought of Ike at all?"

"I thought of him later. When you said you'd rather go to Ventnor or someplace like it, I remembered then that he lived there now."

"And that's when you decided you had to see him?"

"Yeah, it grew on me. I miss him, that's all. It's not about dealing."

"So why's he like you so much?"

"I don't know. He has problems with his own son. His son's about the only person in the business who had trouble working with him."

"But you said you were staying out of it. You said you were gonna get a real job or else finish school or both. You've said a lot of things to me."

"Said it and meant it. Look, why don't you come with me to see him? See for yourself. It's just about friendship, that's all. But friendship's a lot."

"No, I'm not gonna rain on your parade."

"Are you kidding? I want you to come. I'm proud of you. I wanna show you off, okay? I want you to get to know Ike. He doesn't need me to push his merchandise. Believe me, the guy has a fleet of workers and behind them a fleet of wannabe workers."

"Oh geez, I'm so impressed. It's almost like meeting Einstein, I guess."

"Come on, you don't have to be sarcastic. I'm sure you'll like him. And I really want you to come with me. I mean it."

She looked at him with a serious expression in her hazel-green eyes. It was strange. He had almost the same color eyes as her but hers expressed so many more emotions.

"I must need my head examined to stick with you."

"What?"

"What? You're a drug dealer. You're gonna get busted. Just like every dealer I've ever known. And you're gonna get me busted too."

"What are you talking about?"

"I must love to have tragedies happen to me. They got a word for people like me?" she said, getting out of bed.

He stared at her body in awe. Couldn't believe sometimes that she was his lover and knew then that he wanted her as his wife one day. But he couldn't tell her yet. Maybe later on when they'd finally gone to Atlantic City.

"So what have you decided?" he said.

"I'm coming with you, you know that. But I gotta get ready first."

One other thing he loved about Rina, she always looked great when they went out. Not just good but appropriate for the occasion too. It took her a lot of time but it was worth it. This time it wasn't so bad because he hadn't smoked, which would make the time seem longer, but had taken a 'lude he had in his pocket just to take the edge off waiting. Somehow Quaaludes and Atlantic City went together like a sunset over the ocean, he thought.

While she was primping, mostly with her hair and makeup, he found Ike's address in his old address book. He wondered if he should call first but decided it would be more fun to surprise him. Then he wondered what he'd say if Ike wanted him to do a deal. Could he really say no to Ike? But anyway, that could wait for later. He knew Ike wouldn't ask him in front of Rina, especially with her dressed kind of conservatively in a light pink dress and her brand-new beach shoes that she bought back in Fort Lee. She was a classy woman and Ike appreciated class. He was lucky, unimaginably lucky, to have Rina as his girl, he knew that. So what if she'd had to hook for a while years ago? The woman had been handed a nightmare life right from the start, her own father doing her when she was only twelve.

"How do I look?" she asked, emerging from the bathroom with a big smile.

"Like heaven."

"Now you're the one who's not talking," she said to him in the car.

They were less than a mile from Ike's house and he was thinking how nice her perfume smelled and how nice it would be to smell her when they made love later and then, for a moment, wondering why he was visiting a criminal like Ike, however benevolent his personality might be.

"You feeling nervous about seeing him?"

He shrugged. "A little."

"Go ahead, have a hit. I'll have one too. It won't kill us."

"You mean that?"

"Yah, of course. I ain't a cop. Pull over into that alleyway by the Italian restaurant. We can do it there."

They took their emergency traveling joint from the glove compartment, lit up, and each took two hits.

"It's hard to stop, isn't it?" he said. "When the pot's so good."

"We can do the rest later, after we see Ike," she said, suddenly looking sad.

"What's the matter baby?"

"You know, it isn't easy for me even being near Atlantic City. You know why I went there in the first place, don't you? I told you about my father."

"Yah, of course you told me."

"I mean, why'd he have to fuck me, huh? What kind of guy does that to his own daughter when I wasn't even thirteen yet? He was already getting plenty of women on the side, you know, what'd he need me for?"

"Try not to go down that road, okay?" he said. "The pot will only make it worse."

"I just feel nervous lately, anxious, like something very bad's gonna happen. Do you understand? Like I'm gonna die soon, or something. Do you know what I mean? Maybe it's just because we're so close to A.C."

He knew exactly what she meant. Lately, a lot of the time when he was straight he felt like he was going to die soon too, a feeling only the right drugs could take away, but he didn't want to tell her that. "Kind of," he said.

"I wish we were back in bed in Fort Lee doing it together. That's what I wish."

"We can drive back right after we see Ike. I'd like that too."

"Really?"

"Yeah, really," he said, although he still wanted to see the beach, if only for a few minutes, where he once swam with his father. Maybe he could go there alone for ten minutes while she stayed in the car or else while she was in the motel in Ventnor packing (if they really were going to leave right away), though he wished somehow they could go there together.

"I like that all the time," he added to reassure her, "being in bed with you. Even in my grave I'll want it with you."

"No kidding?"

"No question about it."

"So you're not thinking of ditching me here and taking up with some loose bimbo you meet in a casino?"

"No way, course not. It's just you I want, always."

"That's not the pot talking, is it? You don't just love me when you're on drugs, do you?"

"Course not. I love you all the time. So, you feeling better now?"

"Yeah," Rina said, taking his hand and squeezing it.

"Okay, we're only a block from Ike's. I think we should go see him now, okay?"

"Sure," she said. "I'm ready."

He noticed the tight, smallish white beach houses of Ventnor were suddenly sparkling. He felt blissed out. He looked at her and thought she was feeling the same thing.

"What are you feeling?" he said to her when they were two houses from Ike's. There was a strong breeze blowing in from the sea and it moved her hair in an attractive way.

"Like my problems are a million miles away."

He gave her hand another squeeze. "Me too."

Then they started to walk up the steps to Ike's house, the largest one on a block where a number of low- to mid-level Mafia reputedly owned homes.

He rang the bell, hoping he wasn't too stoned, but still glad that he'd smoked. He waited, then rang a second and third time. It probably took Ike longer to get around now that he was in his early seventies. Stacy continued to wait until he felt a pair of eyes staring at him through the peephole. An unfamiliar voice said, "Who is it?"

He felt then that he'd made a mistake and should excuse

himself and leave. Instead, he said, "I came to see Ike. It's Stacy."

A few seconds later the door opened. The man who let them in was huge, both taller than Stacy by three or four inches and heavier by fifty to seventy pounds. He was wearing a loose T-shirt that said *Hell Busters* on it, loose light blue, low-slung jeans, black boots, and lots of tattoos on his arms and neck, making Stacy think he might be Ike's bodyguard.

"Hey," Stacy said. "This is Rina."

Rina nodded and said a soft hello. There was something bird-like and sad in the little sound she produced.

"I'm Dom," he said, without extending his hand. "Ike ain't here. Wanna beer?"

"Sure," Stacy said.

"You too?" Dom asked.

"Yes, thanks," Rina said, a little nervously.

Dom left the room and came back with the drinks, walking in a herky-jerky halting kind of way. Neither Stacy nor Rina felt they could risk looking at each other so both stared straight ahead.

"Sit down," Dom said, pointing to the generic-looking couch in the living room. "Take a load off." They sat down on the couch, Dom on a straight-back chair facing them. While they made small talk about the weather Stacy strained to see something that would remind him of Ike but couldn't. The furniture was much cheaper and more ordinary than Ike's would be. Ike was a man who liked nice things.

"Want another?" Dom asked.

"No thanks," they replied in unison. Stacy couldn't help staring at Dom's tough, inscrutable face—a collage of scars, wrinkles, and stubble. He was definitely on some drug but Stacy couldn't tell which. "So you have any idea when Ike will be back?"

"He's not coming back. Ike's gone forever, I'd say, wherever *forever* is."

"That's too bad. I'm an old friend of his and I just thought I'd drop by."

"Yeah, I know who you are," Dom said, in a voice both matter-of-fact and sullen.

Stacy looked harder at him, but there was a blurred haphazard quality to Dom's face as if it had run away from itself.

"You don't remember me, do you?" Dom said.

"I feel embarrassed but I can't say—"

"I'm Ike's kid, remember now?"

"Sure, he talked about you a lot."

"I'll bet he did. Ike's not here though. I run things now."

"Oh, I didn't come about business."

"Really? You sure about that? I remember you were very interested in business. I remember you muscling me out of a number of deals. Yeah, you wanted to get my territory in Atlantic City, and goddamn it if my old man didn't give it to you."

"That was so long ago."

"Was it? I remember it real well and I ain't even gone to college like you did. See how much I know about you? I have an excellent memory."

Stacy shrugged reflexively. "Well, I'm not in the business now. Anyway," he said, looking at Rina, "I think we should get going now. Thanks for the beers."

"Really? I think you're still trying to give me the business is what I think," Dom said, putting down his empty beer can with emphasis, next to the three other empty cans on the little white Formica table beside him. Stacy stared hard at him as Dom slowly withdrew a gun that his T-shirt had previously hidden. "I was wondering when I'd see you again, college boy. I was thinking of visiting you, but I couldn't find you. You must have been working on something big you wanted to keep secret from me and Ike, but now presto/chango you've come right to me."

Seeing the gun, Rina let out a little gasp.

"Shut up," Dom snapped, softly but authoritatively, moving his eyes snakelike for a moment in her direction.

"What's going on?" Stacy said.

"What's going on is what your late, great friend Mr. Ike would call a *superior opportunity*. For me anyway," he said, laughing. "See, I can speak fancy too."

"I don't understand why you're upset."

"Upset?" Dom said, looking around the room incredulously, as if he were appealing to an audience. "You think I'm *upset*?"

"Your father likes me. I'm a friend of his. We never had a problem."

"Oh, I know he *liked* you, matter of fact he fuckin' loved you. I told him you weren't worth a shit in the ground but he didn't believe me. But it don't matter what he thought anymore, does it?"

"What do you mean?"

"Weren't you listening, bright boy? Old Ike is dead. He's worm food now, so it don't matter what he said or thought. I run things now. I run all his things: the business, this house, this gun," he said, waving it in the air briefly like a pennant.

"What happened to Ike?" Stacy blurted.

Dom looked down at the floor for a second. "Cancer. You heard of that, ain't you?"

"My father died of cancer too," Stacy said.

Dom nodded curtly. "That so? You think that makes us brothers or something?"

Stacy realized then that Dom was definitely on some kind of powerful drug. He didn't know what it was, only that it was strong.

"So I can see you're upset but—"

"*Upset*?" Dom said in the same incredulous voice, as he looked around the room again. "You in love with that word or something? I ain't upset. Just 'cause I took out my piece to show you? I'm just having fun. If you knew me you'd understand. But you never bothered to know me. Bet you wish you had now."

"Hey you." He pointed the gun at Rina. "Show me your tits. I feel like seein' something pretty."

She looked at Stacy uncertainly for a second but he said nothing, felt his face was frozen as if he'd had some kind of neurological attack.

"Come on," Dom said, pointing the gun at her. "I wanna see 'em now."

She took off her dress in a few seconds. She was wearing a black bra he'd bought her from Victoria's Secret.

"Take your top off too. What're you, deaf?"

She took off her bra. Maybe someone would walk by and stop it, Stacy thought, a cop or someone from the neighborhood. Even if the neighborhood really was all Mafia, they liked order and quiet, didn't they, and wouldn't want any unnecessary trouble or attention, certainly not a loose cannon like Dom, who could never fit in with them. Never.

"You know how to dance?" Dom said to her.

She looked at Stacy again and he nodded to show it was okay with him.

"I can't," she said.

"You can't? Course you can. Every girl knows how to dance. I'm sure you know how to dance, yeah. I've heard about you. Fact is, I'm pretty sure I've seen you too. Yeah, I've seen all the dancers. *Summer Wave* I think your name was. I could have sworn that was your name in Atlantic City."

"That's not my name."

"It's not your name now, but it was once."

"No, it wasn't ever my name."

"I think it was. I've got a really good memory for tits, especially unusual ones. Yeah, I remember your nipples, honey, remember 'em well. So, do me a dance."

She shook her head back and forth then looked at Stacy. "I can't."

"What's the problem? Is it Bozo over there?" he said, pointing the gun briefly in his direction. "I can get rid of him in a second."

"No, no, it's not him."

"Hey, Bozo, tell the little lady to dance for me, okay? Tell her *now*."

"Leave her alone," Stacy said, more weakly than he wanted to sound.

"Hey." Dom moved toward him and punched him hard in the stomach. "You don't tell me what to do, *ever*."

"Okay," Rina said, beginning to dance. "I'm doing it."

"See, I told you you could. Now bring it a little closer to me."

Stacy was slumped over the chair.

She looked at him hesitantly, not knowing what to do, just like a little girl, he thought, as if the shock of the situation had drained her of her years.

"Don't look at Bozo to see what to do," Dom said. "Bozo's a clown, a sad little clown who don't know what to do. You want to live to dance again, you bring your tits to me now!" He pointed the gun at her again and she started to cry.

Stacy tried to sit up in the chair. There was a sharp pain in his ribs. He must have been hit more than once because his stomach hurt too.

Dom was hooting now like a cowboy at a rodeo as Rina continued to dance for him while she cried. Angel dust, Stacy thought, Dom must be on some kind of angel dust or maybe meth.

She looked at him one more time, while Dom was unzipping his pants.

"Hey, no staring at Bozo. I already told you that. Bozo don't have what you need, bitch. He's just got a little clown dick that don't give nothin' to no grown-up woman like you. You get on your knees now and open your mouth. I'm about to fill you up like you ain't ever been filled before." Dom laughed as he grabbed her head and, holding it firmly, put himself inside her. Stacy stared in disbelief for a few seconds then got up from his chair and charged at him with his head down, but Dom was surprisingly agile, moving away like a matador and then hitting Stacy on the head with his gun two times. Stacy landed on the floor but felt like he was still falling, like a pebble would keep falling in the depths of the ocean. Then he no longer saw anything.

When he woke up she was driving. She told him they'd left Dom's house almost two hours ago, that Dom was worried he'd killed him. Then she told him that she'd stopped at the motel and thrown their things in the car as fast as she could. "If you want me to, I'll take you to a hospital."

"No," he said, noticing that she was staring straight ahead (had barely looked at him once). She was also talking in an even, expressionless voice like a zombie. Then he wondered if Dom had finished in her mouth, but knew he could never ask her. Hated himself for even thinking about it. He felt a pain in his head and ribs though it wasn't as bad as he'd remembered.

"I gave you a lot of ibuprofen," she said, as if reading his mind.

"Thanks."

It grew quiet in the car, as if quiet could grow like a spreading plant. It got so quiet Stacy felt like they were in some other kind of machine seated far apart, a Ferris wheel perhaps, somehow equipped to travel on the road.

No one wanted to hear the radio—they agreed on that without even talking about it. Nor did they speak about possibly stopping for food. He felt sorry that she had to be straight now, but she was afraid to drive a long distance on any kind of drug, and she wouldn't let him drive, saying he was too beat up to do it.

After an hour or so, his thoughts about Dom faded a bit and he began thinking about Atlantic City and how he'd never gotten to go to the beach where he'd swum with his father, though that was the reason why he'd wanted to go there in the first place. It was funny, Atlantic City wasn't what you'd call one of the beautiful places in the country like the Grand Canyon or Niagara Falls. It was probably beautiful once, of course, but that had all ended with the boardwalk and the casinos. It was as if that once beautiful Atlantic City had sunk and was now like Atlantis, the "lost island" he'd read about as a kid.

Rina began crying, but softly, as if they were tears shed during a dream. "I'm not going home with you," she said. "I'm going to drop you off and stay with my sister in Brooklyn."

"Don't do that, please."

"No, I am," she said, with tears running down her cheeks now. "You'll be all right . . . I mean, you can't want to sleep next to me tonight, or *ever*, so what's the point of pretending?"

"What are you talking about?"

"I'm trash, Stacy, I must be. That's why trashy things keep happening to me, don't you get it? That's why you take drugs all the time, 'cause you're depressed about being with me."

"Hey, stop it. Stop talking like that, okay? That's crazy talk. You think I blame you for what happened? If there's any blame, I blame myself for bringing you with me when I went to see Ike. You're innocent, Rina, totally innocent. I shouldn't have gone to see Ike. I really just wanted to see where my father took me swimming."

"Why didn't you then?"

"I don't know. I should have. Look, pull over, get on the soft shoulder, will you?"

"Why?"

"Just do it, okay? I wanna feel some real air while I talk with you."

"You're sure you're strong enough to get up?"

"Yeah, I'm sure," he said, though when they got out of the car he felt light-headed and took one of her hands in his. "I want us to forget about what happened. It was horrible but now it's over and none of it was your fault."

"Are you high?"

"I'm not, no, no, I'm not," he answered, still holding her hand.

She didn't say anything. He could hear the cars whizzing past them in the dark, their headlights flying by like little bonfires.

"Are you losing it? Are you all right?"

He had been shaking but he wasn't now. He decided he would never ask her about what happened with Dom. "I'm not losing it," he said. "But if you talk about leaving me, I will lose it. So don't ever say it."

She looked at him and nodded. "Yah, okay, I'll try to believe you."

"Good, that's good." He looked down at the ground for a moment. When he glanced up he saw a single car pass by with only one headlight. It was as if the car were headed to hell all by itself, he thought.

"Stacy, let's go back to your place. That's what I really want to do," she said. "I'm sorry I called it a tomb."

"It *is* a tomb, no question about it, but it's our tomb, isn't it?"

"Our tomb," she said with a little laugh. "Yeah, I guess it kinda is."

Welcome to West Ga. Regional Library F
You checked out the following items:

1. New Jersey noir
   Barcode: 31057011264424
   Due: 2/22/12 11:59 PM
2. The New Funk & Wagnalls illustrat
   Barcode: 31057000027279
   Due: 2/22/12 11:59 PM
3. The Australian echidna
   Barcode: 31057902148041
   Due: 2/22/12 11:59 PM

VGRL-HQ 2012-02-08 15:22
You were helped by

AUGUST: FEEDING FRENZY

BY ALICIA OSTRIKER

Jersey Shore

Pink dawn, tide coming in: big fish driving mullets up
        into jetty rocks and onto sand, pulling back
in the undertow, jaws agape for small
fry they devour by the hundreds, water
whorling, gulls circling and dipping—

my two little granddaughters gleefully watching.

PART III

Commerce & Retribution

Gerald Slota

A BAG FOR NICHOLAS

BY HIRSH SAWHNEY

Jersey City

Shezad Ansari—or Shez to his customers, fans, and friends—had once been a successful musician. He'd played keyboards in a psychedelic grunge band called Cold Warrior, which released a *Billboard* Hot 100 single in '98. The next few years were good to Shez. Sandra, a film editor, finally agreed to marry him. He went to parties with distinguished actors and directors. He acquired a taste for champagne, caviar, and cocaine. But those days were long behind him. He was now thirty-eight and living, once again, in Jersey City.

He lived alone in the one-bedroom Newport condo his father had bought in 2001 and bequeathed him just two years later. Shez had two sources of income: royalty checks from Cold Warrior's first album, which covered his property taxes and utilities, and cash profits from the three-and-a-half- and seven-gram baggies of marijuana he sold to the local bourgeoisie. This side business took care of his grocery bills and bar tab.

An unexpected phone call from his ex-wife Sandra made Shez decide it was time to stop selling pot. She called him on a Monday in late February and said she had a real job for him, playing the Hammond B-3 organ on a soundtrack for an independent film. The film's director, who'd won a Sundance grant, owed her a favor. All Shez had to do was show up to a meeting in Brooklyn that Thursday, and the job was practically his. He told himself that Sandra's phone call was the start of a new leaf. He grew excited for his renaissance. Life as a normal, functional adult suddenly seemed possible.

Thursday came, and Shez hadn't sold a bag or restocked his supply of bud in three days. He woke up at noon and entered the bathroom. Mildew clouded the transparent shower curtain, and balls of hair and dust littered the floor. Shez powered up his father's old transistor radio. WBGO was playing a Lou Donaldson song. He'd fallen in love with the track during his first and only year at Rutgers. He placed his hands on the sink, confronting his hangover in the mirror. The bags under his eyes were puffy from last night, and from countless other solitary nights. A tight ball blazed in his stomach. He was no longer inspired by the thought of a new beginning.

He tugged one of his thick black curls toward his cheek. His hair didn't need cutting, but his beard was another story. It was unruly, a black and gray bird's nest, and it made him smile with a mixture of disgust and pride. He looked psychotic, like the shoe bomber. He opened up the medicine cabinet and reached for his stainless steel hair clippers. His father's expired beta blockers rested beside them though the man had been dead for five years.

Shez was trimming his beard when his phone began to vibrate. He pulled it out of his sweatpants pocket. He recognized the number but ignored the call. Then a text message arrived. *Shez*, it read, *this is Nicholas. I need a favor.*

Nicholas was a novelist who lived in Hamilton Park with his corporate-lawyer wife and toddler. Shez sold him a quarter-ounce every six weeks or so, and Nicholas sometimes invited him in for a glass of single malt and a conversation about jazz or the Grateful Dead. Shez didn't text back. He was done with that game.

The phone buzzed for a third time while Shez was using a razor to shape his mustache. "Jesus Christ," he muttered. He pressed a button and brought the device to his ear. "I'm sorry," he said, "but I can't help you out."

"Shez, hey," said Nicholas. "How's it going, man?"

"Fine, but I'm in the middle of something."

"I really need one of those hats, man. The situation is, like, desperate."

Shez smiled. The covert words people used to talk about weed amused him. In fact, so many things about the trade were pleasing. It was more than just a way to earn his spending money. It was a pastime. It was a pursuit. It was the way in which he interacted with the world. "No more hats," he said. "Not one left."

"Really?" Nicholas sounded skeptical.

"Really."

"That sucks, man. I've got this old buddy coming to town and—"

"Look, I can't help."

"He really wanted to meet you," said Nicholas. "He's seen you play live before."

Shez sighed. He was softening. "How much do you need?"

"A quarter-sized hat."

"Just a quarter?"

"Yeah, but I can give you a lot for it."

"How much?" Shez asked. He had a number in his mind: two hundred.

"Two-fifty," said Nicholas.

"I don't know," said Shez. "I have a real busy day."

"Three hundred," said Nicholas.

"Okay. I'll be there before five."

Shez hadn't touched his keyboard in several weeks, and he'd been gearing up to practice whole tone scales the entire afternoon, like Monk used to do. But now he had other plans. He had to get out to Sardul Singh, his oldest and best friend. He had to score a bag of herb for Nicholas. He put on his green, holey cargo pants and his blue hoodie. He stuffed Nirvana's *Unplugged* CD into his backpack and left the apartment.

In the elevator, a pretty Indian woman rested her ringed fingers on a baby stroller. He tried to smile at her, but she wouldn't meet his eyes. The building was filled with so many fresh-off-the-boat Indians. Most were in their thirties and here to crunch numbers for a year or two. He often saw them on the roof deck, getting loud and laughing without even drinking anything. They reminded him of junior high school students.

It was Shez's father who'd relished conversing with these "bright-eyed youngsters." He was born in Delhi but migrated to Pakistan in '47. He loathed Pakistan with every atom in his body but had an undying love for all things Indian. This attitude had always struck Shez as simplistic.

He stepped out into the winter afternoon. Sunlight leaked through a few fissures in the sky, reflecting off the sooty, crystalline snow. He squinted, and his wrinkles deepened. He began to walk toward Newark Avenue, where his car was parked. After clearing the gaggle of skyscrapers, he passed the old power station, which looked like the orphaned offspring of a dilapidated factory and the gothic German castles he'd admired on his only European tour. Trees grew inside the building, and birds nested in them during springtime.

"Fuck," he said out loud. He had reached his turquoise Corolla, and a boot was clamped to the car's front wheel. A ticket rested underneath its windshield wiper. It was already two o'clock, and he had to be in Brooklyn at seven-thirty sharp. He knew what he should do: get the boot off his car, tell Nicholas to go fuck himself, and get ready for his meeting.

A number 80 bus turned onto Newark. Shez remembered that the 80 would take him right to the courthouse, just a block or two away from the old neighborhood. He imagined Sardul's house and the pungent odor of marijuana. He didn't want to smoke it, he just wanted to weigh it. To place it in a sandwich bag, then roll, lick, seal; roll, lick, seal. The baggie would become a tight cylinder, ready for purchase, for a new home.

He turned around and bounded up Newark, making it to Jersey Avenue a few seconds before the bus. His blood was pumping, and he was wheezing. His anxiety about tonight had disappeared. The vehicle opened its doors, and he boarded. The bus charged up Newark Avenue, clearing downtown and rising toward William H. Dickinson High School, his alma mater. Shez had recently Googled himself and discovered that he was listed as one of the high school's notable alumni on its Wikipedia page.

He got off across from the courthouse and started walking down Oakland Avenue. He was home, back in the old neighborhood. The route to Sardul's house didn't pass his old house, which his parents had sold when they moved to the Newport condo. It did take him by the shop, though. He paused in front of the place for just a few seconds. It hadn't changed much. It was still called Courthouse Convenience, and the same bail bondsman sat to the left of it. A Peruvian restaurant had replaced the beauty salon on the right.

His father had bought the store from a distant cousin when Shez was six. It was 1980, and the family had been in the country two years. Running the shop was boring for Shez's dad, who'd been an up-and-coming barrister in Lahore. He sat behind the register six days a week, rereading treatises by John Stuart Mill, listening to talk radio, and constantly sipping liquor from a coffee mug.

The business's only bad year was '87, but that was a bad one for everyone. Bands of disgruntled white men were beating brown immigrants with baseball bats and kicking them into comas. The family lived in fear, and they were right to be afraid. Shez's father went to open up the shop one morning and found a swastika painted on the metal gate. They'd also sprayed the words *Dotheads go home* in red letters. "Ignorant idiots," said his dad. "We're Muslims—we don't wear dots on our heads."

His father agreed to pay Shez and Sardul ten dollars each to clean the graffiti every time it appeared, but the first time Shez cleaned it up himself. He spent a couple of hours slapping on a coat of metallic paint and then walked into the store to find his dad on the floor behind the register. His father's mug was cracked, and an almost empty bottle of Johnnie Walker Red Label rested on the counter. Shez crouched down and propped his father up against the wall, convinced more than ever that he had to get far away from this place.

He climbed up the steps of Sardul's detached Beacon Avenue home. The place was a standard two-story abode, encased in aluminum siding. An American flag swayed beside its front door. Shez and Sardul used to drink wine coolers on the house's roof, staring out at the blinking tops of the Twin Towers. They were in junior high school and dreamed of living in those towers one day. Shez rang the doorbell and looked at his watch.

It was a quarter to three. If he was quick, he would have time to hand over the bag to Nicholas and even change his clothes before his meeting. He decided he'd put on one of his father's tweed jackets, and a little excitement began to pulse in him again. He imagined sipping a glass of red wine and expounding on the history of the electric organ. Sandra's movie director friend, whoever he was, would be impressed. His ex-wife's lips would form an amused, wistful smile. These thoughts reignited the tight ball in his stomach. The anxiety returned, and with it, shame. Why was he back here? For money he'd blow at the bar by Sunday?

The door opened, and Sardul's aunt greeted him. "Welcome, son, welcome." Aunty was a slender, tall woman with a striking dime-sized nose ring. She dyed her hair jet-black, though Shez could make out her silver roots. "You look good," she said, "nice and clean cut." She always spoke to Shez in Punjabi, and he responded in English.

"You're the one who looks good," he said. "You couldn't be a day over forty."

"Always a charmer," she said, smiling. "Like your father. How's Mom?"

"Good, Aunty, I spoke to her just last week."

"Sardul's parents love being back in Delhi, and your mom

seems happy in the Gulf. Me, I couldn't do it. This place is my home."

He followed her into the family room, which contained plush pink sofas and a high-definition television, all purchased by Sardul, all paid for in cash. Shez noticed that Aunty was wearing her burgundy nurse's aide uniform. "I thought you quit," he said.

"Your friend says I shouldn't work. But I need my independence; I need something to do." Aunty grabbed a glass from a granite counter and took a long gulp. She drank a mixture of ginger ale and beer every afternoon. "Have a shandy," she offered.

"No, Aunty, I'm fine."

"Suit yourself," she said. "Your friend's in his quarters." She got close to Shez and gave him two loving slaps on the cheek. "I have to go do some shopping." She put on a coat and walked out the door.

He climbed the carpeted staircase and arrived at Sardul's door, which had two stickers on it. One was from the previous year's presidential campaign and said the words, *Got Hope?* The other said, *9/11 was an inside job.* Shez wasn't very political, and he had little patience for Sardul's conspiracy theories. He knocked on the door and opened it before getting a response.

His friend was sitting on a pink recliner that matched the downstairs sofas. He wore a plaid flannel shirt, and baggy, ironed jeans fell over his construction boots. He was playing Rock Band, and the Beatles song "Get Back" was on. He was leaning into a solo. "What's up, fool?" asked Sardul. "Wanna play?"

"Nah, I'm cool." Shez loved "Get Back," especially the Billy Preston keyboard solo. He couldn't desecrate such masterful music.

Sardul pressed pause and put his toy guitar down. He got up and gave Shez a one-armed hug. Sardul was at least six inches shorter than Shez, and a few patches of adolescent acne still blemished his round face. A long black braid streamed out of the back of his Yankees cap.

"Want one?" asked Sardul. He nodded at the handblown glass bong on his coffee table.

"I can't," said Shez. "Got a job interview tonight."

"Really? Where?"

"In Brooklyn. It's for a movie. A soundtrack."

"Let me guess. Sandra set it up for you?"

"Yeah, so?"

"So you need to stop dealing with that bitch." Sardul reached for the bong and filled its chamber with smoke.

"Watch it, man. I used to be married to that bitch."

Sardul extracted the bowl from the bong and cleared the chamber. Water gurgled, and a stream of smoke shot into his lungs. "She's not a bad person. She's just bad for you." Smoke escaped from his nostrils and lips as he uttered these words.

"She's trying to help me out. She's trying to do me a favor."

"You ever ask yourself why? She has a new man. She's pregnant. She just wants to be able to enjoy her co-op and her nanny without feeling guilty about your drunken ass."

Shez sighed and shook his head. "I guess I'll have a small hit."

"It's good shit," said Sardul. "From BC this time."

Shez smoked, then licked his lips. "It's like fruity or something."

"Exactly. It tastes like fruit, and it's got blue hairs. We're calling it Blueberry Bud."

"Yo," said Shez. "I need a little of this Blueberry Bud."

"Yeah, no kidding. You only come by when you need a re-up."

Shez giggled.

"What's so funny?" asked Sardul.

"Nothing," he lied. He was amused, though. Sardul was imitating the TV again. These days it was *The Wire*. It used to be *Goodfellas* or *Scarface*.

Sardul walked toward a door on the wall behind his television. "Whatever," he said. "You laugh like a little girl." He opened the door and, like a gentleman, motioned for Shez to pass through first. Sardul followed, closing the door behind him.

* * *

Sardul's office was more of a large closet. An imposing metal desk hulked against a wall and a filing cabinet stood next to it. The cabinet contained time sheets and invoices from his roofing business, which didn't function during winter. Sardul sat down on his Aeron chair and reached for the safe underneath his desk. Shez stared at a framed photograph of him and Sardul at the 1999 MTV Music Awards. Both of them were wearing tuxedos, and Sardul dangled an arm around Shez's neck. He was holding up two of his fingers, as if to say, *Wassup, homie?* not *Peace.*

Sardul had rung Shez's doorbell when the boys were nine, just a few weeks after Sardul's family had moved to America. He had on one of those little-kid turbans and asked if Shez wanted to play. Shez taught him how to play stickball, and they became best friends.

Shez took some distance in high school, when he wanted to cease being just another dorky Jersey dothead. His walls stayed up until he got his first whiff of success, when he realized he needed a friend he could trust. He needed someone who would be happy for him, not envious. Sardul didn't hold any grudges. He held Shez's hand through the divorce. He was in the hospital when Shez's dad was on a respirator, and when he died.

The safe door swung open, and Shez's heart started pounding. He admired Sardul's penchant for neatness. Wads of tens and twenties were neatly stacked at the bottom of the safe. Then came four large Tupperware containers of high-grade marijuana and a digital scale. Shez always flinched at the sight of Sardul's Glock, but Sardul promised him he didn't keep it loaded.

"So what you need?" asked Sardul. He took out the scale, and then the pot. The room began to smell skunky.

Shez was about to answer, but Sardul cocked his head toward the door.

"What is it?" Shez asked.

"You hear that?"

"No. I don't hear anything. You're just stoned." Shez listened and did hear footsteps, though.

Sardul took his gun out of the safe. The doorknob began to rattle. The door opened.

Sardul's aunt was standing there, smiling.

Sardul sighed and shook his head. "Jesus, you scared the shit out of me." He put his pistol in his pocket. "What is it?" he said, switching to Punjabi.

"I need money," the woman answered.

"For what?"

"To feed your big belly."

"How much?"

Aunty held her thumb and index finger a centimeter apart. Sardul opened his safe again and handed her a wad of twenties. She put them in her coat pocket and walked out the door.

"Knock next time!" Sardul screamed after her.

"I don't need to knock in my own house," she called back.

Sardul closed the door and locked it this time. "So, what do you need?" he said again.

"A quarter."

Sardul handed Shez a Tupperware container filled with a quarter-pound of pot.

"Not a QP," said Shez. "A quarter-ounce."

"I thought you said you were done, by the way."

"I am. I'm just doing someone a favor."

Sardul pushed his scale in front of Shez, and Shez placed marijuana on it until the number 7 appeared in red. He closed the Tupperware and handed it back to his friend, but Sardul began to scowl and shake his head.

"What?" said Shez.

"I always tell you—round up, not down. I've got a rep to maintain."

Shez threw on another bud, and 8.2 grams now rested on the scale.

Sardul nodded in approval. "You're a talented man," he said. "But business just isn't your thing."

Shez stood with his hands in the pockets of his hoodie at a bus stop near the corner of Newark and Central. The wind had picked up and the temperature had dropped. Two Filipino women in high heels emerged from the nearby probation office and lit up cigarettes next to him. They shivered and linked their arms together. A bus arrived and carried them away. He was waiting for the 86, but it never came. He looked at his watch: 4:45. Shit, he thought. He was cutting it close.

The reality of his day and decisions suddenly became clear to him. He wanted to play music again, but his simple life of pot and royalty checks was cozy. He wanted to change, but just thinking about change was draining. He had sabotaged himself. Again. He felt ashamed.

An 80 bus pulled up, and Shez asked the driver if something was wrong with the 86. The driver told him the 86 didn't stop here. Shez decided he would take the PATH to Grove Street and walk to Hamilton Park from there. He could deliver the bag and get right back on the train. He would make it to his meeting with time to spare. He took the marijuana out of his backpack and slipped it underneath the elastic of his boxers. They often searched Shez's bags on the train because of his beard and skin tone, but they never searched his body. The baggie chafed his penis as he walked toward Journal Square.

He entered the terminal and waited on the platform amidst a crowd of tired brown and black faces. Everyone stared up at the TV screen streaming outdated weather reports and incorrect train times. Trains heading to Newark arrived and left on the other side of the tracks, but all trains to New York were behind schedule. Shez tensed up again. Time wasn't on his side.

A train bound for the World Trade Center finally arrived, and he got on board. It was one of those new trains, the ones with shiny blue interiors. A couple of seats were empty, but he stood by the doors. A man standing across from Shez stared at him. He was wearing a suit and had a silver stud in his left ear. He had wide shoulders and a leather briefcase. Shez put his backpack on the ground, and the man's eyes followed the bag.

Shez's phone began to buzz. He removed it from his cargo pants. Nicholas had sent him an SMS. *You coming or what?* it read.

The shame Shez had been feeling suddenly turned to anger. He was angry at himself, and pissed at Nicholas. He looked at his watch. It was 5:12. Maybe he could do everything—drop off the bag and even pick up his tweed jacket. But what was the point? He didn't owe this customer—ex-customer—anything.

The train barreled toward Grove Street, and Shez started punching in a message. *Sorry man, can't help you. No more hats . . . Ever!* He pressed the send button, but the phone told him his message didn't go through. He noticed his signal strength was low—only one bar left, and even that bar began to flash. He held the phone up toward the ceiling of the train, hoping for a stronger signal. He noticed the businessman with the earring was still staring at him.

He tried sending again with his arm closer to the window, but the text refused to go through. His arm dropped to his side, and he sighed. He felt eyes bearing down on him. He looked up and saw the businessman glaring at him. The man's green eyes were wide. The man's face was clenched.

"Do you have a problem?" Shez asked him.

"Yeah, I do, actually," said the man. "What were you just doing?"

"Why?" Shez wanted to unleash his anger, but remembered the pot in his crotch.

"Because it looked a little suspicious."

"It's none of your business what I was doing."

"Yes it is. My safety is my business."

"What?" said Shez. "You've got to be kidding me."

"I'm not kidding, and I wouldn't mess around if I were you. What do you have in that bag?"

Shez began to sweat. The train pulled into Grove Street, and he was relieved. He disembarked, but the man followed him onto the platform. Shez saw the man walk toward a cop, and he headed for the staircase. He began to climb the stairs, the seven— no eight—grams of pot pressed against the skin near his groin. He was almost at the turnstiles. If he could make it through, he'd be free. He was on the last step when a voice called out.

"Excuse me!" it shouted. "Sir, hold up. Sir, stop where you are. Police!"

Shez froze. Then he slowly turned around.

"Get back here," the cop said.

Shez obeyed him.

The cop, a black guy, made Shez stand beside a door at the far end of the platform. The businessman waited a hundred feet away from him talking to another cop, a white guy. The black cop searched Shez's backpack. He pulled out the Nirvana CD, and then a couple of old issues of *DownBeat*. "A jazz fan," he said.

His words comforted Shez. Things might end up okay. They might not find the pot. If they let him go, he promised himself he would never sell a dime of pot again. He would get this job and move on with his life. His hopefulness vanished, however, when he saw a third cop walking a German shepherd down the stairs. The burning in his stomach made his moistening pits feel particularly cold.

The new cop and the canine walked toward Shez.

The black cop asked Shez to put his hands against the wall and widen his legs. He patted him down thoroughly but didn't touch his groin. The cop with the dog instructed the animal to give Shez a sniff.

I'm fucked, Shez thought. If this fucking dog barks, I'm busted.

The dog sniffed his shoes, his pants, then his hoodie.

Shez tried to send it subliminal messages. *Don't bark, doggie. I'm your friend, doggie.*

The dog didn't bark.

"Looks like this one isn't carrying any bombs," said the black cop.

"Come on, boy, let's go," commanded the dog cop. Man and canine went back up the stairs.

"Does this mean I can leave?" asked Shez.

The black cop shook his head. "You're going to have to wait for just a few more minutes. It's your name. It's similar to one that's on a watch list."

"You think I'm a terrorist?"

"No, but I'm sure as hell going to check." The cop took out a key and opened the nearby door, which led to an office with a crappy computer and an old phone.

Shez looked at the wall clock. It was six-thirty.

"Have a seat," said the cop.

Shez obeyed him again.

The cop started playing solitaire on his computer. Shez stared at his feet and thought. He thought about asking whether he should consult a lawyer. He thought about asking if he could use the phone to tell Sandra he was going to be late. His father wouldn't have been afraid to do one or both of these things, but Shez knew the best thing was to stay quiet.

The phone rang at 7:34, and the cop answered it. "Okay," he said, "that's what I figured." He put down the phone and looked at Shez. "You're okay; you can go. But I'd think about changing that name if I were you."

Shez surfaced in front of Grove Point. He walked toward the Dunkin' Donuts and pulled out his phone. His meeting should have started fifteen minutes ago. He dialed Sandra.

"Where are you?" she asked.

"I'm sorry," he said, "but I'm going to be a little late."

She asked him how late.

"I can get there in forty-five, an hour max. You're never going to guess what—"

"Forget it," she told him. "I don't want to know."

"Should we reschedule?" he asked, but he knew the answer before she responded.

"I'm done, Shez." She ended the call.

He walked down Newark Avenue and entered his bar. He held up a finger, and the bartender poured a Jameson. He called up Nicholas and told him he'd be there in a little while. Tomorrow he'd go back to Sardul's and get a full quarter-pound.

GLASS EELS

BY JEFFREY FORD

Dividing Creek

etween a spreading magnolia and a forest of cattails that
ran all the way to the estuary stood Marty's dilapidated
studio. The walls were damp, and low-tide stink mixed
with turpentine and oils. It was late on a Saturday night in early
March. They drank beer and passed a joint. Len spoke of insom-
nia, a recent murder out on Money Island, and a buck he'd seen
with pitch-black antlers. Marty told about a huge snake on the
outside of the studio window and then showed Len his most recent
paintings—local landscapes and a series of figures called *Haunted
High School.*

"That chick looks dead," said Len, pointing at a canvas with a
pale girl in a cheerleading outfit, smoking a cigarette. In the background loomed an abandoned factory, busted glass and crumbling
brick. A smokestack.

"She's haunted," said Marty. "I gotta sell a couple of these in
the next gallery show in Milville on Third Friday. I need enough to
fix the roof. We're fuckin' broke."

"I heard there was a guy in a van buying glass eels before day-
break in the parking lot behind the burned-out diner on Jones
Island Road," said Len.

"The state banned it back in the '90s, didn't they?" Marty
asked.

"Yeah, *they* banned it," Len said and laughed. "I heard one
kilogram is going for a thousand dollars. That's two pounds of eel
for a grand."

"How many eels is that?"

"You gotta remember," said Len, "they're only two inches long, see-through thin. So you have to do a fair amount of dipping to bring up two pounds, but not enough to call it work."

"Are you saying we should do this?"

"Well, we should do it just once. Think of your roof."

Marty nodded.

"Shit, I could use the money for my prescriptions," said Len.

"How much can you make in a night?"

"Most guys do about a kilogram and a half to two. Some do a little better. But there are times when a person'll bring in twenty or even more."

"How?"

"They know a spot no one else knows, a certain creek, or gut, or spillway, where saltwater and freshwater come together and the glass eels swarm. And I was thinking today, after I heard that they were going for a grand, that there was a place my father would take me fishing for eels at the end of July. We'd barbecue them."

"How long ago?"

"Thirty years."

"You think we could find it?"

"Nothing changes around here," Len said. "Myrtle's Gut. Down the end of your own block out here. At the marina, we get in a canoe and paddle a little ways and there's a big island of reeds. It's pretty sturdy to walk on, but the water is everywhere and if you take a wrong step in the dark you could fall in up to your neck. There used to be a trail through the reeds into the middle of the island. Sort of at the center is a spot where this creek comes up from underground and winds its way for three turns, once around a Myrtle bush, on its way out to the Delaware."

"That ain't real," Marty said.

"Yeah," said Len, "that's what it is. A freshwater creek that runs out to the reed island beneath the floor of the bay and then surfaces."

"And the eels that go there swim underground up into the freshwater streams?"

"Eels will do anything they have to do to get where they're going. On their way back out to sea to spawn, if a creek dries up, they'll wriggle right across the land. Years ago on a full moon night in August you could club eels passing through. It was an event. The guy who owned the best meadow for it had a stand nearby that sold corn dogs and lemonade. Everybody clubbed a couple. There were guys there who'd take your eels and smoke them for you for a half dollar."

"Sounds *Lord of the Flies*."

"The underground protects them on the way out, so why not on the way in?"

"How do you see them at night when they're so small?"

"They're like tiny ghosts, especially in the moonlight."

"So we go out there in a canoe?"

"We'll need a couple of coolers and some nets, a couple of flashlights."

"I can't run, man. If we get caught, there's no way I can run."

"Forget it, no one's gonna see us. Nobody gives a shit. The last time I saw a cop down here was about a year and a half ago when Mr. Clab's coffin went on a voyage. Remember, they found it on the beach next to the marina?"

"The cop said there was an underground stream beneath the cemetery that washed the box out to the bay."

"You see," said Len, "there's your proof of what I'm saying."

Len and Marty sat on the damp ground beside the spreading myrtle bush at the second bend in the gut. There was a breeze. Between them lay a pair of lit flashlights like a cold campfire. They were dressed warmly with hats, gloves, and scarves. Beside them were coolers and nets. Len took out a joint and said, "We gotta wait for the moon."

"Why?"

"The tide. The moon's gonna rise in about five minutes, nearly full, and in a half hour it'll be a good way up the sky and big as a dinner plate. The eels will come in with the tide."

"It's dark as shit out here," said Marty.

"Nice stars, though," said Len. He passed the joint.

Marty took a hit and said, "The other night, after you left, it started raining hard. I went up to bed. When I got under the covers Claire's back was to me. I knew she was awake. I told her what you said about the eels, and I told her if something happened where I got caught she would have to bail me out. A few seconds passed and, without turning around, she asked, 'How much can you make?' 'Maybe a couple of thousand,' I told her. The rain dripped in. She said, 'Do it.'"

Len laughed. "That's what I call a working marriage." He leaned forward and took the pint from Marty's hand.

"Do you think Matisse ever did this?" asked Marty.

"I don't think Matisse was ever a substitute teacher."

"The other day they sent me to teach English in a separate school for all the truants and delinquents. They call it the Hawthorne Academy. Jesus, it's the worst. Fights, a couple an hour. Crazy motherfucker kids. They're being warehoused by the state until they reach the legal age and can be released into society."

"Haunted High School," said Len. He pointed into the sky. "Here comes the moon."

"Nice," said Marty.

They sat quietly for a long while, listening to the flow of the gut and the wind moving over the marshland. Len lit a cigarette and said, "I saw a guy in town this afternoon. I think I remember him from 'Nam."

"Oh lordy, no Vietnam stories. Show some mercy."

"I'll just tell you the short version," said Len.

"Never short enough. When do the eels show up?"

"Listen, I saw this guy, Vietcong. We never learned what his real name was but everybody on both sides called him *Uncle Fun*. I was shown black-and-white photos of him. We were sent into the tunnels with an express mission to execute this guy. The tunnels were mind-blowing, mazes of warrens, three, four floors, couches, kids, booby traps. He was a fucking entertainer, like a nightclub act, only he played the Vietcong tunnel systems instead of Vegas. He told jokes and sang songs. For some reason they wanted us to cancel his contract asap."

"You're a one-man blizzard of bullshit," said Marty.

"Fuck you. Intel said that at the end of every performance he laughed like Woody Woodpecker."

"What was he doing downtown this afternoon, trying out new material in the parking lot of City Liquors? You been taking your pills?"

"Shit, they're here," said Len. "Grab a net."

The moon shone down on the bend in the gut and the water bubbled and glowed with the reflection of thousands of glass eels. Len and Marty scooped up dripping nets of them like shovelfuls of silver.

"Do we need to put water in the coolers to keep them alive?" asked Marty.

"Are you kidding? They're tough as hell. They'll keep for hours just like they are."

"The black eyes creep me out."

"A glass eel the size of a person would be the Holy Ghost."

Marty drove his old Impala. Len was in the passenger seat. The nets were in the back, the coolers in the trunk. They headed north, away from the marina, past Marty's house, and turned at the cemetery onto a road that went over a wooden bridge. It led to a narrow lane lined with oak and pine. The deer looked up, their eyes glowing in the headlights.

"You know that giant tree up at the end of the road here, where you make the turn? The one with the neon-orange pentagram on it? Star with a circle around it. What's that all about?" asked Marty.

"That's Wiccan, I think. Nature witches. They've been here for a long, long time. They mark the important crossroads."

"Witches?"

"I've run into a few. You hear stories about spells and shit, but I never witnessed any of that. They just seem like sketchy hippies."

"Me and Claire call it the Devil Tree. Which way am I going here?"

"You want to make a left. Then, in a quarter of a mile, make a right. I hope the buyer's there again."

"How much do you think we've got?"

"I'd say about eight grand. Maybe more."

"Jeez."

"These eels have never been successfully bred in captivity," said Len. "When it comes to eels you can only take."

"You trying to make me feel guilty?"

"Yeah, but fuck it, we need the cash. The parking lot of the old diner is up here on the right just past these cattails."

Behind the burned-out shell of Jaqui's All-Night Diner, in a parking lot long gone to weeds, Len and Marty stood before the open back doors of a large van. Inside was a lantern that gave a dim light. Behind the lantern, a teenage girl sitting on a crate aimed a shotgun at them.

"We'll see what you have," said a heavyset man to their right. He wore a tweed suit jacket and had a pistol tucked into the waist of his jeans. Before him on a makeshift wooden platform was a large antique balance scale, one end a fine net, the other a flat plate holding four-kilogram cylinders of lead.

"Snorri," called the buyer, and a huge guy with a crew cut, wearing a shoulder holster, appeared from around the side of the van. "Pour these gentlemen's eels, I have to weigh them."

Snorri lifted the first cooler and carefully poured out the eels into the net of the scale. The weighing took awhile. Every time the scale moved it creaked. The wind blew strong and whipped the reeds that surrounded the parking lot. The girl with the shotgun yawned and checked for messages on her phone.

"That's the last of them," said the buyer, clapping his hands. "One more calculation, though. I subtract for the water the eels have on them. I only pay for eels, not water." He laid three small white gull feathers on the flat plate of the scale and leaned over to read the difference. "You have a little more than nine kilograms here. I can give you eight thousand."

"I heard it was a thousand a kilogram," said Len.

"One hears what one wants," said the buyer.

"I know from a reliable source that last night you were paying a grand."

"Supply and demand," said the buyer.

"Explain it," said Len.

"Eight grand or I can have Snorri explain it to you in no uncertain terms."

The girl in the van laughed.

"We'll take the eight grand," said Marty. "Chill out," he said to Len. "We're talking eight grand for an hour and a half of fishing."

"Okay," said Len.

Snorri stepped back, taking the gun from its holster. The buyer leaned into the van and stuffed eight stacks of banded hundreds into a yellow plastic grocery bag. He handed the bag to Marty. "Check it."

Marty held the bag open and counted the stacks in a whisper. He reached in and felt the money. He lifted the bag and smelled it. "Thanks," he said.

"An hour and a half," said the buyer. "That's very fast for what you brought in."

"We don't mess around," said Len.

"Where were you?"

"Over west," said Len, "in the woods by the bay south of Greenwich."

"Can you be more specific?"

"Have Snorri explain it to you," said Len, and laughed on his way back to the Impala.

They got in the car. Marty backed out past the remains of the diner and onto the road. "Why'd you have to be such an asshole with the guy? I thought they were gonna shoot us in the back with every step I took."

"They're not gonna shoot us. Think about it, they need us. If we're getting a bit less than a grand for a kilogram, imagine what the buyer is making per kilogram from aquafarms in Asia."

"Too many guns for me."

"Quit your cryin', we've got four grand apiece. You can get your roof fixed and I can medicate. Harmony will reign."

"I'm happy for the four grand," said Marty. "In your honor, I'm gonna paint a series, maybe eight canvases, each a scene from the career of Uncle Fun."

"Put him in a tux and make him look like a North Vietnamese Bobby Darin."

"Hey, there's somebody behind us."

Len looked over his shoulder. "We'll know soon enough if it's a cop. When you get to the Devil Tree, keep going, don't make the turn. Head down the road a ways and then turn back by the old glass factory. We can lose him in the dunes."

"Could just be somebody out driving."

"I kind of doubt it," said Len. "We've got eight thousand dollars in cash here and it's three in the morning on one of the loneliest roads in the world. When you get to the tree, hit the gas. We'll see if he keeps up."

"I can't drive fast at night. I can't see dick."

"You gotta lose this fucker now."

The Impala suddenly accelerated. Len whooped and called, "Faster!"

Marty was hunched up over the steering wheel, peering into the dark.

"They're definitely on our asses," said Len. "Turn in at the glass factory."

"I don't know where the turn is. You're gonna have to warn me."

"Okay, okay, okay . . . Now!"

Marty cut the wheel. The back tires skidded sideways and the car did a 180. He put it in reverse, turned around, and they were headed into the maze of sand dunes.

"Go to the right," said Len. "That's where it gets crazy."

"You know your way through here?"

"Nobody knows their way through here. I used to play here as a kid and I'd get lost and turned around all the time."

"How's that gonna help us?"

"Make a left after this next dune. Twenty minutes of driving around in this bullshit in the dark and that guy's gonna forget all about us and go home. Just keep dodging him for a while and then I'll get us back to the road."

"That plan sucks."

"That's its strength."

"Oh shit," said Marty, "I'm past empty."

"You're kidding," said Len, and leaned over to look at the dashboard. "Oh man."

"I forgot to gas up."

"That's just fuckin' dandy."

"It's running on fumes, should I try to make it back to the road?"

"No, go deeper in. We'll hide somewhere with the lights out. Make as many crazy turns as you can."

"I don't like it."

"When the car craps out, shut up. We're gonna run silent, run deep."

The Impala died in a cul-de-sac bounded by three enormous sand dunes.

"Kill the lights," said Len. "Crack a window so we can hear better and then turn everything off."

"That guy's probably home having a beer right now, cursing us 'cause we gave him the slip."

Len unzipped his jacket and reached down the front of his shirt. He cocked back his chin and pulled out a large scabbard and knife on a leather strap around his neck. Taking the strap off, he removed the knife, ten inches with a hunting blade and grip guard, and stowed it up his jacket sleeve, hilt first.

"What's that for?"

"Whatever," said Len. Then he whispered, "I remember, once we had Uncle Fun surrounded and he managed to give us the slip . . ."

"Run silent," said Marty.

They sat quietly in the dark. Off to the east an owl called.

Len and Marty stood ten yards in front of the Impala. Three guys in black hoodies and ski masks surrounded them. The one in front of them held a .22 pistol with a homemade silencer on it. Marty shivered and clutched the yellow grocery bag. The moon was gone from the sky. Dark clouds raced and it smelled like rain.

"What you two have to learn is that if you harvest glass down here, you need to pay us 15 percent of your take," said the guy with the gun.

"Are you ladies pro-eel or something?" asked Len. "I mean the outfits. You look like eels. It's the first thing I thought when I saw you."

"Nobody's pro-eel, asshole. We're pro-cash. We poach the poachers. Like the food chain."

"That silencer have a wipe?" asked Len.

"What difference does it make? I could shoot you with a cannon out here and nobody'd know."

"Listen, I was born down here," said Len. "I have as much right to these eels as you do."

"Wait, man, listen," said Marty. "It's just like a tax. Everything has a tax on it. So we pay for eight grand—twelve hundred or something. Let it go and let's get out of here."

"I'm not paying anything," snapped Len. "He can suck my glass eel."

"That's it for you," said the guy in the mask, and raised the gun.

Len ducked as the shot sounded, the gruff sudden cough of an old man. When he sprang up, he had the knife in his hand. In one swift motion he slashed the blade across the wrist of the masked man's gun hand. The sharp metal bit in deep and severed the tendon. The gun dropped. The guy screamed. Marty, pissing his pants, turned and ran.

Len took a backhanded swipe and the blade tore open the throat beneath the ski mask. Blood poured and the scream turned to a gurgle. Len pivoted to follow Marty and was hit in the left side of the head with a baseball bat. He staggered sideways a few steps before his feet went out from under him. The masked guy with the bat took off after Marty while his remaining partner stood over Len and drew a .22 pistol with a silencer from the pocket of his hoodie. Len's jaw was busted and jutting to the side. He blinked and grunted. The cough of the gun sounded twice.

Marty worked like crazy to climb the dune but he got nowhere. Finally, he turned and lay back against the slope. He held the bag of money out toward the two masked men that stood only a few yards below him. One kept a flashlight trained on the painter. The other carried the pistol.

"I just wanted to fix my fuckin' roof. Take the money."

"We're gonna throw your bodies in an eel pond," said the guy with the flashlight. "In August, when the old ones head to the Sargasso to spawn, you'll go with them." He laughed high-pitched and insane.

Marty quit weeping. "Uncle Fun?" he asked. "Is it you?"

"This loser's lost his mind," said the gunman to his partner. "I'll give you Uncle Fun," he said to Marty, and pulled the trigger three times.

MEADOWLANDS SPIKE

BY BARRY N. MALZBERG & BILL PRONZINI
Rutherford

Listen to me. Please listen. Everything I'm about to tell you is the gospel truth.

I can't live with this terrible secret any longer. It's been thirty-five years, but I've never stopped thinking about what I did. Not for a single day. It's all there, every detail burned into the walls of my mind. It could've happened yesterday, that's how clear it is.

I see him alive, not just that night before the bullets tore into him, but the way he was when he had the power. Big man, bigger than life, bigger than death everybody thought, shouting words and slogans, promises and lies in his giant's voice. King of Labor, King of the Long Labor Con. The job action. The sit-down strike. The secondary boycott. The sick-in. All of that and so much more until they threw him in the slammer for jury-tampering.

James Hoffa, that's right.

And then came the Nixon pardon that set him up for another run at the union presidency. He should've known it wasn't going to happen. No one was stupid enough other than Brother James himself to think he'd get the deal past his successors, as hard-nosed a bunch as they were. Should've known they'd take him out by any means necessary.

I was the means.

I picked him up that night in my car. Just me and him, nobody else. He thought we were going to a secret hush-hush meeting with some bigwigs in Rutherford—

Sure, I know he was last seen in the Detroit area, but that was the day *before*.

They set him up by calling him back to Jersey on the QT. Nobody but Big Billy and me and a couple of others knew that the only meeting he was going to was with God or the Devil.

So anyhow, I drove him to the closed-up garage I owned. That's where I emptied my Colt automatic into him, six shots grouped in his chest like it was a bull's-eye target.

Then I put on overalls and gloves, dragged his body down into the grease pit, and dismembered it with a hatchet and a hacksaw. Awful job. Awful. But that was the way the big boys uptown wanted it done, don't ask me why.

I can still see him lying there dead after I put those six rounds into his chest. Still see the pieces of him after the butchering was done, all the bloody pieces, all the King's parts: legs, arms, torso, head—my last view of the Great Man before I stuffed the pieces into six separate plastic bags and put them into the trunk of my Buick.

Jimmy H. alive, Jimmy H. dead, Jimmy H. in pieces. Nothing left but chopped-up clay, the torso weighted with lead pellets, bouncing and thudding in the trunk as I raced along the Turnpike to the new Meadowlands stadium.

That's what I said, the Meadowlands.

How did I get in? I had a key to the gate, that's how. Back then I had connections, guys who'd do me a favor without asking questions and then keep their mouths shut. The refineries five miles to the south would have made quicker work of the remains, but butchering him was bad enough, I couldn't burn him up too. The Meadowlands was better. Home base. Burial instead of cremation.

The state of New Jersey is where America comes to die. You don't think so? Remember Paul Simon? The cars on the New Jersey Turnpike, each filled with people in search of America. I was one of them that night, in a Buick with a dismembered slab of America in my trunk and the rising yellow clouds from the refineries staining the night around me.

Oh, I remember, all right. Every detail after three and a half decades. Arriving at the deserted stadium site. Opening the Buick's trunk in the moonlit dark to get the shovel. Digging six holes all across the south end zone—

Don't laugh. It's not funny. I'm telling you just what I did: dug six holes, six graves for the six pieces of Jimmy H.

If New Jersey is where America comes to die, then the end zone was the perfect burial spot for Brother James. Hell, it would have been perfect for the Wobblies, Mother Jones, the '37 Ford strikers, hundreds of others like them. You see what I mean?

Once the bags were planted, the holes covered up and smoothed out, I stood leaning on the shovel, gasping in the cold, like an exhausted actor taking a crooked bow after a command performance. Thinking that the whole business hadn't been so bad, that I'd gotten it all done pretty quick. A speed run from the killing to the cutting up to the driving to the burying. Thinking that was the end of it.

But it wasn't. Not for me. I should have known it wouldn't be because even then I could see the pieces spread out deep under the end zone turf, as if I had X-ray vision. The flesh that would decay in summer heat and winter ice. The scattered bones that would crumble to dust.

I didn't stay there long. It was almost dawn and the almost-finished stadium was glowing in the restless early light. Soon there'd be workers, traffic. I couldn't afford to be seen in the area.

I drove the Buick straight back to the garage, backed it inside, and took care of the cleanup. Washed the blood down the grease pit drain with a hose. Used some solvent to remove a couple of stains in the trunk. Burned the overalls and gloves and my filthy clothes in the incinerator out back. When I was done, there wasn't a trace left.

My house was half a mile from the station. Jane was waiting for me when I got there.

Where were you all night? she said.

Never mind, I said. It's none of your business.

You look terrible, she said. What have you been doing?

Nothing, I said. What else could I have said to her? Oh, nothing much, babe, just out murdering the boss, cutting up the boss, burying the boss.

I walked past her, heading toward the shower. This is a filthy place, I said then. It's always filthy. Why don't you ever clean it up?

She didn't like that. She hadn't liked anything about me for a long time. Even thirty-five years later I can feel her contempt, her suspicion. I guess I can't blame her. Living jammed close together in that little house, not just her and me but the kid too, none of us getting along with each other, fearing Big Billy and the uptown boys, torn apart by secrets. She left me not long after that night, you know, just as soon as the kid got out of high school, and for all I know she's dead now. The kid too—I haven't seen or heard from him in twenty years.

But I'm getting off track. After I had my shower and put on some of my better threads, I drove into the city to report to Big Billy.

Disposing of Jimmy H. was the nasty part of the assignment, but facing Big Billy wasn't much better. You remember him? Sure. He's long gone now, most of the uptown boys are long gone, but back then he was a force. I did a lot of jobs for him before that night, but none like the one with Brother James. None that was even close.

An hour later I was standing in Big Billy's office, surrounded by concrete, his hard little eyes boring into mine.

I dumped him, I said. It's finished business.

Don't tell me dumped, Big Billy said. Don't tell me finished business. Where did you put the sucker?

You really want to know? I said. You told me handle it any way I want, just make him disappear. So that's what I did.

I got to know, he said, so I can tell them uptown.

Well, they didn't want to know uptown, he'd told me that before. He wanted the information only for himself. But if you didn't want to end up like Jimmy H., you did what Big Billy told you to. And you never lied to him.

So I told him the truth. I put him where they'll never find him, I said. The Meadowlands Stadium. Under the south end zone.

I thought he'd say that was a perfect spot, I couldn't have come up with a better one. I thought he'd say, Good job, you'll get a bonus.

Get the fuck out of here, he said, and don't come around no more.

That was the last I ever saw of him. But that was all right with me. I didn't want any part of his operation after that night, any more than he wanted me to be part of it. I'm still above ground, so he must not have talked to the boys uptown. Or if he did, they decided I'd done the job right even if Big Billy didn't think so. Nothing ever happened to me because I was right: they never found Jimmy H.

It seems simple when you look at it that way. But it's not simple. New Jersey is not a state of simplicity, the sinkhole town of Rutherford not a site of easy answers. New Jersey is a place of secrets, complex, rotten with tangled branching vines and rivers of ancient, heaving blood. Somebody said that to me once, I don't remember who.

Well, anyhow, that's about it. They tore the stadium down after thirty-some years and still they didn't find what was left of Brother James, that's how good a planting job I did. I don't know how they could've missed finding the skull, some of the bones, but I guess they were in a hurry and careless with the demolition.

If it didn't make me sick now, thinking about it, I'd have to laugh about the turf wars between the Giants and all those other teams right there in the shadow of that end zone, in the end zone itself, players after they scored a touchdown spiking the ball down right above where the boss's head was buried—

What's that you said?

No, I sure as hell didn't make all of this up. You got no right to say that. I told you before, it's the gospel truth. Give me a Bible and I'll swear on it—

What do you mean, New Jersey is full of mooks like me, little guys with big ideas? I was never a little guy, I had connections, I knew secrets. That's how I got the job to take out the boss. One of the biggest jobs ever, horrible as it was, and my disposal idea was just as big. Smart. I couldn't have got away with it for thirty-five years if it wasn't big and smart.

Yeah, I got away with it, but I couldn't get away *from* it. You cops can't imagine what a burden it's been on me all that time—not the Meadowlands part, the killing and butchering part. How much of a toll it's taken. That's why I'm here now, that's what I been trying to get across to you. I can't live with it anymore. The nightmares, the awful bloody images—

What? No! This isn't another false confession. It's my one true confession. Don't you see, don't you get it? Those previous confessions of mine . . . substitutes, surrogates. I couldn't make myself tell what I did to the boss, so I copped to other murders, other crimes instead.

I was trying to pay my debt with phony claims so I could finally have some peace. But now I know the only way to stop the haunting and the hurting is to reveal my secret, New Jersey's secret, America's secret—

What're you doing, lieutenant? Who're you calling?

Oh Christ, no, you can't send me back to the Pines. I don't belong in that place. I'm not crazy any more than John the Baptist was crazy.

Please, you have to believe me! I shot Jimmy H., I dismembered his body, I buried the pieces in the end zone at the Meadowlands Stadium. I did, I did!

KETTLE RUN

BY ROBERT ARELLANO

Cherry Hill

Ernie passes through the living room on his way to the kitchen. His father lies on the sofa, his head on the arm-rest, his hair that hasn't been combed in weeks, his hand balancing a breakfast beer on the sofa back. How carefully he holds it. "Hey, Pops."

"Hey youself."

A girl in a gold leotard tumbles over a blue floor on TV. "What you watching?"

"Olympics."

"Olympics are over."

"Then reruns."

He sees the bottle of rum his father finished last night on the kitchen table. Ernie pinches three cigarettes from the Marlboro box and grabs his backpack. "See ya later, Pops."

He drives. Boxy brown Buick Skylark, his father's car. The only advantage to the move is that Ernie drives. In Florida the age was sixteen but in Jersey it's seventeen, so he is ahead of his class. He drives to school, drives Pervert home, and drives his father around. Too many DWIs.

He stops by A&P for breakfast: Donut Gems and OJ. At the edge of the parking lot he squeezes the tobacco from one of the Marlboros onto the back of Kevin Klausen's algebra homework. He cracks the door to let the shreds fly away in the wind and looks to make sure there's nobody near the Buick, then pulls a baggie from his jacket pocket and unzips the top. The fragrance hits him and he crumbles a bud onto the sheet, making a crease and funneling the shake down into the empty paper tube. He twists the tip and flicks the rattail against his thigh until the grass is tamped down to the filter, then he gives the end one more twist and yanks off the paper wick.

He starts the car, pulls out of the lot, pushes in the lighter knob, and puts the joint in his mouth. Just the filter between his lips gets him in the right state of mind. By the time the lighter is hot he is going thirty-five on Springdale Road. He smokes, cracking the window to keep air circulating so the smell doesn't get in his hair, and flips on the radio to The Apple instead of 'PLJ because they play Twisted Sister and he's sick of hearing "Born in the USA" all day.

Ernie drives into Cherry Hill and picks up Pervert. It's a warm autumn morning and the windows are rolled down on Kresson Road when they breeze by the sign for Cherry Hill East High. "Hey, you just passed the school." He shows Pervert the baggie. "Where'd you get that!"

"I'd tell you, but I'd have to kill you."

"You fucker! I knew I smelled something. You already smoked one without me."

"You want to blaze or not?"

"Hell yeah! Let's go back to that old Girl Scout camp."

"There's two more cigs in the glove compartment. Get to work."

They roll up the windows and drive up the long, steep hill on the outskirts of town while Pervert twists a couple of rattails. They turn on Kettle Run, pass Tull's place, and on into the pines, the pines, the pines. Ernie pulls onto the dirt road to the abandoned Girl Scout camp and weaves between the junk and the trees. He parks in front of the old bunkhouse and they smoke, Pervert alternating hits of pot with blasts from his inhaler.

They get out of the Buick and take turns firing rocks at bottles. "Hey, Ernie! Look at that fish!"

"This river is full of them."

"How do they swim when it's so shallow?"

"They skip."

"I gotta take a shit."

"Again? Jesus Christ, Pervert, why don't you tell your mom to buy a fuckin' toilet?"

Ernie sits cross-legged by the river. Sunlight reflected makes wavery projections on the rocks. His mouth is dry and cottony like the fake-sheepskin lining of his jacket. This water here is cleaner than any ditch in Miami, but still there are cows that graze upriver so he knows he better not drink.

When he first got to Cherry Hill, before he was labeled a loser, it had almost looked like Ernie might become a cool kid. Tío Tony told him: "No es como Miami where everyone Cubano and live outside. Aquí te dan pequeñas pruebitas: *Joo comuniss o American? Joo like Coca-Cola o guava juice? Hambooger o taco? Bruce Espring-steen o Julio Iglesias?* En Miami la gente knows the difference entre los Marielitos y los Cubanos de buena familia, pero aquí no. No en this estate. Aquí en Nueva Jersey joo gotta get esimilation."

In Cherry Hill it was all guesswork, all these little tests they gave you on the stupidest things. Ernie figured it out pretty quickly that if he could guess what they were thinking he would get past the bullshit and assimilate.

Kevin Klausen, the jock with the hottest girlfriend, invited him over to his house after school and they sat on a leather sec-tional in a big family room and played Atari. Ernie liked Kevin and wanted to be his friend. Kevin's mom offered snacks. "Want an apple or a peach?"

Which one sounded less tropical? "An apple." Mrs. Klausen smiled.

For lunch she made sandwiches. "Want cheese or peanut butter?"

"Peanut butter." Definitely peanut butter.

She was actually a bit nervous, giving him all these little *prue-bitas*, nervous he was a crazy Scarface, maybe, but also nervous *for* him. He was her token something-or-other. She wanted Ernie to succeed. To assimilate. When Kevin's mom brought them Nutter Butter sandwiches with the crusts cut off, Ernie smelled her perfume and looked at her hips in red corduroy and thought she was too pretty for this planet. Cherry Hill, he thought to himself, is heaven.

Then one day he was hanging out after school with a bunch of the popular boys, jocks and cools, on the brick wall outside the equipment shed, flicking matches and talking about getting some firecrackers. Somebody's big brother was taking the train to Chinatown at the end of the month, and Ernie put in a dollar for some bottle rockets.

Talk turned to fucking. A couple of the boys agreed that Mrs. Klausen was a woman anyone would willingly fuck. For a mother she was downright fuckable. One kid put the question to Ernie. "I'd fuck her. Wouldn't you?"

He didn't have much concept of what would really be involved in a fuck, but Ernie knew that this woman, unrivaled among the mothers of Cherry Hill for the sweetness of her perfume and for her shapeliness in bell-bottoms, was someone he would like to hug, and hug was near enough phonetically to fuck that, given the opportunity, he would give it a try. Ernie said, "Yes."

Kevin walked up. "Hey, Kevin, Ernie wants to fuck your mom."

"Boat person, you suck! Why don't you go back to Cuba?"

Ernie flushed. "My parents came over on plane" was all he could say. He could have added that it had been more than twenty years ago and he was born in Florida, but that wasn't the point. It's 1984, and everyone, even kids, knows what kind of trouble Ernie's people have been causing for the past four years since that hillbilly Carter invited them all to come over on their inner tubes.

There was that predatory gleam in Kevin's eye. "Hey, Fidel, why don't you go smoke a cigar?" All the boys laughed. It could have been Speedy Gonzalez, Ricky Ricardo, Pepé Le Pew, or any other caricature of alien origin, but it happened to be Fidel. "Fee-del! Fee-del!" The other boys joined in the rhyme. "Fee-del! You smell!" At that moment, Ernie knew he was never going to play with these kids again. He wanted that dollar for his bottle rockets back.

The next day Kevin started picking on Ernie in gym and making him do his homework. Now Ernie's only friend is somebody everyone calls Pervert.

Pervert comes back to where Ernie is sitting. "You look like a Indian." He rinses his hands in the river, cupping them and slurping some water.

"Cows shit in that water."

"I don't see no cow shit."

"You don't see it, that's the point, but upriver there's big cow patties getting dissolved."

"I don't taste it." Pervert shrugs, slurps some more. "Let's blaze this last one before we go to school."

"Then we won't have one for after."

"We'll pick up a soda can at lunch and I'll make a pipe for the roaches. I can't take fuckin' English class without being majorly baked."

Suddenly, out of nowhere comes a big pickup truck, a black F-250 roaring up the dirt road with blackout tinting on the side windows. Ernie sees through the windshield who's in the passenger seat. "Tull—what the fuck is he doing out here?"

Pervert groans. "Are you sure it's him?"

"Oh shit! And Keith's driving." Keith, a mean fucking twenty-year-old.

Pervert sinks in his seat. "Shit."

The F-250 stops, blocking the Buick, and Tull gets out. Tull in filthy, fuzzy slippers, bright orange gym shorts, and sleeveless sweatshirt, dingy gray like a river, his doughy upper arms seeded with blackheads. Count these to avoid looking at his bloodshot blue eyes, his candle-stub nose, odd plugs of hair not definable as a beard. "Not you fuckin' homos."

Ernie does the talking. "We're not homos."

Tull bellies up to where they're sitting. An oily matt of hair bursts from each armpit, tucked up in there like two cheeseburgers. "Then what's the fuckin' problem?"

"No problem." Offer them a hit. Or don't offer them a hit. They've got the best shit. "Just smokin' weed."

"Whose weed you smokin'?"

"What do you mean *whose weed*?"

"Someone's been topping our plants." Ernie wants to say, *What plants?* but it makes too much sense: them being out here in the Pine Barrens, their aggressive roll-up. This is where they grow. Ernie shoots Pervert a look, sees him shaking, and knows he stole some pot. It *is* a fuckin' problem.

Keith gets out of the truck. Handsome, sleepy-eyed Keith. "Give me your keys." Shit. Give them your keys and they got your car. And then you're stuck. Here. The lonely quiet of wind blowing high in the pines. The far whoosh of cars out on Kettle Run.

Ernie gives him the keys. Keith goes back and checks the Buick, looking in the glove compartment, under all the seats, popping the trunk, even looking under the spare in the wheel well. Tull shakes Ernie down, checking all the pants pockets. He finds the little bag of weed in Ernie's jacket. It's just the Marlboro rattail and a couple of cured buds, what's left of a nickel bag Ernie got from Keith. Tull keeps it.

Pervert is next. Tull works him over roughly and Pervert squirms like he's getting tickled. None of this makes sense. Tull is their loser friend, but he goes at Pervert savagely—front pockets, back pockets, jacket. He finally plunges his hand down Pervert's underwear and Pervert squeals. Ernie watches as Tull pulls out a wadded-up piece of paper—Kevin Klausen's homework. Tull unfolds it, holds it up for Keith to see. Ten or twelve big buds, freshly cut. "You little shits."

* * *

Yesterday they stopped by Tull's trailer before school. A homemade sign on the gate features a cameo of a handgun: *Tresspassers shall be greeted by Smith n Wessin*. Pervert got out, the cold odor of exhaust in the air. He swung open the gate and Ernie pulled the Buick up the drive. Pervert shut the gate and got back in. They drove up to the trailer and Ernie cut the engine. Vicious dogs barked and growled from a ruined cage choked by wisteria vines.

They had met him at Luigi's playing pinball, another loser from another generation. Tull had largely given up socializing with people his own age and concentrated on a world of never-ending adolescent pleasures: marijuana, video games, and BB guns.

Tull's trailer door had *No Soliciting*, *NRA*, and *FOP* stickers. Pervert punched out the secret knock, five steady taps and one more delayed—the "Aqualung" riff. Closed curtains quivered at the far end of the trailer. Tull would look out all four sides before throwing two padlocks and lifting the four-by. Pervert snorted. "You could break through these walls with a rusty can opener."

Tull opened the door and they were hit with the smell: onions, rotten bananas, and marijuana. "You leeches. You mooches." They came in. "You wanna smoke?"

"Only if you are."

"Fuckin' couple of kiss-ass bloodsuckers, you know I smoke all day. Here, clear this bowl." Tull didn't pack them greens, but his pipe, passed without ceremony or comment, was amply resinous. With Tull this guaranteed a dark, funky mind-blow. "Wanna shoot?"

They hiked into the pines behind the trailer, Pervert wheezing from the walk. They shot at rats and empty cans of Tab and Pabst.

Tull said, "You know, you could kill someone with a pellet gun."

Pervert snickered. "Yeah, if you hit him over the head with it enough times."

"You want to try something really hard?" Tull reached into his shorts and pulled out a handgun.

Pervert shrieked. "Sweet!"

"Forty-four caliber. You ever hold such a thing?"

"I want to try it."

"Fifty cents a bullet. You can shoot two for a dollar."

"You want to try, Ernie?"

"I don't know. I'm pretty fucked up." He was thinking, *I don't like this.*

Ernie plugged his ears and Tull took the first shot, knocking over a big rock. Even with fingers pressed tight against his skull, the concussion punched Ernie in the chest and left his heart pounding to get out. It was louder than an M-80, maybe as loud as an M-160—a half-stick of dynamite. Ernie's buzz turned black. He wanted to be out of there.

Pervert took the second shot, blowing a huge chunk off a pine trunk and knocking himself on his ass in the deadfall and rotting leaves. "Holy fuck! Fuckin' awesome!"

Tull grinned. "You ever hold anything like that?"

Let's get out of here, thought Ernie. *Let's go back and say we never saw this.*

Back in the Buick and out the gate, Pervert showed Ernie a handful of roaches and pot crumbs he had picked from the carpet in Tull's trailer.

"I don't know why you do that, Pervert."

"He doesn't even notice."

"He puts his naked ass on that rug, you know."

"Roll up your window."

"Check the glove compartment. My pops should have a cig in there."

Pervert came out with a loose Marlboro and pulled a piece of paper from Ernie's notebook: Kevin Klausen's homework. "That kid's an asshole, Ernie. Why do you do his shit?"

"You have no idea what it's like to get sat on in front of all the girls in gym."

"Weren't you guys friends for a while?"

"Supposedly, for about a week, until I became a loser."

"Like me." Pervert pinched the tobacco out of the cigarette and started tearing open roaches onto the back of Kevin's homework. "Go down Kettle Run. There's a place used to be a Girl Scout camp."

"We got time?"

"You got study hall first period and I got gym, and I'm excused." Pervert refilled the empty paper tube with shake and pushed in the lighter knob. They saw the decaying wooden sign for the Girl Scout camp and Ernie pulled the Buick behind an old bunkhouse by the river.

"Roll down your window so our clothes don't smell."

"Your clothes always smell, Ernie."

"Oh yeah?"

"Yeah, like Fidel Castro's crotch."

They blazed, Pervert alternating hits with the inhaler. The sun and the weed made the maple burn redder. Pervert climbed out of the Buick. "We still got some time, right?"

"Took us twenty minutes to come out here and now it's quarter to ten."

"Don't turn this into fuckin' algebra homework, Ernie, just tell me whether I've got time to take a shit."

"What! Where?"

"Over there in those trees."

"How you going to wipe?"

"Whatever ain't poison ivy."

"You sure you know the difference?"

Pervert went singing around the back of the bunkhouse. "*Leaves of three, let'm beeeee . . .*"

At the time Ernie didn't think twice about it, but Pervert took so long they would end up late for second period. "Jesus, Pervert, took you for fuckin' ever."

"Rome wasn't built in a day."

"What'd you use to wipe?"

"Kevin Klausen's algebra."

"What!" Ernie punched his arm. "You asshole!"

Pervert wrapped his arms around his head and curled up squirming in the passenger seat. "Peace! Peace! Peace!"

A day later they're back at Girl Scout camp and Ernie watches Pervert. He wants to look Pervert in the eye, but Tull is holding him tight by his jacket collar shaking him and shouting in his face, "Little shit! Where's the rest?"

Pervert is shivering, crying. "There ain't no rest." A wet spot spreads down the leg of his jeans and Ernie looks away.

Keith gives Ernie a drowsy look. "You follow us out here yesterday?"

"No."

"You sayin' your friend did it alone?" No. That isn't it, either. But Ernie isn't in a position to contradict. Keith speaks up to the sky. "The way I see it, one of 'em or both of 'em is lyin'. And they ain't been sellin' it yet cuz the shit ain't cured. So somewhere there's about six pounds of pot we can still get back into the right-ful hands." Tull, with his gaze fixed on piss-pants Pervert, is intent on Keith as if listening to his own inner voice. "Why don't you have a talk with that one and I have a talk with this one and the first one to tell us the truth gets to see his mommy again? I'm sure when these kids see what a bad choice they made, we'll get back whatever they haven't already smoked. And then they can tell us about how they found it."

They break off like pairs of dance partners, Pervert with Tull and Ernie with Keith. Keith pulls Ernie by the wrist and leads him around the back of the bunkhouse, another twenty steps to a thick hedgerow that seems impenetrable, but Keith pushes aside a heap of vines and they duck into a small clearing in the trees.

Here they are, the gigantic cannabis plants, about twenty of them, all taller than Ernie and bearing big, beautiful buds with dark-purple hairs, getting irrigated from the river through siphons.

Ernie can see three stunted plants. The stalks have been cut cleanly with a pocket knife near the top. Nobody could expect this to go unnoticed, but it seems to have been done deliberately, with care: not brute vandalism, more like a tithe.

Keith sits Ernie gently on a stump and stands over him with one foot up like a cop confiscating firecrackers. "It's not a ton of money, when you consider all the work and worry, and I don't feel like harvesting today. Forecast puts first frost two weeks away. Let those plants bud another ten days and it doubles the take." He's not trying to be intimidating; Keith is just thinking out loud when he says, "It might end up better to keep you missing awhile."

Ernie's voice trembles. "I swear I won't tell anyone. I'll forget we ever came out here. Could I please have my keys?"

Keith answers very slowly. "We. Both. Know. That. Can't. Happen."

Ernie looks up at the abandoned Girl Scout bunkhouse as if something from this vestige of happier days might come to his aid, but the windows are long gone from the empty boxes and the bunkhouse looks down on the scene with hollow eyes. Suddenly he hears Pervert scream, "Wait! No!"

An explosion startles them both. For a second Ernie and Keith stand frozen looking at each other before Keith pushes through the vines and runs around the bunkhouse. Ernie follows.

When he comes around the front of the bunkhouse, Ernie sees Tull with his .44 standing over Pervert who's facedown on the ground, motionless, blood spreading a stain beneath his body, soaking the earth.

Keith speaks evenly: "Tull, you dumb fuck. You greasy, dumbass fuck."

"The little shit shouldn't've tried to run!"

"Goddamnit, give me that fuckin' gun." Keith takes the weapon and goes to the truck. He comes back and hands Tull a shovel. "Dig."

"Fuck that! Make this little shit do it."

Keith doesn't have to repeat himself. The look he gives Tull is enough to say they will have to discuss it later. Tull shakes his head, starts digging. "Shit's fucked up."

Ernie can't believe what he sees. A minute ago Pervert screamed and now Tull is digging a hole. He imagines Pervert's mom in town right now with her hair piled up in a beehive, thinking about Pervert by his real name, Morgan, washing his socks, washing his underwear, skidmarked Pervert underwear getting bleached for another day that will never happen. He imagines Pervert just yesterday knocked on his ass in the woods behind Tull's trailer, that look of surprise on his face, squirming in the sticks and leaves, shouting, *Fuckin' awesome!*

When they arrived late for second period yesterday, Ernie got bumped from behind at his locker—Kevin Klausen.

"Where's my homework?"

"I cannot tell a lie. Pervert used it to wipe his ass."

"He WHAT?"

"Tell Mr. Trees you lost it. I can redo it for him tonight."

"How did it get into Pervert's hands for him to wipe his ass with?"

"I give him a ride to school some days."

"You fags butt-fuck in the backseat that early in the morning? Next time you keep it in a binder or something. I don't need that punk knowing where my grades come from."

Ernie took the Visine, gave himself two drops in each eye, and he was ready for gym. He suited up even though it was asking for punishment. Mr. Connelly called roll military style. "Álvarez, Ernesto."

"Here." The cool boys followed this with sneezes of *Spic* and coughs of *Faggot.*

It was the day for dodgeball, a euphemism for Smear the Queer because that was how it worked out after teams got picked, the big jocks having a blast making the losers and faggots hit the deck and taking bets on who could raise a redder welt.

Back at his locker, Ernie heard softly in his ear: "Hey, boat boy, I hear you do homework." A girl. *Wait wait wait wait wait wait*: *Carleen Delmonte—Kevin's girl.* She looked so good in those jeans, the ones with the little question mark on the pocket, it made Ernie's heart ache.

"Who said that?"

"Mr. Moore."

"The science teacher? He knows?"

"He told me, *Connie*—he thinks my name is Connie—*if you need help with homework, ask the Spanish kid.*"

"Science, huh?"

"I'm not asking you to do it for me. I just need a little tutoring. You could come over."

I can come over, Ernie said to himself. Boat boy is coming over to Carleen Delmonte's house.

Ernie's father sat at the kitchen table with his head in his hands. His nose, marbled with wasted capillaries, poked out between tobacco-yellowed fingers. It was the afternoon hour when sense returned for just long enough to give him the idea to jettison it again, because all sense brought with it was recollections of other afternoons before exile made Ernie's mother crazy.

"Hey, Pops." His father parted his hands and waved his fingers. "Can I take the car tonight?"

"What you doing?"

"Studying for school tomorrow."

"Tomorrow Saturday."

"Tomorrow's Friday."

"Okay, okay."

What was left for them? All his father wanted was to be left at home alone. Ernie was too old for hide-and-seek, and it had never been about playing fair, never his father's turn to seek. What was hidden were bottles, all sizes and colors, in toilet tank, shoe box, guitar case—these were the easy hiding places—inside breaker box, under toolbox tray, above ceiling panels, beneath linoleum tiles. His father would literally tear the house apart to hide them. Ernie used to feel triumph at finding one, but he had given up for the futility of ever winning, of beating the fatigue that was beating them both. And his father began leaving the empties around, not so much as a sign of conquest but of resignation: *See, this is me.* So it was almost as friends again that they recognized each other across the kitchen table yesterday afternoon: *Let's be easy on each other today.*

"Pops, when's it going to lift?"

"Hay cosas en la vida—los estresses, ¿no?—que son demasiados soportar solo, pero uno las tiene que soportar. ¿Comprendes?"

"Maybe you don't have to withstand them alone."

"Son míos. Son *yo.*"

"We could talk about it." His father waved it away like always. It was understood that he genuinely lost his voice when the subject came up. Ernie believed him. It happened to him too. Hearts break slowly, which is why we can look tragic news in the eye at the moment of shocked certainty and say, *This is happening to me.* Got to face it or stab yourself in the heart, because no painkiller will ever lift without making you face it all over again. Ernie didn't have the courage to stab himself, and yet he wasn't sure he had the heart to face it, and nobody could tell him how long it was going to take. He couldn't even guess.

When he knocked on the door a large man answered, South Jersey redneck, shirtless, tattooed, a faded Confederate flag erupting from his chest. "What do you want?"

A woman called over the TV: "That's him, Larry, the tutor from Carleen's school."

"Hello, Mrs. Delmonte."

"That's not my name, honey. Call me Glynnis." The mom was sunburned with a peroxide permanent, those same bright eyes as Carleen and still nicely built. "Come back to the couch, Larry, the 'mercial's over." Larry turned and walked back to the TV. Hellfire engulfed his big shoulders, flames licking the 609 on the back of his neck.

Carleen came out wearing those question-mark jeans and a close-fitting pink sweater. Her eyes were drowsy-pretty with a pencil twirled in her hair. She led Ernie back to her room, Prince hanging over her bed with his shirt off. "You got a curfew?"

"Nah. My dad doesn't give a shit."

"What does he do?"

"Drink, since the divorce. My uncle moved us up here thinking he'd be able to turn him around, but so far nothing's changed except the weather. What about your dad?"

"No fuckin' idea."

"That's not him answered the door?"

"Who? Fuckhead? He's not my dad, but I've never known my mom without a boyfriend. Your mom got a boyfriend?"

"No. I mean, I don't think so. She's crazy down in Miami."

Ernie thought about her getting in trouble with the apartment manager. She would lock herself out and the man would let her in and see all these newspapers and half-empty cans piled up to the ceiling, smell bad odors coming from her room. Anyone crazy enough to go out with her was probably locked up in his own apartment somewhere. Maybe right next door.

They didn't talk for a minute while Carleen pulled out her books. She had sharpened three pencils to needle points and they sat there lined up beside the blue binder all her friends had signed and scribbled the initials of guys they liked on.

"How long you been going out with Kevin?"

"Like, never long."

"Really?"

"At Cherry Hill East, you got to look like you're going out with a jock or the cheerleaders call you dyke or slut. I picked Kevin 'cause he doesn't try to touch me. Probably a fag."

"Wow." Ernie had never thought of that.

"I do have a boyfriend, but he's older. Mom would kill me if she knew I was going out with a guy in his twenties, but who the fuck is she to talk with the scumbags she chooses?"

The natural next question would have been *Have you fucked him?* but asking it would put Ernie in the same category as the school nurse and guidance counselors, people she might actually tell this kind of thing to who nevertheless would never get to fuck her. Instead, he decided he should appear uncurious like someone she might like. Anyway, her boyfriend was in his twenties, so of course they'd fucked.

"Hey, boat boy, you smoke, right?"

"Nah. Sometimes my clothes smell like my dad's Marlboros 'cause we live in a small house."

"No, I mean pot."

"Uh . . ."

She narrowed her eyes and widened the smile. "I know you do. I can see it in your eyes."

Ernie smirked. "I thought Visine takes the red out."

"Not what I mean."

Carleen went over to her jewelry box and took out a tampon box. "One place Fuckhead won't look." She pulled out a lighter and a smokeless one-hitter.

"Cool, where'd you get that?"

"My boyfriend got it at Spencer's in the mall."

"They sell those at Spencer's?"

"In the back part."

"Shit, they won't even let me in there."

She cracked the window and took a hit, blew the smoke outside, and handed him the one-hitter still hot, still wet with her spit. Ernie hit it and tasted the brass that a second ago had been between Carleen's lips. It was really good weed. "Where do you get this shit?"

"My boyfriend grows it."

"Maybe we should get started on this homework."

"Forget the homework, boat boy. You drive, right?"

"Uh-huh."

"Can you give me a ride somewhere?"

She told her mom, "Me and Ernie are just going to Luigi's." She hadn't wanted him to do her science homework. Carleen hadn't even wanted any help with it. She just wanted someone her age to take her out of the house so that she could hook up with her older boyfriend.

They made a left on Tomlinson Mill Road and drove north to a world he didn't know was out there in the pines. The light was dying and the mile markers went by unnoticed under the hypnotic spell of the long straightaway. The blue glow in the sky off to the right came from the last light of the day reflecting off the Atlantic.

She told him to pull into the last driveway on the left. "Flash your lights twice before getting out of the car. Don't forget or they might have to shoot your ass."

What the fuck was he getting into? He pulled in next to a black pickup, stepped out of the Buick, and followed Carleen up to the house.

The door opened before they got to it and Ernie saw a familiar ugly face—Tull's. He pretended he didn't know Ernie. Inside, the boyfriend Keith sat at a table with a bunch of baggies and a postal scale. The baggies were full of pot. Carleen sat on his lap and kissed him like Ernie never saw anyone kiss except for in the movies. Keith spoke without looking at him, her jeans on his lap. "You drive?"

"I just moved here from Miami."

"You want some pot?"

"I don't have any money."

"Figures." Keith pulled a couple of buds out of a bag and gave Ernie what was left. "I'll take her home later. You know how to get back to town?"

"Yeah, I think so."

"Don't have to tell you not to come around here again or say anything about this. I know who you are. If I get any unauthorized visits, you know what?"

Tull finally spoke up: "We're the town murderers. We'll chop you up in little bits and scatter the pieces in the Pine Barrens for the wolves to eat."

Keith acted like he hadn't heard this. "You know the Betsy Ross Bridge?"

"Yeah."

"That's where we'll go."

Ernie knew it was time to leave. It had gone all right. He had a baggie of pot. Tull followed him to the door. "Careful out there in those pines. UFOs come out of hiding when you're high."

Now Keith and Tull are both looking at Ernie but not looking at Ernie, everything sideways, not looking him in the eye with everyone knowing that with one kid dead, another kid a witness, and nobody else but killers at an abandoned Girl Scout camp, something must come next.

Three tops. How much did he say that was? Six pounds? It doesn't make sense. Where could Pervert have put it? Not folded in Kevin Klausen's algebra homework. They had been out here only one other time. No way Pervert came back; nobody but Ernie or Pervert's mom would ever drive him anywhere. No way Pervert could have hauled more than an ounce or two out of here in his underwear. Two days in a row and he at best got a handful of buds. And Ernie knew Pervert: that's all he would have tried for, would have lied for. Always wanted to get over, never liked to share, fat little klepto. But it was nothing to get shot for.

Keith puts a hand on Ernie's shoulder and walks him back around the bunkhouse. He has Tull's gun. Ernie's adrenaline is flowing, his heart and his head going a thousand miles a second. He thinks of his mother talking to herself in her apartment in Miami. He thinks of his dad drinking at the kitchen table in Cherry Hill. He thinks of Carleen in first period, of how good she looks in those jeans. If only he could communicate with one of them. I'm here, Carleen, at the old Girl Scout camp off Kettle Run. Help.

Keith takes him back through the hedgerow to the clearing and the stump. Why had they come out here? It had been stupid to return. This is where it ends, at a forgotten Girl Scout camp in the Jersey Pinelands, by a river, with the leaves all rotting around him. Ernie is trying to guess: What does Keith need to hear? This is the stump where I will go down, unless I can figure out the answer. Remember Tull's trailer. He spelled trespassers wrong. Twitchy fuckin' Tull, and now Pervert is dead. Fuck, Pervert, why'd you try and run, you fuckin' fat asthmatic fuck?

That's when Ernie sees: he didn't try and run. *Go down Kettle Run. There's a place used to be a Girl Scout camp.* How'd he know that yesterday? It was after they had gone to see Tull.

"Keith . . . I think I've got it, Keith."

Driving back to Cherry Hill last night, Ernie had smelled a whiff of Carleen's perfume on his shirt. He wouldn't have thought shit about the scent at a store, but now that he connected it to her pink sweater and question-mark jeans he planned on sleeping with this shirt on. He planned on wrapping it around his head. Would she say hi to him in the hallway? He didn't care. He wasn't a sentimental little shit. He wouldn't even brag to Pervert about it. Something as pure as this belonged in a very quiet space. The best way never to lose something is to take it out carefully on special occasions, turn it very delicately in your hand, and put it back away without wasting a second, keep it in a safe place, someplace Fuckhead would never look.

It was Tull who told Pervert about the plants, baiting Pervert to come out here because he knew he could frame him and get away with a few extra pounds for himself. Then he brought Keith out to catch Pervert and Ernie, and only Pervert had known the setup.

Now Keith comes back around the bunkhouse and Tull is

almost done digging. "Took for fuckin' ever." Tull looks up, sees Keith holding the gun, sees Ernie watching. "What the fuck?"

Here comes your answer.

NOIR, NJ

BY Paul Muldoon

Paramus

When I wake up in a strange bed
Beside a girl called Pam
I try to play the whole thing down
And give my name as Sam
It's clear I'm way out of my depth
It's clear that she's dropped a dime
It's clear that even I suspect
I'm guilty of some crime
I know those goons by the streetlamp
Are champing at the bit
I last saw them on board the train
Before we took a hit
And jumped the observation car
Only to lose our way
In a nightmarish railroad yard
Somewhere near Noir, NJ

When I squint through the slatted blinds
Pam orders juice and eggs
She'll let a man do the legwork
While she works on her legs
It's clear her husband was a wimp
It's clear he had no spine
It's clear she lit that cigarette
To give the goons a sign

I know that it's a rule of thumb
A gumshoe's fingered me
When ladies who're high maintenance
Meet lighting that's low key
They're just so many femmes fatales
Who have been led astray
And now lure plainclothesmen et al
Back there to Noir, NJ

When a sergeant with a scattergun
Meets a shamus
Halfway up the stairs
Somewhere between Paterson
And Paramus
They redefine the parameters
And bid us welcome, hey, hey, hey,
Welcome to Noir, NJ

When I flash forward through the murk
Of who did what to whom
I'm pretty sure I don't deserve
To die here in this room
It's clear that I've been double-crossed
It's clear that I've been framed
It's clear Pam's husband was half deaf
From how they shout his name
I know I'll be reduced to pulp
She'll gulp with her orange juice
If I don't reassert myself
She'll kick in my caboose
It's not too late to be hard-boiled
Like the eggs on Pam's tray
Though even her pistol would recoil
At what happened in Noir, NJ

PART IV

GARDEN STATE UNDERGROUND

Gerald Slota

TOO NEAR REAL

BY JONATHAN SAFRAN FOER

Princeton

On the first day of my forced sabbatical, I noticed a car driving down Nassau Street with a large spherical device extending from its top. It looked like the past's vision of the future. I assumed it was part of some meteorology or physics or even psychology experiment—another small contribution to our charming campus atmospherics—and I didn't give it much thought. I probably wouldn't have even noticed it in the first place had I not been taking my first walk for walk's sake in years. Without a place to get to, I finally was where I was.

A few weeks later—exactly a month later, I was to learn—I saw the vehicle again, this time crawling down Prospect Avenue. I was stopped at a corner, not waiting for the light to change, not waiting for anything that might actually happen.

"Any idea what that is?" I asked a student who was standing at the curb beside me. Her quick double-take suggested recognition.

"Google," she said.

"Google what?" I asked, but wanting far more to know what she thought of me, and how other students on campus were talking about and judging me.

"Street view."

"Which is what?"

She sighed, just in case there was any doubt about her reluctance to engage with me. "That thing above the car is a camera with nine lenses. Every second it takes a photograph in each direction, and they're stitched together into a map."

"What kind of map?"

"It's 3-D and can be navigated."

"I thought you used a map *for* navigating."

"Yeah, well."

She was finished with me, but I wasn't ready to let her go. It's not that I cared about the map—and if I had, I could have easily found better answers elsewhere. But her reluctance to speak with me—even to be seen standing beside me—compelled me to keep her there.

I asked, "No one minds having all of these pictures taken all the time?"

"A lot of people mind," she said, rummaging through her bag for nothing.

"But no one does anything about it?"

The light changed. I didn't move. As the student walked away, I thought I heard her say, "Fucking pig." I'm virtually positive that's what she said.

A few days earlier, while eating pasta out of the colander, I'd heard an NPR piece about something called "the uncanny valley." Apparently, when we are presented with an imitation of life—a cartoon, a robot-looking robot—we are happily willing to engage with it: to hear its stories, converse with it, even empathize. (Charlie Brown's face, characterized by only a few marks, is a good example.) We continue to be comfortable with imitations as they more and more closely resemble life. But there comes a point—say, when the imitation is 98 percent lifelike (whatever *that* means)—when we become deeply unsettled, in an interesting way. We feel some repulsion, some alienation, some caveman reflex akin to what happens when nails are run down a blackboard.

We are happy with the fake, and happy with the real, but the near real—the too near real—unnerves us. (This has been demonstrated in monkeys as well. When presented with near-lifelike monkey heads, they will go to the corners of their cages and cover their faces.) Once the imitation is fully believable—100 percent believable—we are again comfortable, even though we know it is an imitation of life. That distance between the 98 percent and 100 percent is the uncanny valley. It was only in the last five years that our imitations of life got good enough—movies with digitally rendered humans, robots with highly articulated musculature—to generate this new human feeling.

The experience of navigating the map fell, for me, into the uncanny valley. Perhaps this is because at forty-six I was already too old to move comfortably within it. Even in those moments when I forgot that I was looking at a screen, I was aware of the finger movements necessary to guide my journey. To my students—my former students—I imagine it would be second nature. Or first nature.

I could advance down streets, almost as if walking, but not at all like walking. It wasn't gliding, or rolling or skating. It was something more like being stationary, with the world gliding or rolling or skating toward me. I could turn my "head," look up and down—the world pivoting around my fixed perspective. It was *too much* like the world.

Google is forthright about how the map is made—why shouldn't they be?—and I learned that the photos are regularly updated. (Users couldn't tolerate the dissonance of looking at snow in the summer, or the math building that was torn down three months ago. While such errors would put the map safely on the far side of the uncanny valley, it would also render it entirely uninteresting—if every bit as useful.) Princeton, I learned, is re-shot on the fourth of every month.

I wanted to walk to the living room, find my wife reading in her chair, and tell her about it.

The investigation never went anywhere because there was nowhere for it to go. (It was never even clear just *what* they were investigating.) I'd had two previous relationships with graduate students—explicitly permitted by the university—and they were held up as evidence. Evidence of *what*? Evidence that past the appropriate age I had sexual hunger. Why couldn't I simply repress it? Why did I have to have it at all? My persistent character was my character flaw.

The whole thing was a farce, and as always it boiled down to contradictory memories. No one on a college campus wants to stand up to defend the right of an accused harasser to remain innocent until proven guilty. The university privately settled with the girl's family, and I was left with severely diminished stature in the department, and alienated from almost all of my colleagues and friends. I believed they believed me, and didn't blame them for distancing themselves.

I found myself sitting in coffee shops for hours, reading sections of the newspaper I never used to touch, eating fewer meals on plates, and for the first time in my adult life, going for long, directionless walks.

The first night of my forced freedom, I walked for hours. I left the disciplinary committee meeting, took rights and lefts without any thought to where they might lead me, and didn't get back to my house until early the next morning. My earphones protected me from one kind of loneliness, and I walked beyond the reach of the local NPR affiliate—like a letter so long it switches from black pen to blue, the station became country music.

At some point, I found myself in the middle of a field. Apparently I was the kind of person who left the road, the kind of person who walked on grass. The stars were as clear as I'd ever seen them. *How old are you?* I wondered. *How many of you are dead?* I thought, for the first time in a long while, about my parents: my father asleep on the sofa, his chest blanketed with news that was already ancient by the time it was delivered that morning. The thought entered my mind that he had probably bought his last shirt. Where did that thought come from? Why did it come? I thought about the map: like the stars, its images are sent to us from the past. And it's also confusing.

I thought that maybe if I took a picture of the constellations, I could e-mail them to my wife with some pithy thumb-typed sentiment—*Wish you were here*—and maybe, despite knowing the ease and cheapness of such words, she would be moved. Maybe two smart people who knew better could retract into the shell of an empty gesture and hide out there for at least a while.

I aimed the phone up and took a picture, but the flash washed out all of the stars. I turned off the flash, but the "shutter" stayed open for so long, trying to sip up any of the little light it could, that my infinitesimally small movements made everything blurry. I took another picture, holding my hand as still as I could, but it was still a blur. I braced my arm with my other hand, but it was still a blur.

On the fourth of the next month, I waited on the corner of Nassau and Olden. When the vehicle came, I didn't wave or even smile, but stood there like an animal in a diorama. I went home, opened my laptop, and dropped myself down at the corner of Nassau and Olden. I spun the world, so that I faced northwest. There I was.

There was something exhilarating about it. I was in the map, there for anyone searching Princeton to see. (Until, of course, the vehicle came through again in four weeks, replacing the world like the Flood.) Sitting at my kitchen counter, leaning into the screen of a laptop I bought because, like everybody else, I liked the way it looked, I felt part of the physical world. The feeling was complicated: simultaneously empowering and emasculating. It was an approximate feeling had by someone unable to locate his actual feelings.

I asked myself: Should I go on a trip?

I asked: Should I try to write a book?

Should I apologize? To *whom* should I apologize? I'd already apologized to my wife in every way possible. To the girl's parents? What was there to apologize *for*? Would an apology retroactively create a crime?

There were the problems of shame and anger, of wanting to

avoid and manufacture encounters like the one with the student at the streetlight. I needed to be away from judgment, and I needed to be understood. There was nothing keeping me. I'd never been enthusiastic about teaching, but I'd lost my enthusiasm for *everything*. I felt, in the deepest sense, uninspired, deflated. I'd lost my ability to experience urgency, as if I thought I was never going to die.

I took a left on Chestnut, and suddenly heard something beautiful. *Heard*, so I wasn't in the map. This was real. The music was coming from someone's earphones, a student's. She was wearing sweatpants, like the athletes do after their showers after practice. It was a beautiful song, so beautiful it made me ecstatic and depressed. I didn't know how I felt. I didn't know how to ask what the song was. I didn't want to interrupt her, or risk a condemnatory look. I kept a fixed distance. She entered a dorm. There was nothing to do.

Afraid of forgetting the tune, I called my phone, and left myself a message, humming the bit I could remember. And then I forgot about it, and after seven days my phone automatically erased saved messages. And then, too late, I remembered. So I took my phone to the store where I bought it and asked if there was any way to recover an erased message. The clerk suggested I send the SIM card to the manufacturer, which I did, and seven weeks later I was e-mailed a digital file with every message I'd received since buying the phone. I found nothing remarkable in this, felt no even small thrill in the confirmation that nothing is ever lost. I was angered or saddened by its inability to impress me.

This was the first message:

Hi. It's Julie. Either you're hearing this, and therefore deserve to be congratulated on having entered the modern world, or—and this seems equally likely—you have no idea what the blinking red light means, and my voice is hanging in some kind of digital purgatory . . . If you don't call me back, I'll assume the latter. Anyway, I just walked out of your office, and wanted to thank you for your generosity. I appreciate it more than you could know. You kept saying, "It goes without saying," but none of it went without saying. As for dinner, that sounds really nice. At the risk of inserting awkwardness, maybe we should go somewhere off campus, just to, I don't know, get away from people? Awkward? Crazy? You wouldn't tell me. Maybe you would. It goes without saying that I loathe awkwardness and craziness. And the more I talk about it, the worse it gets. So I'm going to cut my losses. Call me back and we can make a plan.

That was how it began. Dinner was my suggestion, going off campus was hers. It was a pattern we learned to make use of: I asked if she wanted something to drink, she ordered wine; I wiped something nonexistent from her cheek, she held my hand against her face; I asked her to stay in the car to talk for another few minutes . . .

The final message was me humming the unknown song to myself.

I went to Venice in the map. Never having been to actual Venice, I have no idea how the experience measured up. Obviously there were no smells, no sounds, no brushing shoulders with Venetians, and so on. (It is only a matter of time before the map fills out with such sensations.) But I did walk across the Bridge of Sighs, and I did see Saint Mark's Basilica. I walked through Piazza San Marco, read Joseph Brodsky's tombstone on San Michele, window-shopped the glass factories of the Murano islands (bulbs of molten glass held in place at the ends of those long straws until the next month). I looked out at the digital water, its unmoving current holding vaporettos in place. I tried to keep walking, right out onto the water. And I did.

Only someone who hasn't given himself over to the map would scoff at the deficiency of the experience. The deficiency is the fullness: removing a bit of life can make life feel so much more vivid—like closing your eyes to hear better. No, like closing your eyes to remember the value of sight.

I went to Rio, to Kyoto, to Capetown. I searched the flea markets of Jaffa, pressed my nose to the windows of the Champs-Élysées, waded with the crows through the mountains at Fresh Kills.

I went to Eastern Europe, visiting, as I had always promised her I would, the village of my grandmother's birth. Nothing was left, no indication of what had once been a bustling trading point. I searched the ground for any remnant, and was able to find a chunk of brick. I download images of the brick from a number of perspectives, and sent them to a friend in the engineering department. He was able to model the remnant, and fabricate it on a 3-D-rendering printer. He gave me two of them: one I kept on my desk, the other I sent to my mother to place on my grandmother's grave.

I went to the hospital where I was born. It has since been replaced with a new hospital.

I went to my elementary school. The playground had been built on to accommodate more students. Where do the children play?

I went to the neighborhood in which my father grew up. I went to his house. My father is not a known person. There will never be a plaque outside of his childhood home letting the world know that he was born there. I had a plaque made, mailed it to my younger brother, and asked him to affix it with Velcro on the sixteenth of the following month. I returned to his house that afternoon and there it was.

Instead of dropping myself back down in Princeton, I decided to walk all the way home. It is quicker to walk in the map, as each stride can cover a full city block, but I knew it would take me most of the night. I didn't mind. I wanted it that way. The night had to be filled. Halfway across the George Washington Bridge I looked down.

Nothing ever happens because nothing *can* happen, because despite the music, movies, and novels that have inspired us to believe that the extraordinary is right around the corner, we've been disappointed by experience. The dissonance between what we've been promised and what we've been given would make anyone confused and lonely. I was only ever trying to inch my imitation of life closer to life.

I can't remember the last time I didn't pause halfway across a bridge and look down. I wanted to call out, but to whom? Nobody would hear me because there's no sound. I was there, but everyone around me was in the past. I watched my braveness climb onto the railing and leap: the suicide of my suicide.

On the fourth of the next month, I walked beside the vehicle. It was easy to keep pace with it, as the clarity of the photographs depends on the car moving quite slowly. I took a right down Harrison when the car did, and another right on Patton, and a left on Broadmead. The windows were tinted—apparently the drivers have been subject to insults and arguments—so I didn't know if I was even noticed. The driver certainly didn't adjust his driving in any way to suggest so. I walked beside him for more than two hours, and only stopped when the blister on my right heel became unbearable. I had wanted to outlast him, catch him on his lunch break, or filling up at the gas station. That would have been a victory, or at least a kind of intimacy. What would I have said? *Do you recognize me?*

I went home and turned on my computer. Everywhere you looked in Princeton, there I was. There were dozens of me.

Hi, it's me. I know I'm not supposed to call, but I don't care. I'm sad. I'm in trouble. Just with myself. I'm in trouble with myself. I don't know what to do and there's no one to talk to. You used to talk to me, but now you won't. I'm not going to ruin your life. I don't know why you're so afraid of that. I've never done anything to make you think I'm in any way unreliable. But I have to say, the more you act on your fear that I will ruin your life, the more compelled I feel to ruin it. I'm not a great person, but I've never done anything to you. I know it's all my fault, I just don't know how. What is it? I'm sorry.

I was spending more time each day inside of the map, traveling the world—Sydney, Reykjavik, Lisbon—but mostly going for walks around Princeton. I would often pass people I knew, people I would have liked to say hello to or avoid. The pizza in the window was always fresh, I always wanted to eat it. I wanted to open all of the books on the stand outside the bookshop, but they were forever closed. (I made a note to myself to open them, facing out, on the fourth of the next month, so I would have something to read inside the map.) I wanted the world to be more available to me, to be touchable.

I was puzzled by my use of the map, my desire to explore places that I could easily explore in the world itself. The more time I spent in the map, the smaller the radius of my travels. Had I stayed inside long enough, I imagine I would have spent my time gazing through my window, looking at myself looking at the map. The thrill or relief came through continual reencounters with the familiar—like a blind person's hands exploring a sculpture of his face.

Unable to sleep one night—it was daytime in the map, as always—I thought I'd check out the progress on the new dorms down by the water. Nothing could possibly be more soul-crushing than campus construction: slow and pointless, a way to cast off money that had to either be spent or lost. But the crushing of the soul was the point. It was part of my exile inside of the map inside of my house.

As I rotated the world to see the length of the scaffolding, something caught my attention: a man looking directly into the camera. He was approximately my age—perhaps a few years older—

wearing a plaid jacket and Boston Red Sox hat. There was nothing at all unusual about someone looking back at the camera: most people who notice the vehicle are unable to resist staring. But I had the uncanny sense that I'd seen this person before. Where? Nowhere, I was sure, and yet I was also sure somewhere. It didn't matter, which is why it did.

I dropped myself back down on Nassau Street, drifted its length a few times, and finally found him, standing outside the bank, again looking directly into the camera. There was nothing odd about that, either—he could have simply walked from one location to the other, and by chance crossed paths with the vehicle. I rotated the world around him, examined him from all sides, pulled him close to me and pushed him away, tilted the world to better see him. Was he a professor? A townie? I was most curious about my curiosity about him. Why did his face draw me in?

I walked home. It had become a ritual: before closing the map, I would walk back to my front door. There was something too dissonant about leaving it otherwise, like debarking a plane before it lands. I crossed Hamilton Avenue, wafted down Snowden, and, one giant stride at a time, went home. But when I was still several hundred feet away, I saw him again. He was standing in front of my house. I approached, shortening my strides so that the world only tiptoed toward me. He was holding something, which I couldn't make out for another few feet; it was a large piece of cardboard, across which was written: YOU WON'T GET AWAY WITH IT.

I ran to the actual door and opened it. He wasn't there. Of course he wasn't.

As computing moves off of devices and into our bodies, the living map will as well. That's what they're saying. In the clumsiest version we will wear goggles onto which the map is projected. In all likelihood, the map will be on contact lenses, or will forgo our eyes altogether. We will literally live in the map. It will be as visually rich as the world itself: the trees will not merely look like trees, they will feel like trees. They will, as far as our minds are concerned, *be* trees. Actual trees will be the imitations.

We will continuously upload our experiences, contributing to the perpetual creation of the map. No more vehicles: *we* will be the vehicles.

Information will be layered onto the map as is desired. We could, when looking at a building, call up historical images of it; we could watch the bricks being laid. If we crave spring, the flowers will bloom in time lapse. When other people approach, we will see their names and vital info. Perhaps we will see short films of our most important interactions with them. Perhaps we will see their photo albums, hear short clips of their voices at different ages, smell their shampoo. Perhaps we will have access to their thoughts. Perhaps we will have access to our own.

On the fourth of the next month, I stood at my door, waiting for the vehicle, and waiting for him. I was holding a sign of my own: *YOU DON'T KNOW ME*. The vehicle passed and I looked into the lens with the confidence of innocence. He never came. What would I have done if he had? I wasn't afraid of him. Why not? I was afraid of my lack of fear, which suggested a lack of care. Or I was afraid that I *did* care, that I wanted something bad to happen.

I missed my wife. I missed myself.

I did an image search for the girl. There she was, posing on one knee with her high school lacrosse team. There she was, at a bar in Prague, blowing a kiss to the camera—to *me*, three years and half a globe away. There she was, holding onto a buoy. Almost all of the photos were the same photo, the one the newspapers had used. I pulled up her obituary, which I hadn't brought myself to read until then. It said nothing I didn't know. It said nothing at all. The penultimate paragraph mentioned her surviving family. I did an image search for her father. There he was.

I entered the map. I looked for him along Nassau Street, and at the construction site where I'd first seen him. I checked the

English department, and the coffee shop where I so often did my reading. What would I have said to him? I had nothing to apologize for. And yet I was sorry.

It was getting late. It was always the middle of the day. I approached my house, but instead of seeing myself holding the sign, as I should have, I saw my crumpled body on the ground in front of the door.

I went up to myself. It was me, but wasn't me. It was my body, but not me. I tilted the world. There were no signs of any kind of struggle: no blood, no bruises. (Perhaps the photo had been taken in between the beating and the appearance of bruises?) There was no way to check for a pulse in the map, but I felt sure that I was dead. But I couldn't have been dead, because I was looking at myself. There is no way to be alive and dead.

I lifted myself up and put myself back down. I was still there. I pulled all the way back to space, to the Earth as a marble filling my screen in my empty house. I dove in, it all rushed to me: North America, America, the East Coast, New Jersey, Princeton Borough, Princeton Township, my address, my body.

I went to Firestone Library to use one of the public computers. I hadn't been to the library since the investigation, and hadn't even thought to wonder if my identity card was still activated. I tried to open the door, but I couldn't extend my arm. I realized I was still in the map.

I got up from my computer and went outside. Of course my body wasn't there. Of course it wasn't. When I got to Firestone, I extended my arm—I needed to see my hand reaching in front of me—and opened the door. Once inside, I swiped my ID, but a red light and beep emitted from the turnstile.

"Can I help you?" the security guard asked.

"I'm a professor," I said, showing him my ID.

"Lemme try that," he said, taking my card from me and swiping it again. Again the beep and red light.

He began to type my campus ID into his computer, but I said,

"Don't worry about it. It's fine. Thanks anyway." I took the ID from him and left the building.

I ran home. Everyone around me was moving. The leaves flickered as they should have. It was all almost perfect, and yet none of it was right. Everything was fractionally off. It was an insult, or a blessing, or maybe it was precisely right and I was fractionally off?

I went back into the map and examined my body. What had happened to me? I felt many things, and didn't know what I felt. I felt personally sad for a stranger, and sad for myself in a distanced way, as if through the eyes of a stranger. My brain would not allow me to be both the person looking and being looked at. I wanted to reach out.

I thought: I should take the pills in the medicine cabinet. I should drink a bottle of vodka, and go outside, just as I had in the map. I should lay myself down in the grass, face to the side, and wait. Let them find me. It will make everyone happy.

I thought: I should fake my suicide, just as I had in the map. I should leave open a bottle of pills in the house, beside my laptop opened to the image of myself dead in the yard. I should pour a bottle of vodka down the drain, and leave my wife a voicemail. And then I should go out into the world—to Venice, to Eastern Europe, to my father's childhood home. And when the vehicle approaches, I should run for my life.

I thought: I should fall asleep, as I had in the map. I should think about my life later. When I was a boy, my father used to say the only way to get rid of a pestering fly is to close your eyes and count to ten. But when you close your eyes, you also disappear.

EXCAVATION
BY EDMUND WHITE & MICHAEL CARROLL
Asbury Park

I
t was a gray, windy Hallowe'en afternoon in Asbury Park. I
was walking along the boardwalk. The beach was completely
empty although the boardwalk was crowded with hundreds
of people dressed as zombies. As Dita explained to me then in her
heavy Slavic accent, the town was competing with Seattle to see
which community could produce the greater number of zombies.
She told me these facts with her rounded, startled eyes and zinc-
white complexion and in spite of her deep, impeded speech, since
Dita stammered. She laughed her contralto laugh, a throttled
abrasion of a laugh—as if her throat were one of those giant pepper grinders restaurants used to be so proud of in the '60s when I'd
first come east after college. After at last she'd finish a sentence
she would hold herself aloft over me (I was a half-foot shorter than
Dita), then twist out a short rasp of a laugh, spice for her bland,
matter-of-fact words. I'd always found being alone with Dita unsettling. Originally from Poland, she somehow reminded me of the
Midwest, its willed warmth, its quietly self-conscious rectitude—
and why I'd left it.

She lived with my favorite former student, Scott, seventeen
years her junior and twenty years mine. Dita and I were age-mates,
we both loved Scott, and we were both teachers and should have
had lots in common except that she resented me for teaching a
subject, creative writing, she didn't believe in—as well as, I suspected, for being able to do it at Columbia. "Such a course does not
exist in Europe," she'd told Scott. Scott had never been shy about

reporting her harshest judgments of me. Since he'd graduated and finally left New York, quite awhile ago, most of my conversations with Scott had taken place over the phone—wide-ranging, cheerfully anguished chats continuing at times into the early-morning hours. (I think we were both usually drinking while we talked.) Ours wasn't the kind of relationship you could easily explain to a rational, self-possessed woman like Dita, head of computer sciences at William Paterson University. Scott could do a raucous impersonation of Dita and I only wondered if she'd ever been privileged to hear it herself. "I think your friend is declining, he's a drawnk!" she'd supposedly told him, before going into a complaining Carpathian whine: "Oh, Scawt, you need new friends."

And now that I was alone with her and the two of us were walking along avoiding the growls and silly sinister menaces of oncoming zombies, I realized that Scott had been exaggerating, and that her pronunciation of his name and the diphthongs she'd had plenty of time as an immigrant to get used to weren't as Dracula as we'd imagined. "She thinks you're in love with me," he'd once said, and knowing that he was in all likelihood (like a lot of insecure straight boys who consider themselves failures) fishing for my affection, I had acted the neutral part: "Come on!" And yet now as Dita and I hugged our jackets to our bodies while the cold wind whipped off the Atlantic, I realized too that I'd subscribed to those exaggerations of Scott's to add drama to my staid life—and as a bulwark against my disappointments for not having him. And that Dita understood this. Her clear amber eyes had been seeing everything all along, registering every nuance and contradiction in her lover's character, perceiving me and my motives—but it was all right. She wanted us to be friends, and she needed my help. She'd called me in Manhattan the day before with the news that Scott was missing and begged me to take a train down to the Jersey Shore.

"Scott's been acting strange f-f-for a while," she'd said, meeting me at the station, and I'd thought, When has he not? I was thinking insensitively—anyone weird enough to say that I'd written some of his favorite novels had to have a screw loose—but I provided the necessary, soothing coos and ahs of amelioration as she went over the details of what she knew and stopped herself from crying out—a grind in her throat of sudden emotion, a twist of bitterly recovered stoicism. "Americans are absurd," she'd told him, "believing as they do in eternal happiness. What other country would put the word *happiness* in its constitution?" (How quick he'd been to call me up with that observation.) Yet if anyone ever seemed determined to be unhappy, it was cynical, mocking Scott, barely masking his contempt, I thought, for everyone including himself.

For the first ten years of our friendship his admiration of my first two "difficult" avant-garde novels had been a love-offering. In the last ten it had been a bludgeon he used to hit me with over my already bloodied head. He had almost memorized my first novel in all its queer and complicated syntax, its gaudy pessimism—for bits of gorgeous accent shot through the gray fog banks of prose here and there. It was like De Kooning's 1950 painting in Chicago, *Excavation*, which had reintroduced little pits of color into his huge, asbestos-hued abstractions . . . Now Scott told me that my brain was so soaked in gin that he doubted if I could remember anything instructive about the original process that had helped me produce my one masterpiece, *Antic Twists*. He saw me as a burnt-out hive, the swarm long since flown. A bibulous impostor who shared only a name with the gifted (and, that word, *promising*) author of the past. Scott's contempt for me in recent years only echoed my own for myself. They say that alcoholics become hermits because they don't want to expose their weakness to other eyes—no witnesses, please. That must be why I'd been avoiding Scott more and more. We'd been in touch so little lately that I wondered if he'd kept his promise to Dita to get off the bottle. This wasn't a subject I felt naturally disposed to bring up with the woman who no doubt saw me as one of the worst influences on Scott's life—neck and neck with the parents who he'd claimed in a memoir (his one published book) had abused and neglected him as a kid back in St. Louis.

In the long shadow of an abandoned brick behemoth building, Dita and I stepped off the boardwalk and entered an Italian restaurant. "How long has he been gone?" I asked when we were seated and brought glasses of water. I reached for my straw, unwrapped it, stuck it in the glass, and began fiddling with the cast-off paper. "A week, you said?"

"Five days," answered Dita, and she stopped distractedly to watch my nervous knotting of the thin paper sheath, fluttering her eyelashes as she searched her thoughts, and picked up again: "It was five days ago when I came in and didn't find him in the basement. I've been busy grading my midterms, doing departmental things, attending stupid meetings. I know creative writers don't have so much of these responsibilities, but really when it's so technical and I'm deep into my work, arguing with the other faculty members, finding the time for my own work, a paper I've been trying to write for two years—well, Scott is not always so understanding. And I can't just do everything by conference call. *Work from home more*, he tells me. Such a baby! I don't know if you know the baby side of Scott."

I tried to wrap my head around the image of a Scott who wanted babying, and yes it was there—I could just see it. We infantilize our students, dangling in front of them the chance for glory if only they'd work harder for Daddy. I'd grown wary of coddling Scott awhile back. He had an unpredictable, explosive temper, and even by his own admission he'd turned it at least once against Dita. I could hang up, unplug the phone, but Dita had gone to the emergency room while Scott had landed in a twelve-week anger management course and a year's worth of community service. As charming as it would probably seem during the summer vacations of all those New Jersey families, on a gray day Asbury Park with its open-air intoxication and abandon to Hallowe'en pranksterism appeared ripe for a whole army of community-service volunteers.

Just then, a drag queen in black Victorian funeral garb, complete with a black satin-bowed bustle and a black lace parasol, clomped by outside in high-heeled button-up boots. She stopped and studied us through the glass, her face pancaked in silver and her cheeks rouged a ghastly crimson—and I nodded and smiled faintly as her retinue of ghouls in charcoal morning coats and pinstripe pants leapt up and down about her, clawing the air as though to indicate, *Mistress, let's get them!*

Turning, I asked Dita, "This is your weekend house here in Asbury Park, isn't it?"

"Yes, I have—we have—a condo near the university, but Scott won't go there. It has not so much bad memories as not very happy associations. It was very hard for him to write his book, a purging, and when he was done getting all of that out and I was ready to buy the bungalow—you'll see, it's not much more than that—he wanted to stop taking the d-drugs. He said he had written the need for them out of his b-b-brain and wanted to start over." She smiled jaggedly, her lips not quite flush to her gums. "So, no more drugs for depression, and I thought no more alcohol. I made the mistake of believing depression was all in the head, something people allow to happen, to make their minds up about for or against. It's a prejudice, I suppose, I brought over with me—a mindset you call it."

Still wary of the subject of alcohol, I decided to keep my verb tense in the present and stick to a positive note in my voice, and I said, "I've always thought that considering the things he's been through, overall he's done a pretty good job of staying optimistic."

"Not always."

I raised my eyebrows expectantly.

"Like everyone, good days, bad days. On the bad, all we think about is the bad."

Fury or perhaps a sense of self-righteousness had helped iron out her speech. Her stutter subsided. She shook her head irritably and looked out, the Addams Family having pushed on in search of other fun. The brick behemoth—a dilapidated casino, as it turned out—was covered in graffiti and most of its massive windows had been boarded up. But seagulls, their shrieks penetrating our window, had found exposed panes broken by kids' thrown rocks, and they would alight on the sharp edges of glass, then pick and push their suddenly shrinking bulks through. Note to writerly but currently creatively fallow self: a metaphor for increasingly tightened but still ultimately porous U.S. borders?

"What I meant was, no one wants to be miserable. And lest we forget," I went on, thinking darker thoughts than my tense and tone were letting on, and grimacing and trying to make it look jolly, "Scott does have that marvelous sense of humor . . ."

It had been years since Scott had made me laugh more than a jaundiced, withered snicker. But back when we were still pals—me the arch sorcerer to his eager apprentice, or so he claimed—from his end of the line he could parody Updike in a paean to his dinner of pork and beans, eroticizing it and stringing out his sentence to make himself sound aswim in a sauce of small-town recollections. "That deserves another shot of Elijah," he'd say.

Dita seemed to be daydreaming, resting her chin on her palm, her elbow propped on the edge of the table, and I said, trying to feel her out and see if her deepest fears were matching mine, "You'd be a better judge of it, of course, so do you think Asbury Park has been more or less good for him? Was he writing, last time you talked to him?"

"Hmm, he likes it here," she said more cheerfully. "He comes from St. Louis, as you know. He likes being near the Atlantic. He was claustrophobic in—ih—ih—in—"

"Missouri," I said.

"I always want to say Mississippi. What do they call them, the fly—flyyy—"

"You mean the flyover states . . ."

She ground out more laughter and nodded. "Yes, what I meant. But not nice to say! I've never been home with him. I have never wanted to go. Since we're together, Scott has only returned to St. Louis twice. And every time he leaves, he drags his feet to the airport—because really, those people! Horrible! His family, I'm talking about, see."

"I've never gotten the whole story," I said, but what I meant was the true story, as Scott had always been something of a mythographer, I was sure, exaggerating almost to a gothic degree his bad childhood. There were parts of the memoir I'd winced at. My own narratives had gotten more confessional and autobiographical in inverse proportion to the steep plunge of my reputation. I did believe that when he was fourteen he'd tried to burn his house down and been sent to a mental institute. The details of the group sessions and cigarettes, stale coffee and bullying psychologists, were admirably vivid; the Mexican girl he'd met in there made for great characterization and story value. But the cruelty and the tyranny of the father, the weakness and boozy, unremittingly ironical seductiveness of the slushy mother—the Quaker and the feminist in me had revolted. Still, he'd brought it off in the end: the dramatic running-away, a mite-bit too prison-break flick for me, had led to a lovely, lyrical, often comic sequence, in which he hitches rides with truckers to the East Coast, which felt too original to make up. And when in the epilogue Scott is busking in Washington Square and he meets his future wife, a Japanese tourist, and the two decide to take the Staten Island Ferry together for no particular reason, I bawled out loud—ashamed of myself in my cozy Claremont Avenue apartment for not having believed in the skewed earlier portraits. That's talent too. From my jaded, thoroughly writers-conferenced point of view, I'd known better writers to forge more outlandish poetic licenses for themselves. And anyway, given the chance I might take the fractional germ of truth in those Dickens-grade parents over the father who'd herded us with silence and a mother countering with too much praise, and let it sprout into a doorstop that would rival Jane Eyre for gloom and recrimination. "What you have," I'd told him, "is the basic wad of pie dough you'll be able to use for all kinds of inventions, with scraps left over for tea biscuits." I'd then had to explain to him the reference, what grandmothers made on rainy summer days with their little darlings. To hear Scott tell it, blinking above a pinched smile, he'd never had the luxury of knowing any of his grandparents, not since he was two or three. His folks had been too greedy and jealous to share any kind of love with him, but thanks anyway, Teach. How I'd wanted to wipe that satisfied and assuredly abject smirk off his face, and show him love. After that, he'd satirically sign off in phone messages as *Pie Dough Boy*.

Of course, it was the kind of memory best not shared with Dita, and as it fired its way through my emotions during those fifteen seconds of silence while the waitress dropped the menus in front of us, I smiled wistfully and said, "It must have been hard for him."

"I made him go," said Dita, which considering the guilt trip my head was putting itself through, and from which I was just returning, I misheard to imply that she'd driven him away. "He just drags his feet whenever he has to leave," she added, nodding over the menu, "my little boy! But anyhow, you know what's good here? The pasta primavera."

Her look sizzled with delectation and then she slipped her half-moon readers on, a little too comfortably I thought. "I'll take it," I hooted, "something light for a change."

Getting that call from Dita, I'd thought: He's finally done it. Scott had attempted suicide a number of times and threatened it even more. He had the gradually fading scars on his wrists to prove it, and used them, eyes twinkling lightheartedly (if disingenuously, my uncharitable side whispered), as a springboard for talking about "next time." He was a suicide-ideation junkie, an old shrink of mine might have said. Once or twice I'd gotten quiet during these felicitous warnings, something I'd learned not to do (neither the going-along-with-it-with-drawn-breath-protest-of-shock), because he'd gone hot and savage on me: "You've never really taken me seriously. You know what you are? Envious, man."

Dita and I put in our matching orders, and when the bread came around I grabbed for a piece from the basket, saying, "Whom have you contacted?"

The usual. She'd filed a missing persons report, gone around to her neighbors and asked if any of them had seen Scott lately and when they believed was the last time.

"Scott was friendly to everyone he saw on our street and in our neighborhood, but the thing I kept hearing from them was that even though he'd say hello he would never be the one to start up a conversation. Some said they had no idea who I was talking about."

Did this surprise her? I didn't ask. She talked on, not yet touching the bread.

"Well," she said, "someone who prefers to live in a basement— I guess you knew all that—when there are two whole floors with better light, more comfortable space, and he was the one who did the changes and refurbishing, all by himself—for months!"

I remembered Scott's excitement, infectious I'd felt it to be, when he told me how much he liked swinging a hammer and swashing a paintbrush up and down walls. "And I'm good at it," he'd said, "ha ha! Guess I missed my calling, guess I should change my direction before it's too late, don't you think? Because this is really a lot of fucking fun!"

And I remembered how cautiously I'd stepped out of the way of a trap set to snare me, so he could hold me down while accusing me of more envy and disloyalty.

"Just don't get too comfortable with it," I'd said, hoping he might do just that.

"The floors are original," Dita said, now reaching for the smallest piece of bread, "but Scott did have a friend show him how to sand them down and polyurethane them. I think they did it together, and he was proud." She pursed her lips and pushed them out in a puffy pout I'd seen as a gesture of deflationary equivocation in Prague and Krakow, the default mode for people who'd learned not to expect much from life before getting, some of them, more than they'd ever dreamed of having, then judging it not quite up to snuff.

She shrugged one shoulder and considered tasting the bread.

"I bought it as an investment and a weekend retreat, but I had no idea Scott would take to it so po-po-po-ssessively. Ah—and all the bathroom and kitchen fixtures are new. That we had to contract out. The house was entirely insulated to begin with. The furnace was already good, thank God—I didn't have to replace that. But yes, Scott was proud, as he should be. Together we selected nice colors, but he did all of the painting himself. He did a good job. I didn't expect him to move in permanently, but it did happen gradually. No chance, however, of renting it out in the summer when I'm in Europe with my mom."

I would have caught on the detail of Scott's having a friend to help him with the floors if I wasn't focusing so intently on the fact that she was speaking so openly about her investment. Scott himself had been given to get-rich-quick schemes. Having given up hopes of ever appearing on *Oprah* with another memoir detailing his poor New York years and the disaster of his marriage to the girl from Osaka, who'd slept around, he had decided to embark on a series of kitty detective stories for young readers. Just listening to his plans for that ultimately foundered project was enough to make me quit picking up the phone. He could go on for hours about the police cat (an item he'd found in the local newspaper) that went "undercover" posing as an ordinary household pet to help unmask a fraudulent vet in the area who'd been putting animals to sleep for supposed diseases they didn't have and collecting the absurdly high medical fees from distraught owners eager to do the compassionate thing. I didn't stop to ask if he thought the topic right for his target audience and he never solicited my feedback. He'd quit doing that a long time ago.

Another thing I wasn't sharing with Dita was my knowledge of his wild obsessive loves for very strange-sounding women he met on the streets. It was proof of just how desperate the housewives of New Jersey must be, and how lamentably short the town was on presentable men, that Scott—reeking of cigarettes, face haggard from sleepless nights and overwrought, overpowering emotions, his body skinny and shaking from narcissistic dieting as well as all of the wildly alternating years of booze and sobriety—could seduce almost any female he met on his rare sorties out of his cave.

Dita and I ate our primaveras in virtual silence—the lunch crowd had swelled and in response the management had turned up the music—and for once I was grateful for the pop I abhorred. Every third song, as she indicated, was by local hero Bruce Springsteen. (I'd become a shut-in with my lone Bach Sunday brunches and my loud, Bayreuth-of-one evenings, my fully loaded CD player machine-gunning nightly through the Ring Cycle.)

"Just over there!" Dita shouted, pointing with her fork across my shoulder.

"What?!"

"The Stone Pony," she said, careful to enunciate, "where Springsteen started!"

I turned and saw on the other side of Ocean Avenue a modest white cement-block nightclub, and turned back at her grinning gamely. "Did Scott love Bruce Springsteen?"

"Oh, yes," she said, not tripping over my shift into past tense. "Sometimes I think that's why he insisted we move to Asbury . . . I would almost even say he was in love!"

My sweet, dopey grin curdled into something more tart. "I had no idea!"

"Oh, yes!"

I tried listening to some of the lyrics he was warbling and wailing. I had no idea what he was singing. The transience of idols, I thought, maybe not as transient as human lives. I had no idea what we were doing here—we were getting nothing done, not saying anything to curtail Scott's plight. Neither of us was enjoying ourselves, yet I bobbed my head along to the horn-rich rhythm, as though I were back in a seedy bar on Fire Island in the '60s, dancing to race music with other sweater queens amid the required smattering of lesbians whose presence kept the place from getting raided. I wanted a glass of pinot noir, or something inky and gagging, a Bordeaux—I wouldn't give Dita the satisfaction.

"Catchy words," I said, imagining a double bourbon on the rocks. There was no reason not to have one. Soon we would hear that the body had been recovered—and I'd never have to look at this woman again or hear her scratchy words seeking out vulnerable places, the soft bruises from nighttime bumps in my bathroom, to grind their way into my flesh forever. I pointed up, saying, "I guess it's not for nothing that the guy got famous!"

"What?!"

I was glad that she couldn't hear my joshy, Damon Runyon way of expressing a thought so trivial and insincere, and I leaned forward as the music switched to a syrupy, more hushed ballad. "I'm getting worried. Sitting here, I feel sort of ashamed of us . . ."

"I know," she said, blinking rapidly, "but first I want to show you Ocean Grove."

"Would you like anything," she said when we got to the house, "w-w-water, whiskey?"

"I wouldn't," I lied. "I need to get back this afternoon, to teach an evening class."

"Creative writing," she said drily, keeping a steady gaze on me, "on Hallowe'en?"

"Haw. Not even ghosts and goblins have a holiday on Hallowe'en. And you'd be surprised at how many of those want a master's degree and end up taking my workshop."

"Hang on, I think I'll go up and get more comfortable, slip into my pajama jeans."

After tarry double espressos, she had walked me through a covered passage that cut through the abandoned casino and led to the adjoining community of Ocean Grove where the Methodists still had their summer camps. Along the boardwalk there, hideous condos littered the waterfront in a solid tawdry vinyl-sided wall, yet just in back of them rose the colorful turrets and cyclopean gables of the original Victorian mansions, all kept spit-spot and averting their dignified, make that mortified, stares away from crass modernity.

We half-circled the block then had come upon the modest and charming dollhouse rows where the town's mere middle-class mortals got a slice of the pie. Narrow and all of wood, they were twee; simple keyhole-saw gingerbread latticed the shallow porches. We halted to take it all in. The block was shady, with sun peeking through the elms, and even considering the chill of the advancing day a sense of tranquility hung in the air.

"There's just enough room for two to live civilly and harmoniously together," said Dita, "depending on which two. That one, with the vulgar, superfluous fairy lights strung up, and those dumb crystals getting ready to blind whoever passes by, is where she lives."

"She."

"The girl Scott met," she said, and when I shrugged, then for added effect dropped my jaw, we eased back into a stroll. "In truth, I wasn't angry. He met her one summer or the spring before when I was on sabbatical. Anyway, I was in Europe the whole time."

"In Poland, with your mother and family."

"But all over Europe. Not the point. I wasn't angry, not even the least bit. Not even jealous. He thought I was both. I figured he might have called and told you."

"Absolutely not," I said. "And was it a tortured, passionate, doomed affair?"

"Not at all, Scott was happy. Very happy. And I was happy for him. I thought he might have called you to work it up into some big melodrama in his mind between us, but in fact I was supportive. He wanted me to be jealous, but I was thrilled. He only became angry when I suggested he try living with her. It wasn't necessary—but he could, I said."

"I think I follow you," I responded, lightly chuckling. "That sounds like my Scott too."

"It was the same summer he and his buddy from old times, Kenny, were going to get their duo going. They played on the boardwalk and Kenny, according to Scott, said Scott's songs were the real thing. They hoped to play clubs next. And so on. I met her. Scott was too proud not to introduce us. I really didn't like the idea, I thought it was unnecessary, no good for anybody, but he insisted, and when Scott insists—yes, you get it, no? Should we go up to the house and knock and ask her?"

"You mean if she's seen Scott?"

"No, I suppose not. You're right. If she was hiding him, I would already know. I gave the address to the police and the Monmouth County Sheriff's Department and put it all in their hands. If they can't find it in one of these crackerboxes it's probably not there. Where would she put him, under the floor? He's claustrophobic. And hates the mother."

"She lives with her mother?"

As though she'd been rehearsing for days, yet without much talent for this kind of thing—the contemptuous, continental "nonjealous" bit—Dita droned on at quite a clip.

"How else would she survive? She's too stupid to work, I think in fact retarded."

It came to me: Asperger Girl. I'd come in at the end, having been away in France for the summer. But of course there were other reasons to tuck it out of my memory too.

At the corner of the next block I saw the skeletons of the camp meeting's tent city. As I understood it—Dita was too busy cycling through her own spiritual cleansing to stop and enlighten me otherwise—the Methodists used these frames and foundations to throw their canvas tarps over to serve as roof and walls. At the backs, fully enclosed structures housed kitchen and bathroom. They slept with only a layer of cloth between themselves and the stars, and it was such a model of goodness and decency, fresh air, cold plunges in the Atlantic followed by a round of singing and revival, that I was saddened. I knew that Stephen Crane, the sickly and slight son of stalwart Methodists, had been trundled about New Jersey among relatives as a small boy after his father's death, and that he'd fetched up in Asbury Park and as a young reporter had walked these streets. At least as much as a writer is made, or has been given in life, he also grabs and molds his material. Crane had been handed an early death sentence with his chronic lung ailments and he was dead from tuberculosis before turning thirty. But before that he'd traveled on freighters and covered revolutions, and he wrote one certifiable masterpiece, *The Red Badge of Courage*, about a war that ended six years before he was born, convincing everyone including his betters in England, from James and Wells to Conrad and Ford, that since "Stevie" couldn't possibly be a veteran of the bloodiest conflict in American history, the only reasonable conclusion to draw was that he must be a genius. In Sussex, where Crane was dying and in hock to creditors back home, the greatest English writers of the previous generation had doted on an undersized giant. But no one was going to dote on Scott. I'd once sinned against him, it was true. I'd touched him the wrong way in private, caressing his neck and monitoring his confusion with my dumb puppy eyes, insulting not so much his manhood as his talent and intelligence. I regretted it immediately, and wondered if he'd ever told Dita about it.

"No," she was saying, "let's not bother her. You're right, leave her to the church."

"It's getting cold," I said. "Aren't you cold?"

And we walked back to the car, each embarrassed into silence in our way.

She then waited halfway through the drive to the house before saying, "A-a-after that, I gave him a deadline for moving out. *Wr-wr-writers like deadlines*, I told him. I thought it would light a little fire under his seat. I wasn't mean about it—you know about the difficulties of dealing with Scott. They had a demo, *Songs for*

Andi, so okay, you won't work, get a proper job, but I'm not going to be around forever, mister."

I shifted in my seat to get a fuller view of her face, but Dita did not turn. She was keeping her eyes on the road, chin raised, looking out for a calming object in the distance, and I said, "Well, you've carried the bulk of the burden with Scott, I know."

"All of it," I'd insisted.

I snooped a bit in the downstairs, impressed by the Martha Stewart comfort and carefully coordinated colors that read "mutedly tasteful but unsnooty," a composition which Scott had brought off. Dita descended the stairs, slinking almost, while rolling up the sleeves of a neatly pressed white button-down—and wearing a type of pants I'd never seen before. They had the color and stitched-looking design of jeans, but were made of a soft, stretchy material that clung flatteringly to her hips and thighs. Only at that moment did I begin to believe what Scott had always said, that Dita was full of sexy surprises.

"A-a-and I know, even from what Scott said, but also from reading some of your books—yes, you're shocked that a computer scientist can read words?—but I know that you're a great teacher. I'm ready for a drink. The rest of the day and the evening, I will go back to my funk, and wait by the phone like a good wife. You know, Scott really could not marry me because, irresponsible as ever, he never saw to it to divorce the Japanese."

"So that was it," I said.

"That was it," she said, and wagged her finger in the air and led me to the kitchen. "I will wait for the mister, but only for so long. He has us as he wants us, on the end of a string. But in time, maybe we learn"—she exhibited a maniacal looseness under her own roof, and her language had rounded another bend—"we can let go. Mister doesn't count on that, does he? Maybe he'll be back, maybe not, to see we hold our end of them too?" She swung open a cabinet full of liquor and added, "Please say you'll join me."

Some might have called it tempting fate, but judging from

Scott's description of Dita—yes, he was here with me still—she had undoubtedly surveyed the situation and looked at it realistically. Only Americans, he might have said she would say, insisted on the sunniest, most optimistic view, and cleared the fleet of bottles from his thirsty eyes.

"Just one, then," I said. "I'll have—"

"This is what we make at home in my family," she said, unsquatting and coming up with an old Gallo jug filled with a clear yellowish fluid. "Apricot brandy, only it's not really brandy, it's just what we say, and it's peaches. You can't get good apricots: for that you have to be somewhere else—the closest out in California in a grove, but more ideally someplace in Europe, and most ideally in Galicia," and hauled down two juice glasses.

She explained the process, involving soaking the fruit in vodka for months before straining off the liquor, and said that of course it was more of a schnapps. "You like it?"

There was that blessed snap, a lick from the first belt of the day. I'd been careful that morning to have only coffee, half a pot, and for some hours had even believed in the fiction that I might extend that practice as a short-term habit, experiment, ease back into a routine I'd eschewed as equally hopeless years ago, bowing before the muse humbly as a man wishing to reform, and sweet-talking her and seeing if that got me anywhere. All of it sank foolishly away, my resolve, my hangover logic. Stupid idea. This was lots better, felt a lot more like inspiration. Seduce yourself and screw the muse. Fickle tramp!

We went down to the basement.

"I—I'm afraid I couldn't look at it the way it was," said Dita. "I cleaned it a bit."

Everything had been straightened—the clothes I knew Scott to drop anywhere he pleased and the things he would pick up and look at before tossing them aside, his books, CDs, had all been put away, returned to place. And the area resembled the dorm room of an unusually finicky and fastidious college student. Dita stepped aside. When I turned to look at her with an ambiguously approving sniff that said either she'd done the right thing or I wouldn't have known the difference to begin with, she folded her arms over her chest and, blinking rapidly, arranged her face tentatively, as though issuing a meek challenge or opening herself up to polite suggestions for how she might do better the next time.

"He always was a terrible slob," I allowed, "in that hole down on Rivington."

"I've kept the heat on the whole time," she said, "in case he comes back."

Taped to one painted cinder-block wall was the worn Smiths poster he'd kept as a souvenir of his only transatlantic trip, to London. Once Scott and I had argued about the poetic value of rock lyrics (the Smiths had been his first artistic inspiration when he was still rotting in the "juvie bughouse," as he called it), and guess who'd argued against it.

Our last argument had occurred the fall following that summer he'd described to me over the phone as magical and idyllic, the same sorts of adjectives I'd urged him for years to chase from his writing, though I hadn't begrudged him them then—when he had been in love and was getting back to his music, right before both enterprises had crashed, and he'd argued with Andi for thinking she might be pregnant (she wasn't) and Kenny for sabotaging their chances at getting their duo off the ground (I knew who the real saboteur had to be). Ever paranoid, he'd accused me and some of his classmates of a cabal. He'd cooked up a conspiracy theory in which all of us were envious of his upcoming book, I'm So Sorry—and we'd seen to it that it had gotten nothing more than an "In Brief" notice in the Sunday Times. Never mind that it was enthusiastic, that the book was still in print on a small rock press, and that all of mine were out of print and had never been regarded by any reviewer at the Times as anything beyond entertaining oddities at best and stubbornly extruded excrescences, to cite the cruelest review, at worst. And that I'd sat up night after night with him editing and honing the manuscript, wanting to stroke and congratulate him for work we'd done together but that nonetheless had come from his once-tender heart, in order to prepare it for the first eyes in the business that I knew would take a shine to it.

"You're a pretty ungrateful little bastard," I'd said before easing the receiver onto the cradle, never to pick it up on him again. "You whine and complain while everyone all around you marches in lockstep to see a hint of the sun, before the inevitable black cloud comes racing up to cover it over again. You suck blood and all you give back is bile. I'm sick of you, and I'm sick of trying to help you. You don't want help. You want pity, or I don't know what you want but neither do you, it's something no human is capable of ever giving another because it hasn't been invented—which mean it's absurd, and so are you!"

I smelled the sweetness of mildew—not even Pine-Sol and Air Wick could get rid of it—and I went over to the high ledge of the window above the washing machine where he kept his few books, and where I saw the cracked spines of some of my titles.

"There," Dita rasped. "He was proud, always proud of his friendship with you."

When the call came, it was early on a Sunday morning. The strangest thing. I'd been to a play I enjoyed with friends the night before, and after two glasses of wine with dinner and a single digestif returned home and gone straight to bed—all as though to get me ready. Drinking coffee, I sat in my chair reading, just paces from the answering machine.

When it picked up, I thought after she said her name that she'd begun giggling.

"So he's finally done it," said Dita, composing herself, "our Scott killed himself."

I sat there and listened, keeping my place in the book with my index finger. Then I realized that this was something the callous Scott would tell on himself, laughing, and I let the book fall to the floor in a restrainedly cinematic moment that suggested Bergman.

They'd found him in the Raritan near South Amboy. When he was being cavalier and enumerating his upcoming attempts, he'd listed everything from sticking his head in a gas oven to a rematch with the old razor blade in the bath or sedatives and Amaretto to a witches' brew of every pill he could collect from Dita's medicine cabinet chased down with a cocktail of household chemicals. "Very funny," I'd said. "Now shut the fuck up." But he'd very specifically pointed out that it would not be death by drowning—since he violently disagreed with my taste for Virginia Woolf: "Anything Woolfian's too corny."

Of course, I didn't pick up or call her back. I poured myself another cup of coffee and went into my study and began going through student thesis work.

I was busy all of the following week serving on selection committees and I stayed dry until Friday night, when I went to the movies, where I began crying from the opening credits and heard the first twangs of plaintive pioneer theme music. I wept at the national landscape, and I wept unabashedly when a thief in the story was hanged and townspeople played by extras cheered. When the lights were turned on, I got up and left the theater. I didn't cry for the rest of the weekend.

A few months later, a package from Dita containing a CD-ROM with all of Scott's writings arrived, but it made no difference. I'd already decided what to do in just such an emergency.

LONG BRANCH UNDERGROUND

BY ROBERT PINSKY

Long Branch

Wheel of the tides, wheel of the surf, hot nights.
The clean chrome arms of the taffy-pulling machine
Folding it over and over in figure eights.

Because the politicians decreed all gambling
Illegal without some element of skill,
The Wheel of Fortune got a new name: Skil-O.

Carousel waltzes and polkas, Vito Genovese
On television in his yellow glasses
Denying it all. The shooting of Pussy Russo.

The players who put money on a number
Would get to press a little Skil-O button
That slowed the ticking wheel down, just a little.

Herringbone boardwalk. At night, flourishes of light:
The manic neon chicken in spasms dashing
Into the neon basket, and rising again.

I knew a man whose body wouldn't start breathing
Again the way his doctors expected, after
They pulled their plastic tube back out of his throat.

Crosswise to Ocean Avenue and the boardwalk,
Under the traffic, a tunnel of perpetual shade
Ran from the beach to the pool across the street.

The two young surgeons couldn't get the tube
Back into the guy. By chance, a skilled old doc
Passed by and got it back in, and so he breathed.

Down in the tunnel, the bare light bulbs protected
By their steel cages, sand gritty underfoot—
Conduit shaft between brightness and brightness by day

Or darkness and darkness by night, a passage of shades
Enduring after the boardwalk was destroyed
With its merry-go-round, its wheels and sweets and music.

RUN KISS DADDY

BY JOYCE CAROL OATES

Kittatinny Mountains

T ell Daddy hello! Run kiss Daddy."

He'd been gone from the lake less than an hour but in this new family each parting and each return signaled a sort of antic improvised celebration—he didn't want to think it was the obverse of what must have happened before he'd arrived in their lives—the Daddy departing, and the Daddy not returning.

"Sweetie, h'lo! C'mere."

He dropped to one knee as the boy ran at him to be hugged. A rough wet kiss on Kevin's forehead.

The little girl hesitated. Only when the mother pushed more firmly at her small shoulders did she spring forward and run—wild-blue-eyed suddenly, with a high-pitched squeal like a mouse being squeezed—into his arms. He laughed—he was startled by the heat of the little body—flattered and deeply moved, kissing the excited child on the delicate soft skin at her temple where—he'd only just noticed recently—a pale blue vein pulsed.

"What do you say to Daddy when Daddy comes back?"

The mother clapped her hands to make a game of it. This new family was so new to her too, weekends at Paraquarry Lake were best borne as a game, as play.

"Say *Hi Daddy!—Kiss-kiss Daddy!*"

Obediently the children cried what sounded like *Hi Daddy! Kiss-kiss Daddy!*

Little fish-mouths pursed for kisses against Daddy's cheek.

Reno had only driven into the village of Paraquarry Falls to bring back semi-emergency supplies: toilet paper, flashlight batteries, mosquito repellant, mouse traps, a gallon container of milk, a shiny new garden shovel to replace the badly rusted shovel that had come with the camp. Also, small sweet-fruit yogurts for the children though both he and the mother weren't happy about them developing a taste for sugary foods—but there wasn't much of a selection at the convenience store.

In this new-Daddy phase in which unexpected treats are the very coinage of love.

"Who wants to help Daddy dig?"

Both children cried *Me!*—thrilled at the very prospect of working with Daddy on the exciting new terrace overlooking the lake.

And so they helped Daddy excavate the old, crumbled-brick terrace a previous owner had left amid a tangle of weeds, pebbles, and broken glass, or tried to help Daddy—for a while. Clearly such work was too arduous for a seven-year-old, still more for a four-year-old, with play shovels and rakes; and the mild June air too humid for much exertion. And there were mosquitoes and gnats. Despite the repellant. For these were the Kittatinny Mountains east of the Delaware Water Gap in early June—that season of teeming buzzing fecundity—just to inhale the air is to inhale the smells of burgeoning life.

"Oh! Dad-dy!" Devra recoiled from something she'd unearthed in the soil, lost her balance, and fell back onto her bottom with a little cry. Reno saw it was just a beetle—iridescent, wriggling—and told her not to be afraid: "They just live in the ground, sweetie. They have special beetle work to do in the ground."

Kevin said, "Like worms! They have 'work' in the ground."

This simple science—earth science—the little boy had gotten from Reno. Very gratifying to hear your words repeated with child-pride.

From the mother Reno knew that their now-departed father

had often behaved "unpredictably" with the children and so Reno made it a point to be soft-spoken in their presence, good-natured and unexcitable, predictable.

What pleasure in being *predictable*!

Still, Devra was frightened. She'd dropped her play shovel in the dirt. Reno saw that the little girl had enough of helping Daddy with the terrace for the time being. "Sweetie, go see what Mommy's doing. You don't need to dig anymore right now."

Kevin remained with Daddy. Kevin snorted in derision, his baby sister was so *scaredy*.

Reno was a father, again. Fatherhood, returned to him. A gift he hadn't quite deserved the first time—maybe—but this time, he would strive to deserve it.

This time, he was forty-seven years old. He—who'd had a very hard time perceiving himself other than *young, a kid*.

And this new marriage!—this beautiful new family small and vulnerable as a mouse cupped trembling in the hand—he was determined to protect with his life. Not ever *not ever* let this family slip from his grasp as he'd let slip from his grasp his previous family—two young children rapidly retreating now in Reno's very memory like a scene glimpsed in the rearview mirror of a speeding vehicle.

"Come to Paraquarry Lake! You will all love Paraquarry Lake."

The name itself seemed to him beautiful, seductive—like the Delaware River at the Water Gap where the river was wide, glittering and winking like shaken foil. As a boy he'd hiked the Appalachian Trail in this area of northeastern Pennsylvania and northwestern New Jersey—across the river on the high pedestrian walkway, north to Dunfield Creek and Sunfish Pond and so to Paraquarry Lake which was the most singular of the Kittitanny Ridge lakes, edged with rocks like a crude lacework and densely wooded with ash, elm, birch, and maples that flamed red in autumn.

So he courted them with tales of his boyhood hikes, canoe-ing on the river and on Paraquarry Lake, camping along the Kit-tatinny Ridge where once, thousands of years ago, a glacier lay like a massive claw over the land.

He told them of the Lenni Lenape Indians who'd inhabited this part of the country for thousands of years!—far longer than their own kind.

As a boy he'd never found arrowheads at Paraquarry Lake or elsewhere, yet he recalled that others had, and so spoke excitedly to the boy Kevin as if to enlist him in a search; he did not quite suggest they might discover Indian bones that sometimes came to the surface at Paraquarry Lake, amid shattered red shale and ordinary rock and dirt.

In this way and in others he courted the new wife Marlena, who was a decade younger than he; and the new son, Kevin; and the new daughter who'd won his heart the first glimpse he'd had of her—tiny Devra with white-blond hair fine as the silk of milkweed.

Another man's lost family. Or maybe *cast off*—as Marlena had said in her bright brave voice determined not to appear hurt, humiliated.

His own family—Reno had hardly cast off. Whatever his ex-wife would claim. If anything, Reno had been the one to be cast off by her.

Yet careful to tell Marlena, early in their relationship: "It was my fault, I think. I was too young. When we got married—just out of college—we were both too young. It's said that if you 'cohabit' before getting married it doesn't actually make any difference in the long run—whether you stay married, or get divorced—but our problem was that we hadn't a clue what 'cohabitation' meant—means. We were always two separate people and then my career took off . . ."

Took off wasn't Reno's usual habit of speech. Nor was it Reno's habit to talk so much, and so eagerly. But when he'd met a woman he believed he might come to seriously care for—at last—he'd felt obliged to explain himself to her: there had to be some failure in his personality, some flaw, otherwise why was he alone, unmarried; why had he become a father whose children had grown up largely without him, and without seeming to need him?

At the time of the divorce, Reno had granted his wife too many concessions. In his guilty wish to be generous to her though the breakup had been as much his wife's decision as his own. He'd signed away much of their jointly owned property, and agreed to severely curtailed visitation rights with the children. He hadn't yet grasped this simple fact of human relations—the more readily you give, the more readily it will be taken from you as what you owe.

His wife had appealed to him to be allowed to move to Oregon where she had relatives, with the children; Reno hadn't wanted to contest her.

Within a few years, she'd relocated again—with a new husband, to Sacramento.

In these circuitous moves, somehow Reno was cast off. One too many corners had been turned, the father had been left behind except for child-support payments.

Trying not to feel like a fool. Trying to remain a gentleman long after he'd come to wonder why.

"Paraquarry Lake! You will all love Paraquarry Lake."

The new wife was sure, yes, she would love Paraquarry Lake. Laughing at Reno's boyish enthusiasm, squeezing his arm.

Kevin and Devra were thrilled. Their new father—new *Daddy*—so much nicer than the old, other Daddy—eagerly spreading out photographs on a tabletop like playing cards.

"Of course," the new Daddy said, a sudden crease between his eyes, "this cabin in the photos isn't the one we'll be staying in. This is the one—" Reno paused, stricken. It felt as if a thorn had lodged in his throat.

This is the one I have lost was not an appropriate statement to make to the new children and to the new wife listening so raptly to him, the new wife's fingers lightly resting on his arm.

These photographs had been selected. Reno's former wife and former children—of course, *former* wasn't the appropriate word!— were not shown to the new family.

Eleven years invested in the former marriage! It made him sick—just faintly, mildly sick—to think of so much energy and emotion, lost.

Though there'd been strain between Reno and his ex-wife— exacerbated when they were in close quarters together—he'd still insisted upon bringing his family to Paraquarry Lake on weekends through much of the year and staying there—of course—for at least six weeks each summer. When Reno couldn't get off from work he drove up weekends. For the "camp" at Paraquarry Lake— as he called it—was essential to his happiness.

Not that it was a particularly fancy place: it wasn't. Several acres of deciduous and pine woods, and hundred-foot frontage on the lake—*that* was what made the place special.

Eventually, in the breakup, the Paraquarry Lake camp had been sold. Reno's wife had come to hate the place and had no wish to buy him out—nor would she sell her half to him. In the woman's bitterness, the camp had been lost to strangers.

Now, it was nine years later. Reno hadn't seen the place in years. He'd driven along the Delaware River and inland to the lake and past the camp several times but became too emotional staring at it from the road, such bitter nostalgia wasn't good for him, and wasn't, he wanted to think, typical of him. So much better to think—to tell people in his new life, *It was an amicable split-up and an amicable divorce overall. We're civilized people—the kids come first!*

Was this what people said, in such circumstances? You did expect to hear, *The kids come first!*

Now, there was a new camp. A new "cabin"—an A-frame, in fact—the sort of thing for which Reno had always felt contempt;

but the dwelling was attractive, "modern," and in reasonably good condition with a redwood deck and sliding glass doors overlooking both the lake and a ravine of tangled wild rose to the rear. The nearest neighbor was uncomfortably close—only a few yards away—but screened by evergreens and a makeshift redwood fence a previous owner had erected.

Makeshift too was the way in which the A-frame had been cantilevered over a drop in the rocky earth, with wooden posts supporting it; if you entered at the rear you stepped directly into the house, but if you entered from the front, that is, facing the lake, you had to climb a steep flight of not-very-sturdy wood steps, gripping a not-very-sturdy railing. The property had been owned by a half-dozen parties since its original owner in the 1950s. Reno wondered at the frequent turnover of owners—this wasn't typical of the Water Gap area where people returned summer after summer for a lifetime.

The children loved the Paraquarry camp—they hugged their new Daddy happily, to thank him—and the new wife who'd murmured that she wasn't an "outdoor type" conceded that it was really very nice—"and what a beautiful view."

Reno wasn't about to tell Marlena that the view from his previous place had been more expansive, and more beautiful.

Marlena kissed him, so very happy. For he had saved her, as she had saved him. From what—neither could have said.

Paraquarry Lake was not a large lake: seven miles in circumference. The shoreline was so distinctly uneven and most of it thickly wooded and inaccessible except by boat. On maps the lake was L-shaped but you couldn't guess this from shore—nor even from a boat—you would have to fly in a small plane overhead, as Reno had done many years ago.

"Let's take the kids up sometime, and fly over. Just to see what the lake looks like from the air."

Reno spoke with such enthusiasm, the new wife did not want

to disappoint him. Smiling and nodding yes! What a good idea—
"Sometime."

The subtle ambiguity of *sometime*. Reno guessed he knew what
this meant.

In this new marriage Reno had to remind himself—continually—
that though the new wife was young, in her mid-thirties, he himself
was no longer that young. In his first marriage he'd been just a
year older than his wife. Physically they'd been about equally fit.
He had been stronger than his wife, he could hike longer and in
more difficult terrain, but essentially they'd been a match and in
some respects—caring for the children, for instance—his wife had
had more energy than Reno. Now, the new wife was clearly more
fit than Reno who became winded—even exhausted—on the
nearby Shawagunik Trail that, twenty years before, he'd found
hardly taxing.

Reno's happiness was working on the camp: the A-frame that
needed repainting, a new roof, new windows; the deck was partly
rotted, the front steps needed to be replaced. Unlike Reno's previous camp of several acres, the new camp was hardly more than an
acre and much of the property was rocky and inaccessible—fallen
trees, rotted lumber, the detritus of years.

Reno set for himself the long-term goal of clearing the property of such litter and a short-term goal of building a flagstone
terrace beside the front steps, where the earth was rocky and over-
grown with weeds; there had once been a makeshift brick terrace
or walkway here, now broken. Evidence of previous tenants—
rather, the negligence of previous tenants—was a cause of annoy-
ance to Reno as if this property dear to him had been purposefully
desecrated by others.

During the winter in their house in East Orange, Reno had
studied photos he'd taken of the new camp. Tirelessly he'd made
sketches of the redwood deck he meant to extend and rebuild,
and of the "sleeping porch" he meant to add. Marlena suggested a
second bathroom, with both a shower and a tub. And a screened

porch that could be transformed into a glassed-in porch in cold weather. Reno would build—or cause to be built—a carport, a new fieldstone fireplace, a barbecue on the deck. And there was the ground-level terrace he would construct himself with flagstones from a local garden supply store, once he'd dug up and removed the old, broken bricks half-buried in the earth.

Reno understood that his new wife's enthusiasm for Paraquarry Lake and the Delaware Water Gap was limited. Marlena would comply with his wishes—anyway, most of them—so long as he didn't press her too far. The high-wattage smile might quickly fade, the eyes brimming with love turn tearful. For divorce is a devastation, Reno knew. The children were more readily excited by the prospect of spending time at the lake—but they were children, impressionable. And bad weather in what was essentially an out-door setting—its entire raison d'etre was *outdoors*—would be new to them. Reno understood that he must not make with this new family the mistake he'd made the first time—insisting that his wife and children not only accompany him to Paraquarry Lake but that they enjoy it—visibly.

Maybe he'd been mistaken, trying so hard to make his wife and young children *happy*. Maybe it's always a mistake, trying to assure the happiness of others.

His daughter was attending a state college in Sacramento—her major was something called communication arts. His son had flunked out of Cal Tech and was enrolled at a "computer arts" school in San Francisco. The wife had long ago removed herself from Reno's life and truly he rarely thought of any of them, who seemed so rarely to think of him.

But the daughter. Reno's daughter. *Oh hi, Dad. Hi. Damn, I'm sorry—I'm just on my way out.*

Reno had ceased calling her. Both the kids. For they never called him. Even to thank him for birthday gifts. Their e-mails were rudely short, perfunctory.

The years of child support had ended. Both were beyond eighteen. And the years of alimony, now that the ex-wife had remarried. How many hundreds of thousands of dollars . . . Though of course, Reno understood.

But the new children! In this new family!

Like wind rippling over the surface of Paraquarry Lake—emotion flooded into Reno at the thought of his new family. He would adopt the children—soon. For Kevin and Devra adored their new Daddy who was so kind, funny, patient, and—yes—predictable—with them; who had not yet raised his voice to them a single time.

Especially little Devra captivated him—he stared at her in amazement, the child was so *small*—tiny rib cage, collarbone, wrists—after her bath, the white-blond hair thin as feathers against her delicate skull.

"Love you—I love you—all—so much."

It was a declaration made to the new wife only in the dark of their bed. In her embrace, her strong warm fingers gripping his back, and his hot face that felt to him like a ferret's face, hungry, ravenous with hunger, pressed into her neck.

At Paraquarry Lake, in the new camp, there was a new Reno emerging.

It was hard work but thrilling, satisfying—to chop his own firewood and stack it beside the fireplace. The old muscles were reasserting themselves in his shoulders, upper arms, thighs. He was developing a considerable axe swing, and was learning to anticipate the jar of the axe head against wood which he supposed was equivalent to the kick of a shotgun against a man's shoulder—if you weren't prepared, the shock ran down your spine like an electric charge.

Working outdoors he wore gloves which Marlena gave him—"Your hands are getting too calloused, scratchy." When he caressed her, she meant. Marlena was a shy woman and did not speak of their lovemaking but Reno wanted to think that it meant a good deal to her as it meant to him, after years of pointless celibacy.

He was thrilled too when they went shopping together—at the mall, at secondhand furniture stores—choosing Adirondack chairs, a black leather sofa, rattan settee, handwoven rugs, andirons for the fireplace. It was deeply moving to Reno to be in the presence of this attractive woman who took such care and turned to him continually for his opinion as if she'd never furnished a household before.

Reno even visited marinas in the area, compared prices: sailboats, Chris-Craft power boats. In truth he was just a little afraid of the lake—of how he might perform as a sailor on it. A rowboat was one thing, but even a canoe—he felt shaky in a canoe, with another passenger. With this new family vulnerable as a small creature cupped in the palm of a hand—he didn't want to take any risks.

The first warm days in June, a wading pool for the children. For there was no beach, only just a pebbly shore of sand hard-packed as cement. And sharp-edged rocks in the shallows. But a plastic wading pool, hardly more than a foot of water—that was fine. Little Kevin splashed happily. And Devra in a puckered yellow Spandex swimsuit that fit her little body like a second skin. Reno tried not to stare at the little girl—the astonishing white-blond hair, the widened pale-blue eyes—thinking how strange it was, how strange Marlena would think it was, that the child of a father not known to him should have so totally supplanted Reno's memory of his own daughter at that age; for Reno's daughter too must have been beautiful, adorable—but he couldn't recall. Terrifying how parts of his life were being shut to him like rooms in a house shut and their doors sealed and once you've crossed the threshold, you can't return. Waking in the night with a pounding heart Reno would catch his breath thinking, *But I have my new family now. My new life now.*

Sometimes in the woods above the lake there was a powerful

smell—a stink—of skunk, or something dead and rotted; not the decaying compost Marlena had begun which exuded a pleasurable odor for the most part, but something ranker, darker. Reno's sinuses ached, his eyes watered, and he began sneezing—in a sudden panic that he'd acquired an allergy for something at Paraquarry Lake.

That weekend, Kevin injured himself running along the rocky shore—as his mother had warned him not to—falling, twisting his ankle. And little Devra, stung by yellow jackets that erupted out of nowhere—in fact, out of a hive in the earth that Reno had disturbed with his shovel.

Screaming! High-pitched screams that tore at Reno's heart. If only the yellow jackets had stung *him*—Reno might have used the occasion to give the children some instruction.

Having soothed two weeping children in a single afternoon Marlena said ruefully, "Camp can be treacherous!" The remark was meant to be amusing but there was seriousness beneath, even a subtle warning, Reno knew.

He swallowed hard and promised it wouldn't happen again.

This warm-humid June afternoon shading now into early evening and Reno was still digging—"excavating"—the old ruin of a terrace. The project was turning out to be harder and more protracted than he had anticipated. For the earth below the part-elevated house was a rocky sort of subsoil, of a texture like fertilizer; moldering bricks were everywhere, part-buried; also jagged pieces of concrete and rusted spikes, broken glass amid shattered bits of red shale. The previous owners had simply dumped things here. Going back for decades, probably. Generations. Reno hoped these slovenly people hadn't dumped anything toxic.

The A-frame had been built in 1957—that long ago. Sometime later there were renovations, additions—sliding glass doors, skylights. A sturdier roof. Another room or two. By local standards the property hadn't been very expensive—of course, the market for lakeside properties in this part of New Jersey had been depressed for several years.

The new wife and the children were down at the shore—at their neighbors' dock. Reno heard voices, radio music—Marlena was talking with another young mother, several children were playing together. Reno liked hearing their happy uplifted voices though he couldn't make out any words. From where he stood, he couldn't have said with certainty which small figure was Kevin, which was Devra.

How normal all this was! Soon, Daddy would quit work for the evening, grab a beer from the refrigerator, and join his little family at the dock. How normal Reno was—a husband again, a father and a homeowner here at Paraquarry Lake.

Of all miracles, none is more daunting than *normal*. To be—to become—*normal*. This gift seemingly so ordinary is not a gift given to all who seek it.

And the children's laughter too. This was yet more exquisite.

With a grunt Reno unearthed a large rock he'd been digging and scraping at with mounting frustration. And beneath it, or beside it, what appeared to be a barrel, with broken and rotted staves; inside the barrel, what appeared to be shards of a broken urn.

There was something special about this urn, Reno seemed to know. The material was some sort of dark red earthenware—thick, glazed—inscribed with figures like hieroglyphics. Even broken and coated with grime, the pieces exuded an opaque sort of beauty. Unbroken, the urn would have stood about three feet in height.

Was this an Indian artifact? Reno was excited to think so—remains of the Lenni Lenape culture were usually shattered into very small pieces, almost impossible for a nonspecialist to recognize.

With the shiny new shovel Reno dug into and around the broken urn, curious. He'd been tossing debris into several cardboard boxes, to be hauled to the local landfill. He was tired—his muscles ached, and there was a new, sharp pain between his shoulder blades—but he was feeling good, essentially. At the neighbors' dock when they asked him how he was he'd say, *Damn good! But thirsty.*

His next-door neighbor looked to be a taciturn man of about Reno's age. And the wife one of those plus-size personalities with a big smile and greeting. To them, Marlena and Reno would be a *couple.* No sign that they were near-strangers desperate to make the new marriage work.

Already in early June Reno was beginning to tan—he looked like a native of the region more than he looked like a summer visitor from the city, he believed. In his T-shirt, khaki shorts, waterstained running shoes. He wasn't yet fifty—he had two years before fifty. His father had died at fifty-three of a heart attack but Reno took care of his health. He had annual checkups, he had nothing to worry about. He would adopt the woman's children—that was settled. He would make them his own: Kevin, Devra. He could not have named the children more fitting names. Beautiful names for beautiful children.

The Paraquarry property was an excellent investment. His work was going well. His work was not going badly. His job wasn't in peril—yet. He hadn't lost nearly so much money as he might have in the recent economic crisis—he was far from desperate, like a number of his friends. Beyond that—he didn't want to think.

A scuttling snake amid the debris. Reno was taken by surprise, startled. Tossed a piece of concrete at it. Thinking then in rebuke, *Don't be ridiculous. A garter snake is harmless.*

Something was stuck to some of the urn shards—clothing? Torn, badly rotted fabric?

Reno leaned his weight onto the shovel, digging more urgently. A flash of something wriggling in the earth—worms—cut by the slice of the shovel. Reno was sweating now. He stooped to peer more closely even as the cautionary words came: *Maybe no. Maybe not a good idea.*

"Oh. God."

Was it a bone? Or maybe plastic? No, a bone. An animal bone?

Covered in dirt, yet a very pale bone.

A human bone?

But so small—had to be a child's bone.

A child's forearm perhaps.

Reno picked it up in his gloved hands. It weighed nothing—it might have been made of Styrofoam.

"It is. It really . . . is."

Numbly Reno groped amid the broken pottery, tossing handfuls of clumped dirt aside. More bones, small broken rib bones, a skull . . . A skull!

It was a small skull of course. Small enough to cup in the hand.

Not an animal skull but a child's skull. Reno seemed to know—*a little girl's skull.*

This was not believable! Reno's brain was struck blank, for a long moment he could not think . . . The hairs stirred at the nape of his neck and he wondered if he was being watched.

A makeshift grave about fifteen feet from the base of his house. And when had this little body been buried? Twenty years ago, ten years ago? By the look of the bones, the rotted clothing, and the broken urn, the burial hadn't been recent.

But these were not Indian bones of course. Those bones would be much older—badly broken, dim, and scarified with time.

Reno's hand shook. The small teeth were bared in a smile of sheer terror. The small jaws had fallen open, the eye sockets were disproportionately large. Of course, the skull was broken—it was not a perfect skull. Possibly fractured in the burial—struck by the murderer's shovel. The skeleton lay in pieces—had the body been dismembered? Reno was whispering to himself words meant to console—*Oh God. Help me, God. God!* As his surprise ebbed Reno began to be badly frightened. He was thinking that these might be the bones of his daughter—his first daughter; the little girl had died, her death had been accidental, but he and her mother had hurriedly buried her . . .

But no: ridiculous. This was another time, not that time.

This was another campsite. This was another part of Paraquarry Lake. This was another time in a father's life.

His daughter was alive. Somewhere in California, a living girl. He was not to blame. He had never hurt her. She would outlive him.

Laughter and raised voices from the lakeshore. Reno shaded his eyes to see—what were they doing? Were they expecting Daddy to join them?

Kneeling in the dirt. Groping and rummaging in the coarse earth. Among the broken pottery, bones, and rotted fabric faded to the no-color of dirty water, something glittered—a little necklace of glass beads.

Reno untangled it from a cluster of small bones—vertebrae? The remains of the child's neck? Hideous to think that the child skeleton might have been broken into pieces with a shovel, or an axe. An axe! To fit more readily into the urn. To hasten decomposition.

"Little girl! Poor little girl."

Reno was weak with shock, sickened. His heart pounded terribly—he didn't want to die as his father had died! He would breathe deeply, calmly. He held the glass beads to the light. Amazingly the chain was intact. A thin metallic chain, tarnished. He put the little glass-bead necklace into the pocket of his khaki shorts. Hurriedly he covered the bones with dirt, debris. Pieces of the shattered urn he picked up and tossed into the cardboard box. And the barrel staves . . . Then he thought he should remove the bones also—he should place them in the box, beneath the debris, and take the box out to the landfill this evening. Before he did anything else. Before he washed hurriedly, grabbed a beer, and joined Marlena and the children at the lakefront. He would dispose of the child's bones at the landfill.

No. They will be traced here. Not a good idea.

Frantically he covered the bones. Then more calmly, smoothing the coarse dirt over the debris. Fortunately there was a sizable hole—a gouged-out, ugly hole—that looked like a rupture in the earth. Reno would lay flagstones over the grave—he'd purchased two dozen flagstones from a garden supply store on the highway. The children could help him—it would not be difficult work once the earth was prepared. As bricks had been laid over the child's grave years ago, Reno would lay flagstones over it now. For he could not report this terrible discovery—could he? If he called the Paraquarry police, if he reported the child skeleton to county authorities, what would be the consequences?

His mind went blank—he could not think.

Could not bear the consequences. Not now, in his new life.

Numbly he was setting his work tools aside, beneath the overhang of the redwood deck. The new shovel was not so shiny now. Quickly then—shakily—climbing the steps, to wash his hands in the kitchen. A relief—he saw his family down at the shore, with the neighbors—the new wife, the children. No one would interrupt Reno washing the little glass-bead necklace in the kitchen sink, in awkward big-Daddy hands.

Gently washing the glass beads, that were blue—beneath the grime a startling pellucid blue like slivers of sky. It was amazing, you might interpret it as a sign—the thin little chain hadn't broken in the earth.

Not a particle of dirt remained on the glass beads when Reno was finished washing them, drying them on a paper towel on the kitchen counter.

"Hey—look here! What's this? Who's this for?"

Reno dangled the glass-bead necklace in front of Devra. The little girl stared, blinking. It was suppertime—Daddy had cooked hamburgers on the outdoor grill on the deck—and now he pulled a little blue glass-bead necklace out of his pocket as if he'd only just discovered it.

Marlena laughed—she was delighted—for this was the sort of small surprise she appreciated.

Not for herself but for the children. In this case, for Devra. It was a good moment, a warm moment—Kevin didn't react with jealousy but seemed only curious, as Daddy said he'd found the necklace in a "secret place" and knew just who it was meant for.

Shyly Devra took the little necklace from Daddy's fingers.

"What do you say, Devra?"

"Oh Dad-dy—thank you."

Devra spoke so softly, Reno cupped his hand to his ear.

"Speak up, Devra. Daddy can't hear." Marlena helped the little girl slip the necklace over her head.

"Daddy, *thank you!*"

The little fish-mouth pursed for a quick kiss of Daddy's cheek.

Around the child's slender neck the blue glass beads glittered, gleamed. All that summer at Paraquarry Lake, Reno would marvel he'd never seen anything more beautiful.

ABOUT THE CONTRIBUTORS

Carrie Yury

ROBERT ARELLANO was born in 1969 at Overlook Hospital in Summit, New Jersey, and raised at 228 Kent Place Boulevard, where he shared a bedroom with brothers Manuel and Miguel, a wall with sisters Alicia and Ana Maria, and another wall with parents Manuel and Alicia. His novel *Havana Lunar*, which was a 2010 Edgar Award finalist, and his Southwest noir *Curse the Names* (2012), are both published by Akashic Books.

Kelly Leavitt

RICHARD BURGIN'S fifteen books include the novel *Rivers Last Longer* and the story collections *Shadow Traffic* and *The Identity Club: New and Selected Stories*, which the Huffington Post listed as one of the forty best books of fiction of the last decade. His stories have won five Pushcart Prizes and been reprinted in many anthologies including *The Best American Mystery Stories 2005*. He teaches at St. Louis University where he edits the literary journal *Boulevard*.

Phyllis Rose

MICHAEL CARROLL'S stories have appeared in *Open City*, *Ontario Review*, *Boulevard*, and such anthologies as *The New Penguin Book of Gay Short Stories*. He has twice been nominated for the Pushcart Prize.

Gianluca Gentilini

JONATHAN SAFRAN FOER is the author of the best-selling novels *Everything Is Illuminated*, which was adapted into a film starring Elijah Wood; and *Extremely Loud and Incredibly Close*. His short stories have been published in the *New Yorker*, the *Paris Review*, and *Conjunctions*. Foer's latest book is a work of nonfiction, *Eating Animals*, which was an instant *New York Times* and international best seller. He lives in Brooklyn.

Eric Rosenfeld

JEFFREY FORD is the author of the novels *The Portrait of Mrs. Charbuque*, *The Girl in the Glass*, and *The Shadow Year*. His most recent story collection is *The Drowned Life*. Ford is the recipient of an Edgar Award, a Nebula, a Shirley Jackson Award, and a World Fantasy Award. He lives in South Jersey and teaches early American literature and writing at Brookdale Community College.

Marion Ettlinger

SHEILA KOHLER is the author of eight novels including *Becoming Jane Eyre* and *Love Child*, and three collections of short stories. Kohler was awarded two O. Henry Awards, an Open Voice, the Smart Family Foundation, a Willa Cather, and an *Antioch Review* Prize. She was a fellow at the Cullman Center and teaches at Bennington and Princeton. A film based on her novel *Cracks*, directed by Jordan and Ridley Scott, debuted in theaters in the spring of 2011.

Amelia Beamer/Locus Publications

BARRY N. MALZBERG graduated obscurely in the same Syracuse University class of 1960 of which *New Jersey Noir*'s editor was valedictorian. Less than a decade later, as Malzberg struggled toward modest prominence in science fiction, the valedictorian won the National Book Award in fiction. Not only has she been an inspiration for well over half a century, she's kept Malzberg humble. Extremely humble.

Joanne Manfredo

LOU MANFREDO served in the Brooklyn criminal justice system for twenty-five years. His short fiction has appeared in *The Best American Mystery Stories*, *Ellery Queen Mystery Magazine*, and *Brooklyn Noir*. He has authored three novels, *Rizzo's War*, *Rizzo's Fire*, and *Rizzo's Regards* (forthcoming). Born and raised in Brooklyn, Manfredo and his wife Joanne have lived in New Jersey for many years.

Michael Eastman

BRADFORD MORROW is author of the novels *Come Sunday*, *The Almanac Branch*, *Trinity Fields*, *Giovanni's Gift*, *Ariel's Crossing*, and *The Diviner's Tale*. His anthology, *The Inevitable: Contemporary Writers Confront Death*, coedited with David Shields, came out in 2011 with W. W. Norton, and a collection of short stories, *The Uninnocent*, is forthcoming from Pegasus Books. Morrow is a professor of literature at Bard College, and lives in New York.

Peter Crook

PAUL MULDOON is now Howard G.B. Clark '21 Professor at Princeton University. From 1999–2004 he was a professor of poetry at the University of Oxford. In 2007 he was appointed poetry editor of the *New Yorker*. Muldoon's collections of poetry include *New Weather* (1973), *Mules* (1977), *Quoof* (1983), *Madoc: A Mystery* (1990), *The Annals of Chile* (1994), *Hay* (1998), *Poems 1968-1998* (2001), *Moy Sand and Gravel* (2002), *Horse Latitudes* (2006), and *Maggot* (2010).

Charles Gross

JOYCE CAROL OATES is the author of a number of *noir* works of fiction including *Rape: A Love Story, Beasts, A Fair Maiden, The Female of the Species, The Museum of Dr. Moses,* and most recently *Give Me Your Heart.* She has edited *American Gothic Tales, The Oxford Book of American Short Stories, The Ecco Anthology of Contemporary American Short Fiction,* and *The Best American Mystery Stories.* She has been a resident of Princeton, New Jersey, since 1978.

J.P. Ostriker

ALICIA OSTRIKER has published thirteen poetry collections including *The Book of Seventy,* which received the 2009 National Jewish Book Award for Poetry. *The Crack in Everything* and *The Little Space: Poems Selected and New, 1969–1989* were both National Book Award finalists. As a critic, Ostriker has written several books on poetry and on the Bible. She is Professor Emerita of Rutgers University, and teaches in the low-residency poetry MFA program of Drew University.

Vernon Doucette

ROBERT PINSKY'S *Selected Poems* was published in 2011. His recent anthology, with accompanying audio CD, is *Essential Pleasures.* His honors include the Harold Washington Award from the city of Chicago and the *Los Angeles Times* Book Prize for his translation of *The Inferno of Dante.* The videos from his Favorite Poem Project can be viewed at www.favoritepoem.org.

Robin Reese

BILL PRONZINI has been a full-time writer since 1969. He has published seventy-five novels, including four in collaboration with Barry N. Malzberg and thirty-five in his long-running "Nameless Detective" series. Also to his credit are four nonfiction books, and three hundred short stories of which sixty bear the Malzberg/Pronzini byline. Among his numerous awards is the Mystery Writers of America's Grand Master, which he received in 2008.

Ashley Gilbertson

S.J. ROZAN, author of thirteen crime novels, is an Edgar, Shamus, Anthony, Nero, and Macavity award winner, as well as a recipient of the Japanese Maltese Falcon Award. She's a lifelong New Yorker, which means she grew up within sight of New Jersey, and specifically Newark. She misspent a shameful amount of her childhood at the late lamented Palisades Amusement Park and is a huge Cory Booker fan. Her latest book is *Ghost Hero.* For more information, visit www.sjrozan.com.

Drew Kelly

JONATHAN SANTLOFER is the author of *The Death Artist, Color Blind, The Killing Art, Anatomy of Fear,* and *The Murder Notebook.* He is the recipient of a Nero Wolfe Award, and two National Endowment for the Arts grants. He is coeditor, contributor, and illustrator of the anthology *The Dark End of the Street,* and editor/contributor of *L.A. Noire: The Collected Stories.* He lives in New York where he is currently at work on a new novel.

Anjali Wason

HIRSH SAWHNEY moved to Jersey City in 2009, when he received a fellowship to teach and study writing at Rutgers-Newark University. He is the editor of *Delhi Noir,* published by Akashic Books, which is being translated into French and Italian. His writing has appeared in the *New York Times Book Review,* the *Guardian,* and *Outlook Traveller.* He is working on his first novel.

GERALD SLOTA'S photographs have been widely exhibited throughout the U.S. and abroad. His work is included in collections at the L.A. County Museum of Art and the Whitney Museum of Art. His images have appeared in the *New York Times Magazine,* the *New Yorker,* and *Art in America.* Awards include a MacDowell Artist Residency and Mid-Atlantic Fellowship grants from the New Jersey State Council on the Arts in 2001 and 2009. For more information, visit www.geraldslota.com.

Heather Laszlo

S.A. SOLOMON has published short fiction and poems in the *Dos Passos Review, Exquisite Corpse,* the *New York Quarterly, Lungfull!,* and other journals. Her lyrics for Leonid Andreyev's *The One that Gets Slapped,* a circus-cabaret-drama, were featured in a 2008 production at Colby College. Her brush with New Jersey *noir* comes from her years living and working in Jersey City and Newark. She now lives in New York City, and is a freelance writer and editor.

Gerald Zoner

GERALD STERN, born in Pittsburgh, Pennsylvania, in 1925, is the author of fifteen books of poetry including *This Time: New and Selected Poems,* which won the 1998 National Book Award, and a book of personal essays titled *What I Can't Bear Losing.* He has won the Ruth Lilly Prize and the Wallace Stevens Award, and his *Early Collected: Poems from 1965-1992* was published by W.W. Norton in the spring of 2010.

EDMUND WHITE has written some twenty-five books— memoirs, biographies, novels, travel books, short stories, and essays. Among his best-known novels are *A Boy's Own Story* and *The Married Man*. He lives in New York but teaches in Princeton, New Jersey.

C.K. WILLIAMS'S books have won the Pulitzer Prize, the National Book Award, and the National Book Critics Circle Award, among others. His most recent book of poems, *Wait*, was published in 2010, as was a prose study, *On Whitman*, and a children's book, *A Not Scary Story About Big Scary Things*. He is a member of the American Academy of Arts and Letters, and teaches in the creative writing program at Princeton University.

Also available from the Akashic Noir Series

BOSTON NOIR
edited by Dennis Lehane
240 pages, trade paperback original, $15.95

Brand-new stories by: Dennis Lehane, Stewart O'Nan, Patricia Powell, John Dufresne, Lynne Heitman, Don Lee, Russ Aborn, J. Itabari Njeri, Jim Fusilli, Brendan DuBois, and Dana Cameron.

"In the best of the eleven stories in this outstanding entry in Akashic's noir series, characters, plot, and setting feed off each other like flames and an arsonist's accelerant . . . [T]his anthology shows that noir can thrive where Raymond Chandler has never set foot."
—*Publishers Weekly* (starred review)

BROOKLYN NOIR
edited by Tim McLoughlin
350 pages, trade paperback original, $15.95
*Winner of Shamus Award, Anthony Award, Robert L. Fish Memorial Award; finalist for Edgar Award, Pushcart Prize.

Brand-new stories by: Pete Hamill, Arthur Nersesian, Ellen Miller, Nelson George, Nicole Blackman, Sidney Offit, Ken Bruen, and others.

"Brooklyn Noir is such a stunningly perfect combination that you can't believe you haven't read an anthology like this before. But trust me— you haven't . . . The writing is flat-out superb, filled with lines that will sing in your head for a long time to come."
—Laura Lippman, winner of the Edgar, Agatha, and Shamus awards

MANHATTAN NOIR
edited by Lawrence Block
264 pages, trade paperback original, $15.95

Brand-new stories by: Jeffery Deaver, Lawrence Block, Charles Ardai, Carol Lea Benjamin, Thomas H. Cook, Jim Fusilli, John Lutz, Justin Scott, Maan Meyers, Martin Meyers, S.J. Rozan, Xu Xi, and others.

"A pleasing variety of Manhattan neighborhoods come to life in Block's solid anthology, the latest entry in Akashic's city-themed noir series . . . [T]he writing is of a high order and a nice mix of styles."
—*Publishers Weekly*

D.C. NOIR
edited by George Pelecanos
312 pages, trade paperback original, $15.95

Brand-new stories by: George Pelecanos, Laura Lippman, James Grady, Kenji Jasper, Jim Beane, Ruben Castaneda, Robert Wisdom, Jim Patton, Norman Kelley, Jennifer Howard, Jim Fusilli, and others.

"[T]he tome offers a startling glimpse into the cityscape's darkest corners . . . fans of the genre will find solid writing, palpable tension, and surprise endings."
—*Washington Post*

LOS ANGELES NOIR
edited by Denise Hamilton
360 pages, trade paperback original, $15.95
*A *Los Angeles Times* best seller and winner of an Edgar Award.

Brand-new stories by: Michael Connelly, Janet Fitch, Susan Straight, Héctor Tobar, Patt Morrison, Robert Ferrigno, Neal Pollack, Gary Phillips, Christopher Rice, Naomi Hirahara, Jim Pascoe, and others.

"Akashic is making an argument about the universality of noir; it's sort of flattering, really, and *Los Angeles Noir*, arriving at last, is a kaleidoscopic collection filled with the ethos of noir pioneers Raymond Chandler and James M. Cain."
—*Los Angeles Times Book Review*

BALTIMORE NOIR
edited by Laura Lippman
294 pages, trade paperback original, $14.95

Brand-new stories by: David Simon, Laura Lippman, Tim Cockey, Rob Hiaasen, Robert Ward, Sujata Massey, Dan Fesperman, Marcia Talley, Ben Neihart, Jim Fusilli, Rafael Alvarez, and others.

"Baltimore is a diverse city, and the stories reflect everything from its old row houses and suburban mansions to its beloved Orioles and harbor areas. Mystery fans should relish this taste of its seamier side."
—*Publishers Weekly*